Forty
Testoons

BREAKWATER BOOKS LTD.
100 Water Street
P.O. Box 2188
St. John's, NF
A1C 6E6

Canadian Cataloguing in Publication Data
Printed in Canada
Fisk, Alan, 1950–

Forty testoons

ISBN 1-55081-145-2

I. Title.

PS8561.I79F67 1999   C813.'54   C99–950037-6
PR9199.3.F5365F67 1999

Editor: Shannon M. Lewis
Typesetting: Adam Percy and Heather Hunt
Design/Layout: Jon Holden
Cover Image: "A Sketch of the River Exploits by Lieut. John Cartwright, 1768." (PANL, MG 100, the Cartwright Collection.) Courtesy of the Provincial Archives of Newfoundland and Labrador.

Copyright © 1999 Alan Fisk

ALL RIGHTS RESERVED. No part of this work covered by the copyright hereon may be reproduced or used in any form or by any means—graphic, electronic or mechanical—without the prior written permission of the publisher. Any request for photocopying, recording, taping or storing in an information retreival system of any part of this book shall be directed in writing to the Canadian Reprography Collective, 6 Adelaide Street East, Suite 900, Toronto, Ontario, M5C 1H6. This applies to classroom usage as well.

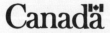 We acknowledge the financial support of the Government of Canada through the Book Publishing Industry Development Program (BPIDP) for our publishing activities.

The Publisher gratefully acknowledges the financial support of the Government of Newfoundland and Labrador that has helped make this publication possible.

Forty Testoons

Alan Fisk

BREAKWATER

To Patrick Hutton. I would never have become a writer without his encouragement, of which he has no recollection at all.

Chapter One

I **have outdone Judas Iscariot, for he was paid** only thirty pieces of silver for betraying his Lord, and I have been paid forty.

The sardonic Dominican friar at the Exchequer in Westminster told me that I should feel proud to be the first man to be paid in the new shilling coins.

"To the priest who is going to the new land," he read from the king's Household Account book, "forty shillings."

He counted them out to me across the table. The light coming from the window behind him made the brand new coins sparkle among his bony fingers. He had an old man's hands though he could not have been aged much more than twenty. The Dominicans are never young.

I admired the bright shillings as he counted them again.

"I've never had new coins before," I told him. "It feels like an honour to be the first man to spend them."

"New coins for a new year," he replied. "We call them testoons, little heads, because they bear the king's head."

He pushed four neat piles of ten coins across the che-quered table which gives the Exchequer its name.

"The king is paying you well for this exile."

"It isn't exile. Newfoundland is an English possession, as English as London or Devon; but the king is paying me well for ministering to the fishing fleet this summer."

"I wish I could do more pastoral work, but the Church has assigned me to financial duties."

Whenever you meet a friar, monk, or priest who is employed on administrative work, they always tell you that they wish they could be working with the poor or the sick, caring for souls instead of scratching on account rolls. It is a strange thing that they never prove it by actually coming forward and volunteering for pastoral work among the unwashed, the unholy, and the ungrateful.

I brought the forty coins across the ocean to Newfoundland in the same great chest in which I keep my Mass kit and my portable altar, the tools of my calling. Being a priest is an easy trade if you do only what you are obliged to do, and an impossibly hard one if you try to do all that you should, because you can never heal all the spiritual wounds that are laid before you every day in the tense whispers of confession.

It is the quiet part of my day now. The fleet is out fishing, and the shore workers have gone into the vast dark forests to cut wood. I am alone here, guarding our encampment, against what or whom I do not know.

I decided to clean out my great chest, which is so old that even my father did not know its age when he entrusted it to me for this summer in Newfoundland. When I opened it for the first time since we landed, I was pleased to find no damage to this thick blank book in which I am writing, or to my goose quills and my ink, and that no one had stolen my forty testoons.

Since I am writing the name in Latin, I write it as *testones*, meaning 'little heads,' just as the English name does, from the head of King Henry VII which they bear.

They were issued in April of this year, the nineteenth year of his reign, 1504 by the calendar. They are the first silver shilling coins ever minted. Why did I bring them here, where no one sells anything and there is nothing to buy?

I am writing in Latin because I suspect that some of the fishermen can read, and I know that a few of the ships' officers can, but I doubt that any of them understand Latin. They have spent all their lives listening to Latin words in church, and even speaking them by rote when the priest requires a response from the congregation, but many have no idea what they are saying, so they have told me.

Latin is a good language for secrets, and I like secrets, as does my father. How do I write my name in Latin? Well, I write it now in English, Ralph Fletcher, priest to the Newfoundland fishing fleet. The name Ralph looks strange in Latin, and I thought about calling myself Radulphus, but then I realised that I did not know the Latin for 'Fletcher,' one who makes arrows. It is my father's greatest shame that our very name proclaims our origins from a family of common craftsmen, but there is no way that a man can change his name. My father would if he could.

I have just gone out of the hut for an hour, weighting down my pen with a beach stone as a defence against the wind which seems never to stop blowing in Newfoundland. An unsecured goose feather might find itself carried all the way back across the ocean to England on those relentless westerlies.

As I closed the door behind me I had to stop it shut with the rock which is kept outside for just that purpose. One of the curiosities of this strange land is that although the wind never stops, the land never changes. The dark trees of the forest and the purple-grey rocks splashed with sad patches of lichen never change. Even the hut which we have built (We? My soft cleric's hands took no part in the work) has the appearance of a natural thing, because it is the same colour as the forest of whose trees it was constructed.

Now that I had resolved to write down my impressions of Newfoundland before I sail home with the fleet at the end of the summer fishing season, I tried to put my observations into words, the precise, correct words, as I was taught to do by my composition master when I was at school at Winchester College.

How much easier it is to find the words in Latin than in English, even though Latin had never been heard in Newfoundland before John Cabot's crew muttered their prayers on that first voyage of discovery seven years ago. Yet somehow this is a land made for Latin, with that language's spareness and austerity and its sense of communicating a deep meaning. I wondered what Newfoundland meant for me and for England, for God must have created it for some purpose which we must find out.

I had turned my back on the shore, looking towards the forest so that I contemplated it with full concentration while I tried to find my words, when Horsfall the under-carpenter came out of the woods dragging a pile of small logs along the ground on a frame attached to his back. "Hullo, Sir Ralph! No work to do?"

Why does everyone call a priest 'Sir,' whether he deserves it or not? I suppose it is a privilege given to the deserving and the undeserving alike, in the same way that the power to turn bread and wine into the body and blood of Christ is given to all priests regardless of whether their manner of life is holy or dissolute.

"Priests don't work, Horsfall. You've all been telling me that since we left England."

"Ah, that's just teasing. You must not have spent much time among rough men."

"I haven't, that's true. You've been working, though. What's all that wood for?"

"Firewood, Father, for the winter crew. You know, the men who overwinter in Newfoundland until the fleet returns in the spring. We'll need a great store of firewood. The winters are bitter here. The first winter crews lost most of their men from cold."

"God help our winter crew, then."

"I hope so, for I'll be one of them. I'm staying."

"You, Horsfall? What will you find to do in the long cold of winter?"

Horsfall began stacking the logs against the front wall of our hut, fighting the gusts of wind which rolled them around as fast as he tried to lay them down in good order.

"It's not I who want to stay. It's Young Martin. He's never been on a voyage before, and he wants to take in all he can of new things and a new land."

"Has he heard the tales of what winter is like here?"

"Oh, indeed, but he won't listen. He's still in wonder at having crossed the ocean, and he wants to be able to say that he's spent the whole year in Newfoundland."

"God grant that he sees the next spring then, and you as well."

"Thank you for not forgetting to add me in that prayer."

Horsfall turned away from me with that sharp shrug which signifies that a man is not interested in my conversation any more. I am accustomed to that shrug of dismissal; I have been seeing it ever since we landed in Newfoundland, and indeed all my life before that. I do not know how to deal with men, and I have no experience of women. I can only hope that my religious training has equipped me to talk properly to God on behalf of myself and my surly flock.

I resumed my attempts to frame the right words to describe the new land, although it is new only to Englishmen, being five and half thousand years old like the rest of the world.

I walked to the far end of the hut and turned right to look at the sea. We are always as aware of its presence as we are of the opposing presence of the forest.

The first sight which meets anyone passing our hut is the fish flakes. These are not fish scales, as my Latin translation would suggest, but are wooden structures on which the cod are spread out to dry after they have been gutted, filletted, and spread out flat in the same way as one opens the leaves of a book. They look flimsy, but they have withstood the gales of what passes for summer in Newfoundland, and the men assure me that they are the same fish flakes which have been in use for several years now. I am not sure that I believe them, but they tell me that one of the tasks of the winter crew is to maintain the fish flakes ready for use in the spring. This may well be one of their jokes at my expense. I sometimes wonder whether they value me more as a priest or as a buffoon.

The fish flakes are the same as the ones in Devon and Dorset from where our fleets come, but instead of looking upon the green hills of southwestern England they face the barren rock of the coast of Newfoundland and the forests which cover the land beyond.

In the seaward direction the view is different as well: Newfoundland is the only place that I have ever been where the sea is blue. Everyone speaks of the blue sea, but around England the sea is always a deep green, close to the colour of these forests. I always wondered why the sea was called blue, but off the coast of Newfoundland the ocean is a deep dark blue. Now I wonder why the sea is green on one side of the ocean and blue on the other.

When I stand by the sea the wind is at my back. In the spring, when the sea is covered by ice, men have been lost because the wind blew them out onto the ice, further and further, towards their death by freezing, while their companions watch them stagger unwillingly to their end, flailing their arms and crying for help which no man could give.

The thought of the ice makes me wish that I had started writing this account earlier, as soon as we landed, or during the voyage out, because the greatest astonishment for me was the icebergs.

I had thought that the sea froze in winter, but it is not so: the ice comes down in the spring, if one can call it spring, in the month of May, a merry month in England but a bitter one in Newfoundland and the northwest seas.

After weeks upon the ocean, the ship had become the whole world, with nothing else to see except water and the clouds overhead, but as we approached the shores of England's newest possession, still invisibly distant, my eye was caught by strange unnatural specks of colour on the horizon.

"What are they?" I asked one of the fishermen who had sailed to the Newfoundland fishing grounds several times before.

"Icebergs. You'll see them clearly later, although we won't come too close. They're great floating blocks of ice."

"But the colours! Look, they're like a rainbow laid out along the horizon. Ice isn't coloured."

"If you say so, Father. You're an educated man who can read the words of scholars and prophets. I can only speak from experience, and I tell you that they're icebergs."

The next morning we passed by the icebergs, and I was able to tell that the fisherman had been right. We came within a land mile of the vast floating palaces of ice, in dull and wet weather, but the colours silenced me with their beauty. The ice was attempting to be white, but it was washed through with blue-green, a colour which seemed too pure and heavenly to be natural, and the edges of the blocks of ice reflected shocks of pink and purple even in the gloomy light.

I believe now that this was the moment when I first truly understood that I had come to a New World, as many men now call these lands on the western side of the ocean. I had not then noticed that the sea was blue instead of green, but I could not fail to be astonished by the icebergs, the first sight I had seen which I could never have seen in England.

Those who have stayed in Newfoundland with the winter crew tell me that sometimes in April the ice covers the sea, and that if you stand on the shore and look east, you see only a sculptured field of ice, so that you can hardly believe that it will ever clear to allow the fishing fleet to come and take the winter crew home.

What else must I describe? Ice, sea, forest, rock, wind, fish flakes, living huts; surely that is not all of Newfoundland for us? No, there is something more which always frightens me. I have written of what the forest looks like from our huts by the sea. When you walk into the forest, and I have never gone far for fear of becoming lost, you are attacked by a disturbing silence.

The trees are small compared to those in English forests. Perhaps the harsh climate and poor soil prevent them from growing larger. What is eerie is the lack of birdsong, and the absence of life. The fishermen tell me that they have never seen a snake in Newfoundland, and that few birds sing here. It is troubling to the spirit that the great silence somehow exists simultaneously with the roar of the sea in the distance and the howling of the wind overhead. How can there be silence in such noise? Yet there is, as though one had walked into a kingdom ruled by unhallowed powers.

So much for the land. What of its people? I have not seen them, and I have not found a fishermen to admit to having seen one, but there are people in Newfoundland.

We have never met the inhabitants of Newfoundland, but other English expeditions have done so. I wanted to meet the three men of Newfoundland whom Sebastian Cabot brought back to England two years ago.

They live in Westminster Palace, and I am told that they now live like Englishmen, but when I was in Westminster for my visit to the Exchequer the officers of the palace told me I would not be allowed to see them. I am sure that they were taken prisoner, or brought onto the ship by a trick and taken to England against their will.

The fishermen with whom I have spoken have seen only strange pieces of carved wood are found along the shore, and broken needles of bone on the floor of the forest among the trees.

Since I have found out nothing about the people who belong here, I must describe instead those who come here every spring from England.

They are all of one class, the fishermen. (No women are ever brought here, and so far as I know no English woman, or indeed any European woman, has yet seen this new continent.) The only distinction is that between the mass of men and the fishing captains, and among the captains there is yet another, and ultimate, distinction: the first captain to arrive on the coast of Newfoundland is called the Fishing Admiral, and holds a pre-eminent position among his fellows.

The fishermen themselves, all from the West Country, are a rough sort of men as one might expect, but because I have been brought up in the Church since infancy this is all as much of a discovery to me as the sight of the new land itself. I am not happy to be among them, but it is my duty as a priest. I would prefer a gentle life among the priests in an old and tranquil cathedral, but I must go where I am sent and do as I am ordered. I can see that this experience may benefit me by teaching me how to deal with all conditions of people, if I am later sent to be pastor of a parish, but I am not sure whether it has been of benefit to my coarse and scornful flock here. How I hope that none of them can read Latin.

It may not be so, because perhaps not all of them have always been fishermen. Harry Chard, the Fishing Admiral, took me aside one day by the sea and asked me what I thought of Gloucester.

"I don't know," I said. "I've never been there. I know only the south and east of England, and not much of that."

"Ah, the city of Gloucester," he replied, as if he had just received a new and unexpected thought. "No, I've never been there either, not as a place." And with that mysterious comment he left me staring baffled at the cold sea while he strolled away with his hands clasped behind his back like a schoolmaster.

At that I finally began to think. I do too much thinking; the men are right, I do too little work, but I was born not to work. I must admit that most of them, in spite of their sinful lives, would make better priests than I would make a fisherman. At least they have the power to lead and master other men, a power which all can see that I lack.

My thoughts led me to the notion that Harry Chard had not been asking about the city of Gloucester, but about the late Duke of Gloucester, who usurped the throne of England under the title of Richard III, and fell nineteen years ago when King Henry VII defeated him. Is Harry Chard a supporter of Richard? Was he an eminent man under Richard, now hiding in the disguise of a master of the fisheries? Was he sounding me out to see whether I was also a sympathiser? These words are dangerous to him and to myself. I must blot them out before we return to England, which we shall do at any day now.

I hate those writers who begin a passage with the words "I now take up my pen again," but indeed I do take up my pen after four days' lapse, including a Sunday. My pen has been repeatedly sharpened, and is so worn and resharpened that it would have earned me a whipping at school, but I must conserve my pens. There are no geese in Newfoundland for me to chase for a new quill, not that I have ever tackled that perilous task myself.

We are waiting for Harry Chard as this year's Fishing Admiral to declare the end of summer. This is not a reference to the climate. I do not believe we ever had a summer as we know it in England. There have been a few warm, sunny days, but most of the time the weather has been like that of a kind autumn or a promising spring. The end of summer means that the fishing season is over and the summer crew sail back to England with all the ships loaded with dried cod to feed the pious every Friday.

Here in Newfoundland the cod feeds both the pious and the impious. The fish merchants do not pay to provide the men with food, so they must find their own, which means fish. The land has hardly any soil, and I wish I understood what the trees grow in. They always remain thin and spindly, and seem never to grow up, like Young

Martin. Everyone, not only Horsfall, calls him Young Martin, although he must be about thirty years old, old enough to remember when Richard was king. I must try not to mention that again; it is a dangerous name for suspicious men to find among your writings.

Young Martin, who, as I say, is not young, is so called because there is something about him which has remained becalmed in childhood while the winds of the years have turned his fellows into tough and ruthless men. His body is fully grown, so much so that he is often called upon for tasks which need a particularly strong man. His mind is that of a man, too; he can speak as well as anyone, unlike the unfortunates who keep the minds and manners of babes all their lives, and who groan and shriek among the monks and nuns who nurse them because even their own families will not.

Young Martin's affliction, if it is right to call it that, is that he is an innocent. He laughs and cries. He will run after an animal which he glimpses darting across the forest floor, and sometimes he breaks into vulgar songs while I am celebrating Mass, not to mock me but in an excess of cheerful spirit.

The men are frightened when he does such things. They live ungodly lives, and have no respect for me as a man, but they fear God and glower at Martin when he behaves wrongly at the Mass.

"Make him quiet, Horsfall," they say, because Horsfall is always able to rule him.

The fishermen are afraid that Martin's antics will bring them to damnation, although I reassure them that the Mass is valid whatever the behaviour of the congregation. After all, the character of the priest does not affect its validity; no matter how sinful and corrupt a man I may be—a subject which I ponder too much for my own good and that of my flock—I can still invoke the Holy Spirit to turn bread and wine into the Body and Blood of Christ.

Yes, the church. I set up my portable altar in one of the huts in which spare fishing gear and food are stored. The hut stinks, but probably no worse than the streets of Jerusalem whose smells must have sidled in through the windows of that famous upper room in which Christ first gave that command to his disciples which they were to do in memory of him. I have tried keeping the door open, so that the incessant wind will remove the smell, but it does not do so, and a smell which cannot be blown away by the winds of Newfoundland will surely offend noses until the Day of Judgement. The wind even blows draughts through the cracks and joins of the huts, and I fear for the winter crew who must live in them until the fleet comes again.

Two more days have passed, with nothing for me to do but to celebrate the Mass for surly and impatient congregations, and to watch the men packing up and carrying boxes, bags, and baskets out to the ships in little rocking dories which were brought out in earlier years. One of the winter crew's duties is to repair them after the season is over.

Any day now Harry Chard the Fishing Admiral will declare the end of summer. I must prepare to leave too. I have little enough to pack. My portable altar and Mass items can be tidied away quickly enough, no doubt a reminder of the days when Christians were a persecuted minority and priests had to be ready to flee in a hurry with all that they possessed or had been entrusted with.

This morning the sun is shining, the wind is gentle, and the sea is oddly calm. The world must feel like this just before a great miracle or revelation. I decided to take a last walk into the forest.

Once again I found myself in that silence which was yet not silence, with the oppressive lack of sound among the trees lying over the rip of the wind and the growl of the sea. It was like the four-level allegory we were taught for understanding the Bible, where the layers of meaning in a sacred text, Literal, Figurative, Anagogic, and Tropological, all express themselves in the same words; and yet it is not the same, for none of the four levels of allegory is stronger than another. They are all equal, but in Newfoundland the forest seems stronger than the sea. I do not understand how that can be.

I seem to be the only man in the fishing fleet who does not fear the forest. I respect it, and never go into it without telling someone that I have done so and how long it will be before I expect to return. Would they search for me? They would, for fear of having no priest to conduct Mass.

There is a thought which keeps coming to me, whether from my own mind or from Satan, which I do not like thinking but which I cannot suppress; it is like a painful memory to which one cries "No!" whenever it returns, as if it could be forbidden from arising. That hateful thought is that the men see me as a wizard, casting spells, and that my portable altar is a place at which magic is daily performed. If there were no priest they would be defenceless before the powers of evil. I keep explaining that this is not so, that God does not grant favours to the righteous any more than to the sinful.

I nearly reminded Horsfall once that the only promise which Our Lord ever made to Christians was not that they would be granted an easy life in this world: He promised them only trouble, whippings, and the hatred of their neighbours. I do not know whether I would be brave enough to preach Christ in the face of such opposition, but I am safe, because all Englishmen have been baptised as Christians even if they do not lead the Christian life. I stopped myself from telling Horsfall that, realising that his simple mind might draw strange and dangerous conclusions from such an idea.

For the first time, I sat down on the forest floor. I listened for animals, but I could hear none. We know that there are catamounts in the woods, great cats with tufted ears. Harry Chard swears that the same cat is found in the north of England, but I have no desire to meet one either in England or in Newfoundland.

I noticed something that I had never seen before: the tracks made by people, pressed into the wet ground. I am no country poacher and have no skill in these matters, but I could tell that at least one person had passed by. The prints showed no trace of a heel, so I wondered whether they could have been left by an Englishman. It rains so often here that I could not judge how recently my unseen companion had passed.

No animals, no men, no birdsong, and no sound; there was nothing for me in the forest. I had been sitting on the twigs and fallen leaves for half a morning. I stood up awkwardly, clawing at the air as if it could help to support me, and trudged back to our huts and the rocky frontier of the sea.

I saw Horsfall piling more wood in front of our hut, and our over-carpenter William Durdle carrying water inside as though for some ritual. It would certainly not be for washing.

Beyond, out to sea, I was amazed by the sight of strange ships, all abreast, with full sails set. Who could be sailing to Newfoundland at this time of the year? Was it a foreign attack? Had some great or terrible thing happened in England, and were these the bearers of that news?

I cried out to Horsfall.

"What ships are those, Horsfall? Who's coming?"

"Nobody is coming, Sir Ralph. Those are our own ships of the fishing fleet. Harry Chard the Fishing Admiral has declared the end of summer."

"But does that mean—"

"Yes, Sir Ralph. That is the fleet sailing back to England. I am staying behind until the spring. I told you that Young Martin and I were going to be in the winter crew."

Horsfall put down his logs, shaded his eyes to look out at the departing ships, and then dropped his hand and stared straight at me.

"We are part of the winter crew, and Harry Chard has ordered that you are to be one of the winter crew too."

"He never told me that!"

"He told us that you knew, and had put yourself in our service, and that you had already been paid forty testoons to stay with the winter crew."

Chapter Two

Two days have passed. The clouds have hung so low that I could believe that I could reach up and touch them, and indeed the crowns of the trees have vanished from sight so that the trunks seem to hang from the clouds like needles from a giant tapestry being woven above our heads. The rain has never stopped, and nor has the wind, so we are all wet and cold. So shall we remain until the spring, I suppose.

I have six companions. Perhaps it ought to be twelve, but, Lord, let me not aspire to allegory above my station.

There is Horsfall, and Young Martin, and William Durdle. There is Peter Slade, a ship's carpenter who will look after the huts and fish flakes, and lead the work of maintaining and repairing the dories. There is Holy Gilbert, a boy of sixteen who obtained his nickname by his piety. He prays constantly, because his widowed mother told him to do so before he set off on this voyage, his first. Horsfall has already made clear to Holy Gilbert, reinforcing his explanation with cuffs and kicks, that his office is to do all the dirtiest work for the winter crew. The last man is Tom Rudge, the oldest of us, perhaps fifty. He is tall and grey-haired and speaks little. He does not move much, either, except when he has to, and then he jerks suddenly and awkwardly. Everything seems a surprise to this man even though he is the one who has seen the most of life.

Lastly, there is myself, Sir Ralph, Father Ralph Fletcher, secular priest, and chaplain to the winter crew. I have the tools of my trade: my portable altar, though its portability will not need to be demonstrated for many months to come while we remain fixed in this place, and my Mass items. I have the voice and hands to perform the Mass, and ears to listen to confessions. I have the guidance of the Holy Spirit, who is always with us even on the coast of Newfoundland. I have a mind that thinks and ponders too much. I have legs to walk me around and around the hut, to the great annoyance of the other men.

Horsfall is always going in and out, and counting stocks of food, and trying and balancing tools in the palm of his hand, but I do not see him doing much actual work yet. Young Martin follows Horsfall around with eyes full of interest and awe. Young Martin watches everything that Horsfall does, so he, too, has done little work.

William Durdle is finding his vocation as our house-keeper, sweeping and cleaning our hut, and trying to stuff earth into all the holes and gaps in the walls and roof through which the wind and rain come. When I wake up in the morning before anyone has opened the door and the inside of the hut is still dark, the light shines in through all the innumerable chinks and apertures, so that it is like a clear night with thousands of stars shining over us.

Peter Slade is making lists of tasks. He is an orderly man. He worried me by begging some paper, and I tore some leaves out of this book to give him. I asked him if he needed a pen, although I did not want to lose one.

"Thank you, Father, but I use this."

He showed me a sort of short black stick which he normally uses to mark the wood in the place where he must cut it. When he writes with it on my paper, he forms the words rapidly and skillfully, although his black stick makes only rough and feathery letters. His ability to write worries me. Surely he cannot read Latin. I do not believe so, because he looks as bored, frightened, and baffled by the Latin words of the Mass as any of the winter crew.

Holy Gilbert does whatever he is told to do, which is whatever nobody else wants to do. It is true that he prays to himself constantly, but I can rarely make out the words, which are often Latin prayers that do not seem to fit the day or his mood.

Another day has passed. I write little because I do little. The men do not exert themselves much, either, by comparison to the labours which they performed during the fishing season. I used to enjoy watching them expertly gutting and splitting the codfish. They do it so fast, and with an swift easy motion which reveals how many years of practice they must have had.

If my congregation is bemused by the Latin of the Mass, I am almost as equally baffled by the words in which they speak of their work. They talk to me of bawns, of strouters, of drafts, and of soundbones, and if I write these words in English it is because I do not know the Latin for them. Perhaps such things were spoken of on the beach at Ostia in the days of ancient Rome, but if so their Latin names have not been recorded by the Latin writers whom I was set to study at school.

I interrupted Peter Slade in his careful making of lists.

"I know what you have to do over the winter, Peter, but what will the other men be doing?"

"Helping me to keep these huts and the fish flakes standing, and making the dories fit for next spring, under my direction."

"Is there no other work?'

"Only the hardest task of all: staying alive through the winter."

"Is it so harsh, then? I have heard stories."

"The stories are true. I have never spent a winter here before, but I have been told the stories by men whom I would trust with my life."

"Then why have you stayed? Were you forced to, like me?"

"No, I am a free man, and I have always been free, though it's cost me much in my life. I put myself forward for the winter crew."

"Why, then, if you've heard all the stories?"

I have always respected Peter Slade, but I had never feared him until then, when I saw him smile at me for the first time. "To see if the stories are true, Sir Ralph."

Two more days have passed, and I continue to learn. I know now that there is hardly any autumn season in this place. The lashing rain had bullets of ice in it this morning, and some small and hard things which stung my face like a swarm of insects. The clouds are darker and heavier, and seem to hang even lower. They pass overhead at such a speed that it is fascinating to watch them slide by. I could be watching a grey and black carpet laid out in wondrous patterns over me.

Why am I here? Is it the will of Harry Chard, fearing that I would betray him for some real or imagined treasonable opinion? Is it the will of God? Is it some condition of my service here, something that the Dominican friar omitted to explain to me when he was handing out my forty testoons? That would be just like a friar. I beg pardon: that is prejudice. Priests, monks, and friars: each class thinks that the other two lead an easy life and are all corrupt.

Has one of these men been left behind to watch me? I realise all of a sudden how easy it would be for them to murder me and to tell my father that I had died of cold or of some disease. Still, they would have done it by now rather than feed me through the winter. I should not be suspicious without cause.

This afternoon, during a break from rain and sleet, I went back into the forest. It is gloomy now for lack of light. We never see the sun and the overpowering rushing clouds steal most of its light from us.

I went back to the place where I had found the tracks. I knew that none of the winter crew had been into the forest since the fleet sailed away, and any fresh marks could not have been left by one of our men.

There was the smell of cold in the damp air, and there were no colours. Even the green of the trees seemed black, their trunks were grey, and the ground was made of black rock and grey mud. I had to kneel in the dim light to examine the tracks in the wet mud. I was sure that I could make out fresh ones, but what did it mean? Had the unknown people who might live in the forest been watching us? Harry Chard had assured me that none of the voyages to this particular anchorage had ever met any of the native people. That might hardly be wondered, if they knew the story of their three compatriots who had been carried off across the ocean and never returned.

It occurred to me that perhaps they were watching me at that very moment. I have been taught that those who live in forests are cunning at hiding themselves.

I stood up and shouted, "Hullo!" There was not even an echo; my voice was absorbed into that mysterious silence that somehow conquered all noise. I shouted "*Salve!*" and "*Pax vobiscum!*" in the hope that they had heard the one common language of all Christian people, except for the Greek heretics. I tried keeping silent, in case I could hear any movement around me, but there was nothing, and yet it was a nothingness that seemed not be empty, just as the silence was full of the sounds of the wind and the sea and the flailing branches of the trees.

I decided that if the people were there, they would reveal themselves to me if they chose. I certainly could not find them in the vastness of the forest, and if I tried I would only become so lost that the winter crew would never find me and I would die in the ice and snow which were soon coming.

I returned to the hut. The days were already ending early, and the hut was black against the cloudy evening sky. I had difficulty finding the door, but when I entered there was enough illumination from the fire and the feeble rushlights for me to see my six companions reclining on their crude bunks like Roman diners at an Epicurean feast. The feast was in fact being prepared: salt codfish, with a few vegetables that William Durdle had managed to grow in the thin and grudging soil.

I stood by the fire to warm myself and dry my cloak. Nobody spoke. I had the impression that I had interrupted a conversation in which my participation was not wanted. The rushlights lit up little more than themselves, but I knew we could not afford any better source of light. Candles are a luxury which are reserved for my altar. My supply of candles must last me until the spring.

I could tolerate the darkness, but not the silence. I could hear the wind outside, and the sea, and it struck me that the silence inside the hut had the same mysterious quality as the silence in the forest. I had to speak.

"Have any of you ever met the people who live here?"

"Nobody lives here," Horsfall replied out of the shadows. "The fishing fleet goes home, and the winter crew don't live here."

"I don't mean Englishmen. I mean the people who have always lived here in Newfoundland."

Holy Gilbert leapt in to show off his knowledge.

"Father Fletcher means the savages. They live by hunting. There are bears and catamounts and other beasts in the land."

"Yes, I do mean them. Have any of you met them?"

The silence fell again, so I had to continue the conversation myself.

"I take it that none of you has. Well, I would like to meet them."

"They are savage brutes," Peter Slade remarked.

"How do you know, if you've never met them?"

"I know what others have told me, and there are those three men in Westminster Palace. Everyone says the same about them. They grunt, and tear at their meat. Their behaviour is like that of wild beasts."

"How can we judge them," I cried, "when it was we, Englishmen acting in our name, who took them by force and carried them away from Newfoundland? What must they say about us, when they're talking with each other?"

Peter Slade tossed a fish tail into the fire, a little triangular speck of darkness flying like a weapon into the flames.

"There are plenty of Englishmen who behave like beasts. I don't need to come to Newfoundland to meet brutal men."

I wondered what he was talking about. He could not mean the fishing crews, because there were no worse than any other men of their kind. I take confession, and although I am forbidden to write of what I hear, I am confident that I am an expert on sin and unChristian behaviour.

I searched for a place to sit in the darkness. As I looked round the hut, it seemed at first that every corner had a face staring out of it, either the colour of the fire which illuminated it, or faint green like an old statue where only the glow of the rushlights fell. I nearly panicked, and suppressed an impulse to count the faces. There should be only six in the hut with me, but for a mad moment there seemed more, and like a foolish innocent I felt a pang of terror that there were more faces, too many faces, and that if there were more than six faces looking at me out of the shadows then some of them could not be human.

I forced myself to look again. In spite of my will, I could not help counting the faces: William Durdle, Holy Gilbert, Horsfall, Young Martin, Peter Slade, and Tom Rudge. Six human faces, all bearing the record of human sin, although Holy Gilbert and Young Martin show fewer marks of it. No grinning demons were lurking in the hut, and certainly no angels.

William Durdle spoke to me.

"Over here, Sir Ralph. I've made a couple of benches for us to sit on. Come and sit between me and Holy Gilbert."

As I shuffled over, afraid to trip over something, I wondered why Peter Slade our ship's carpenter had not made the bench. I suppose he felt it was beneath him as a master of his craft.

I eased myself down between the friendly faces of William Durdle and Holy Gilbert. On the opposite side of the hut, the other four men looked back at us. I thought to myself in apprehension that the whole autumn and winter would be spent like this, three of us sitting on a bench exchanging stares with the other four sitting on the other bench. We shall all go mad, I thought. Perhaps you have to be made to come forward for the winter crew; but then I did not come of my own free will, so I must be the only sane one here.

That made me laugh, and I could not stop until I ran out of breath. Every face in the hut now bore an expression of concern. They were all asking themselves whether I was the first one to go mad, and so soon; the season was not yet winter, and the day had not yet reached sunset. The darkness inside the hut was not yet the darkness of night. Perhaps they had laid bets on who would be the first one to lose his wits. If so, nobody had confessed it to me yet.

Once again Peter Slade took command.

"What is so funny, Father Fletcher? Tell us so we can laugh too. We'll need all the amusement we can find in these next months."

"You wouldn't understand, Peter."

"You may believe that I am an untutored man who has never gone to school, but I am not stupid."

"I didn't mean it in that way, Peter. I just meant that it wouldn't seem funny to you. Anyway, you're not an untutored man. You can read and write."

I had said the wrong thing. The other men all turned to him with interest, and I realised that they had not understood that the marks which he made on paper were writing. I imagine that they thought the writing was some set of symbols used by carpenters. No doubt numbers, letters, and symbols all look alike to the illiterate.

Peter Slade glowered at them all, and then focused his anger on me.

"What if I can read and write?"

"What indeed?" I replied foolishly, baffled for an answer. He had lied in telling us that he had never gone to school, and I had inadvertently shown up the lie. Why had he lied, and why was he so angry?

Peter Slade said nothing, and as I did not know what to say I kept silent too. I knew that this would not be the end of the matter, because the other men would behave differently to him now that they had found out that he could read and write. I would see him differently as well. Who had taught him his letters? Why was it a dangerous secret?

I remembered the Fishing Admiral's strange words about Gloucester, which had also frightened me. Perhaps there was no connection, but I was becoming more convinced that there was much hidden from me, including the real reason why I had been left behind with the winter crew.

William Durdle passed me some salted codfish and cabbage. I muttered a quick Grace and ate the meal. Young Martin gave me a little beer, which I drank gratefully, suspecting that the supply would run out soon and beer would be remembered as a wonderful luxury.

The winter crew, by tradition which had grown up and become inflexible custom in the few years in which there had been winter crews, rationed their drink carefully, so that there was never enough to get drunk on.

There are only two ways to pass the time in such confinement. Since drunkenness was not available to us, we had to make to with the other method, which was story-telling.

Tom Rudge sat up sharply, in that sudden surprised manner of his.

"Evening and autumn have set in, the autumn of the day and the evening of the year. It's time for stories. Who's got a good story?"

"Let's have a tale of yours, Tom," Horsfall suggested. "You're the oldest man here. You must have heard the most stories."

"I have, so I would like to hear a new tale from one of you."

For myself, I would have liked to hear Peter Slade tell the tale of how he had been schooled, but it was no time to make dangerous jokes.

Peter turned my clumsy questioning back upon me. "Father Fletcher must know some stories than none of us have heard. He reads Latin."

"Greek, Hebrew and French, too," I said, and immediately regretted it, because it sounded like a boast. I was only luckier than these men, to have been given a schooling, and not more clever. In another family, I might have become a fisherman, too.

At least if my father had been a fisherman he might not have declared himself so ashamed of me so often. I am one of the few of my station who has been able to study Greek and Hebrew, and to read the Scriptures in the original. That is simply good luck as well. Sometimes I consider myself to be an unfortunate man, and sometimes I consider myself to be extraordinarily lucky.

"Give us a story from another language, then," Tom Rudge said.

I knew I had to grant their request, to show that I felt myself to be one of them, just another member of the winter crew.

I decided to give them a Greek story, and as they waited I heard the roar of the sea again through the walls of the hut. There must be a storm out beyond the coast, and I offered a prayer in my thoughts for the fishing fleet which had left us a few days before, and was now in shelterless open ocean. The sea made me think of the Odyssey, so I resolved to tell them the story of Odysseus and the sirens who lured men to their deaths by their beautiful songs.

The four men opposite me slipped off their bunks and sat on the bench like schoolboys, or like drinkers in a tavern.

Young Martin interrupted me.

"So why was he not lured by them as well?"

"Patience, Martin. I will tell you the end in good time. When the Mystery Plays are played in the streets over a whole day, do you ask to know the whole story from the beginning?"

Peter Slade spoke before young Martin could answer my rhetorical question.

"We already know the end of every Mystery Play!"

"Well, you do not know the end of this one."

I tried to order the story in my mind as if it were a homily which I were preaching. I do not know if my priest's training was intended to help me with this, but it did. I explained the attraction of the sirens, and how Odysseus was desperate to hear them.

"Odysseus ordered his men to tie him to the mast, and then to stop their ears with wax so they could hear nothing. When this was done, they rowed the ship past the rock of the sirens. When Odysseus heard the magical beauty of their songs, he twisted and struggled in his bonds, and cried to his sailors to set him free so that he could jump off the ship and swim to the sirens, but because they could not hear him they kept rowing until they were past the danger. That was how he heard the song of the sirens while preserving his life and those of his men."

I stopped, and waved my empty beer cup at Tom Rudge.

"How was my Greek story?"

"I hope you have others," Tom replied politely.

Young Martin frowned.

"Odysseus heard the sirens, then, in safety."

"That's right. That's the point of the story."

"But," Young Martin persisted, "his men did not."

"No, Martin. Their ears had been stopped to prevent them hearing, so that they could row the ship."

"It's not fair," Young Martin declared. "The captain heard the beautiful songs of the sirens, but the common sailors did not."

"If they had heard the songs, they would have fallen into the sirens' trap. They would have abandoned the ship and the voyage would have been lost."

That reminded me of our ships out there hundreds of miles away in the storm. I offered up another prayer for them.

Young Martin was not satisfied.

"It would have been better if nobody had heard the sirens."

"I have told the tale," I said. "Judge it as you will."

Young Martin slumped on the bench, and nearly fell off it, making Holy Gilbert and Tom Rudge laugh. Peter Slade and William Durdle took no notice, but Horsfall sprang forward to steady Young Martin and make sure that he had not hurt himself.

William Durdle lifted his mug to me in salute, though I am sure that it was already empty.

"Well done, Sir Ralph. I asked you for a story and you have told us one, and a good one, very apt for us in the winter crew."

"How?" I asked, not seeing the connection.

"Because we have all heard the sirens, or we would not be here when everyone else has sailed home. We have all heard a beautiful song, in a different voice, but a song aimed at each man to convince him that he should sit out the winter in Newfoundland and find out what luck that brings him."

I had to disagree with him.

"I didn't hear any beautiful song," I said. "No sirens sang to me. I didn't know I was going to have to stay."

Peter Slade took me up on that.

"You don't, Father Fletcher. You can go."

"How? The last ship has sailed."

"You could leave in the opposite direction, inland. You could walk."

"Walk where? There's nothing in the interior of Newfoundland. No Englishman ever goes there. Where would I find food and shelter?"

"The natives live there."

"I don't know where to find them, and I don't know whether they would take me in. You tell me that they're like brute beasts who eat rough meat. I prefer salted cod-fish and vegetables. What's more, I have a duty to stay. I am your priest. I have been ordered to minister to you."

"You've been paid to minister to us," Peter Slade reminded me.

"Just so. That is my trade, just as you have been paid to work at carpentry."

"I have not been paid forty testoons for my carpentry."

Did everyone in the winter crew know everything about me? I decided to try an attack.

"I'm not going to wander away into the endless forest to die of starvation and cold, or be mauled to death by a catamount. If you want to kill me, you'll have to find another way."

The conversation ended there. Peter Slade and I made an agreement with our eyes to go no further. I could not tell whether he had been impressed by my hint that there was a plot against me, but if there was, I was sure that he was part of it.

William Durdle intervened to make the atmosphere in the dark hut less suspicious and threatening. He was our man for solving problems, and he seemed to have taken it upon himself to assist our survival by making sure that we maintained peace and good fellowship among us until the spring. That should have been my task as their priest and pastor, I remembered, and I was ashamed.

The next morning, Tom Rudge was the first to open the door of the hut, and was almost knocked back by a stroke of sunshine. He gestured towards the light with an expansive wave of his arm, as if it were a wonderful trick of skill that he had performed himself for our amazement and delight.

We all stumbled out into the warmth and brightness. I breathed in the air. Because the forests of Newfoundland seem to be made nearly all of evergreen trees, there were no yellow leaves or bare branches to tell us that the season was autumn.

I could not help crying out.

"Thank you, Lord, for this last gift of summer!"

Horsfall was standing at my shoulder.

"How do you know that God has given it specially for us?"

"He hasn't. It's to be enjoyed by everyone."

Young Martin came up behind me as well.

"It must be for us. We're the only Englishmen in Newfoundland."

I was outraged at this arrogance, even from a simple man like Young Martin. "What about the natives? They live here too."

"They're heathens who don't know God."

"That's not their fault.

Young Martin went on in one of his peculiar streams of logic.

"Well, how do we know that they enjoy sunshine and warmth? Perhaps they run from it. Perhaps they like gloom and cold, which is why they live here."

"Let us leave them in peace," I said, "and concentrate on accepting with gratitude this little happiness which has been given to us."

We all knew that it was probably the final sweet day of the year, before the snows came, and that we might not all live to see a warm day again. Young Martin took Holy Gilbert down to the seashore with the promise of teaching him to swim, but they both fled back to the rocks when they discovered how cold the sea was.

I remarked to William Durdle, who was a veteran sailor, that I was surprised that nobody had taught Holy Gilbert to swim before he went to sea.

"I can't swim," he told me, "and no man who can swim is a true sailor. The old belief is that if fate has chosen you to drown, it is wicked to resist, because you're cheating the sea of a sacrifice. The safety of many is bought, so we're taught, by the payment of a life to the sea from time to time."

I did not know whether I was more shocked by the revelation of this pagan belief still living on in the six-teenth Christian century, or by the sight of Young Martin and Holy Gilbert sitting completely naked on the sun-warmed granite to dry off.

I told myself, in the same tones as others had told me, to stick to my own trade. I celebrated Mass as soon as I could assemble everyone.

Holy Gilbert had the duty of ringing the bell when I elevated the Host. I lifted my arms with that soft weight upon my hands, the very lightness of the yoke of Christ, but the bell did not ring. I turned my head towards Holy Gilbert, and the bell rang shakily.

After Mass I asked Holy Gilbert to come out with me for a private talk.

"Gilbert, you must remember to ring the bell."

"Did I spoil the Mass, Father?"

"No, it is the words and the bread and the wine and the priest's consecration which make the Mass. The bell is only a decoration, but everyone expects it."

"I'm sorry, Father. I was looking at the bell and not at you. I was marvelling at it because it is so pretty and makes such a cheering sound. What is it made of?"

I realised how God had guided his innocent questions.

"It was a present from my father," I told him, and I added with a heavy heart, "and it is made of silver."

Chapter Three

Now I too held the bell up to my eyes. It was simply crafted, and somehow there was a decadent beauty in its very simplicity and lack of decoration. It served its purpose well: when Holy Gilbert rang it it made a sweet, youthful sound. It was the sound that would be made by a bell rung by an angel.

I walked out of the shadows into the sunshine and held the bell out in a beam of light, where it flashed back the sun so that I could not look at it.

Holy Gilbert was baffled and impressed.

"What are you doing with it, Father?"

"Nothing, Gilbert. I am merely admiring it. Perhaps it is too beautiful, and the sound it makes is too sweet and holy and perfect."

Holy Gilbert frowned, struggling with some great thought.

"Father, how can something be too holy? I am a simple—" he paused, frowning again—"*man*," he declared after obviously agonising on whether he was now old and grown enough to claim the title. He must never have called himself a man before. "I do not understand such things. How can holiness be sinful?"

"I don't understand that myself. You lay people think that we priests are infinitely wise and that we know and understand everything."

Holy Gilbert lost his frown and smiled as he had another thought.

"Why did your father give it to you?"

"Ah, well, Gilbert, it is the custom that when a man is ordained as a priest his family give him all the objects he will need to celebrate the Mass."

"But wouldn't the Church provide them?"

"Of course, and if he is a poor man a rich patron will give them in the name of his family. It is a pretty tradition. It is a symbol of the way in which the power to celebrate the Mass, to turn bread and wine into the body and blood of Christ, is a gift from God and not something which the new priest has earned."

Holy Gilbert frowned again as he struggled with another difficult thought.

"So you couldn't give the bell away as a gift, because it was a gift from your father?"

"Who would I give it to, Gilbert?'

Gilbert turned and trotted away. I seemed to have frightened him. I rotated the shining bell in my hands, and the movement made it ring faintly, like a live thing reminding me that it had feelings and imploring me not to hurt it.

The tinkle of the bell also reminded me what wealth I had brought to Newfoundland, silver and gold. The fishermen were all poor men, and the natives, I supposed, were even poorer. Every explorer who has landed on the shores of this new continent and its lands had put one question first to every native that he meets: where is there gold here? The poor innocents have sometimes been tortured and killed for denying any knowledge of gold, or even for not answering a question which they could not understand.

The explorers have discovered one fact through their cruelty, which is that the working of metal is unknown on this side of the ocean, except for gold. They can work gold because it is found free of any ore, and it can be worked without fire. The natives have no metal objects of any kind except for gold ornaments. They have no metal swords or spears, although they have weapons of wood and bone and sinew, living matter refashioned into instruments that hurt and kill.

Perhaps the nobility of gold is that it cannot be used to make weapons. Indeed, now that I consider it, gold is useless. I must be catching the disease of difficult thoughts from Holy Gilbert. It is worse for unholy Ralph Fletcher, ordained priest.

I am already beginning to tire of the company of the winter crew. This is a fault in me, not in them, and I knew it would happen. Dear Lord, I shall be with them for half a year until the fishing fleet returns, and then I must stay for another summer until the fleet goes home again. I still believe that this is the will of God, to teach me to deal with all types and conditions of men.

I have just caught myself thinking that I must reconcile myself to living with the winter crew, because there are no other people here in Newfoundland. Yet it is not so. Somewhere in those endless forests and among those purple hills there are people living as they have done since the Creation. If only I could find them, I could preach the Gospel to them, as the Spanish and Portuguese have done among the hot lands to the south and on the mainland of the continent.

These thoughts are dangerous. I must beware of arrogance. I picture myself remembered as the evangelist of

Newfoundland and perhaps of the lands beyond, in Cape Breton and on the mainland. It is Satan who is giving me these dreams of becoming as famous as St. Augustine, who first brought the faith to England. Even Satan does not have the power to make me believe that there will ever be a St. Ralph with his own feast day in the calendar of the Church. The first day of April would be most suitable, I suppose: All Fools' Day. My Latin name fits better, though. St. Radulphus sounds more imposing, suggesting a commanding man who could bring a whole pagan nation to Christ by the power of his presence and preaching. Alas, I am no Radulphus, but only poor Ralph Fletcher.

Three more days have passed, days of cruel rain and howling wind. I did not know that wind could make so much noise. I have never heard the like in any storm in England, and this has been no storm, merely ordinary autumn weather for Newfoundland.

I sat in the darkened hut with the winter crew. They were telling each other frightening stories of ghosts and witches, of curses and poisoned gifts. Nobody asked me for a holy or a classical story, so I wrote down a plan which I have thought of for passing these long months until the spring.

I was sent here to minister to the fishing fleet. Thanks to Harry Chard the Fishing Admiral, I must stay and minister to the six men of the winter crew as well. (Only six men, half the number of Christ's disciples. Well, that is fair, for I judge myself to be only half a man.)

I may never become St. Radulphus, Apostle to the natives of Newfoundland, with my statue in a thousand churches on this land, and pious women kneeling before it to ask my intercession with the Lord to obtain them favours or relief from suffering. Nevertheless, I have decided that it is my duty to try to establish contact with the natives, and to hope that God will guide me so that I can somehow communicate with them.

Sometimes the tale-teller of the moment would fall silent, watching my goose quill frantically scratching across the paper.

"What are you writing, Sir Ralph?" Tom Rudge asked once.

"Thoughts of my own so that I can arrange them properly."

"Must thoughts be written? I have been thinking all my life without ever having to write."

"These thoughts are only half-thought, confused, like a house or tree seen through a fog. I need to wipe the fog away to see what they mean and what I must do."

"You're saying that this does not concern us."

"No, it doesn't, but I don't mean that churlishly."

"It's we who are the sons of churls. You are a gentleman."

"So my father is always telling me," I replied before I could stop myself. "He wants us to become lords. Being gentlemen is not good enough for him."

Tom Rudge pondered that for a moment, with his face set in that serious and conscientious expression for which I always admire him.

His next words took me completely by surprise.

"Sir Ralph, are you an only son?"

"Yes, I am. I have a sister, but—"

"Your father is disappointed that his name will not be carried forward, and so it will never become noble."

"That's true. He is disappointed in me. I try to explain to him that I did not choose to become a priest, and that it was the priesthood that was chosen for me, but he cannot accept it."

Holy Gilbert intervened unexpectedly from the floor, where he was lying on his belly, kicking his legs up in the air behind him like a little boy.

"Yet your father gave you wonderful gifts for the Mass. The cup, the bell—"

"These gifts are expected from a priest's family, by tradition, if they have the means. Oh, my father could have refused to give me them, but my father knows what is expected of him."

Peter Slade knew what to say to discomfit me.

"You have not given your father what he expected of you."

"No, he wanted me to become a courtier, to make a marriage to a family higher than our own, and to give him sons. None of these things can happen now."

Tom Rudge tried to console me.

"Your sister might yet make a good marriage, and give your father grandsons to make him happy."

"My sister cannot marry. She is an unusual child. I cannot speak about her."

My sister, too, was a disappointment to my father, but at least even he cannot attach any blame to her. I still think of her as a child, and perhaps I always will, because in her mind she will always remain one. She cannot even talk, although she plays with her toys, and although my father keeps her hidden away I believe that she is a treasure. She is so loving and friendly to me.

My sharp words to the men about my sister made them stop questioning me. I took up my pen to start writing again, but when I looked down at the paper I saw that I had no need to write any more words. The plan was finished, written out of some secret place in my spirit while I was hardly aware that I held the pen.

The next morning I wrapped myself in two cloaks and pulled a fur hat down onto my head, and went out into the cold still sunny morning after Mass.

I took my usual path into the woods, taking care to look behind me every few steps to make sure that I did not become lost in the endless forests where nobody might ever find me. Even though I was walking slowly, I was panting from the cold. How long would it be before the snows came?

Finally, after I gone about a mile into the trees, I stopped at the place where I believed I had seen tracks in the mud. I thrust my hand into the tight folds of my cloaks and drew out the silver Mass bell.

When I rang it the sound was astonishing in that silence. I had only ever heard it rung in the Mass, either gently by myself, or reverently by Holy Gilbert. I could have believed that the shock of the noise would be enough to bring the trees crashing down in all directions around me. I seized the clapper to silence the bell, and stood startled by guilt.

Although there were no echoes in that place of wood and starved grass, the aggressive stroke of sound still hung in the air, or perhaps it was only in my own ears, or even yet only in my timid soul. It was, after all, only a little silver Mass bell, and if someone had rung it in a London street nobody would even have noticed it. The difference was the silence, the strange silence of Newfoundland that mysteriously managed to exist in all the noise of wind and sea.

I made sure once again that I knew where I was and that I could find my way back to the shore where the fish flakes and the huts were all we possessed of England. I wondered if any of my companions would have heard the bell over the crash of the sea against the rocks.

If there were truly any natives within a mile of me, they would certainly have heard my bell. What unknown silversmith had performed the perfectly inappropriate feat of making a Mass bell that was so loud? Well, I told myself, I had rung the bell to attract the attention of the natives, so I would try again.

This time I rang the bell hard, and let the clapper strike again and again, for all the world as if I were a seller in the marketplace hawking goods off a stall, instead of a priest using a bell which had been made to announce the moment when bread became the Body of Christ.

I searched into the distance among the trees. The wind blew the branches to and fro like curtains across an open window. The movement of the branches confused my eyes, but suddenly I saw a movement, a flying hint of black and greyish-yellow.

In spite of the wind, I was overcome by an inner stillness so complete that for a moment I seemed to cease to exist, like a mathematical point upon which converged both the sound and light and the hardness of the rocks on which I stood.

"Hullo!" I called. "Will you come here?"

There was no answer, but there was another movement among the trees, slower this time. This time I was sure that the black blur that I glimpsed was a head of flowing black hair, and that the greyish-yellow was a garment; the colour was both animal and somehow not animal.

I scanned the trees, looking to right and left and back again, desperate not to miss any sight which might present itself. Another movement caught my eye amid the green of the branches and the gloom of the tree trunks, but, maddeningly, when I looked again my eyes could not find the point at which I had seen—something. What?

I saw it again, one of those unidentifiable, unknow-
able, indescribable things which one sees from the corner
of one's eyes, those sights which have no name or shape or
colour that one can recall, and yet which one knows to be
real, like an idea in philosophy.

"Please," I called, in my most friendly and conciliato-
ry voice, in the manner which we priests use when accost-
ed by a parishioner who one would prefer to go away. "I
won't hurt you. I'm not a hunter, or a fisherman. Look, I
have no weapons."

I held out my hands, but of course I did hold a
weapon, without knowing it: the little silver bell. I realised
my mistake at once, and thrust the bell into my robes.
These people had no metal of their own; what had they
seen of English metal except knives, arquebuses, swords
and pikes: objects made to hurt and kill.

I offered my bare, giftless hands again.

"Please show yourself. I'm alone."

A great wonder then presented itself to me: a human
face, sliding warily out between the trees as though from
behind a curtain. The face was brown, like the faces carved
on the wood of churches, and as fixed in expression.
Suspicious, questioning dark eyes regarded me from under
straight black hair.

I stepped one pace forward.

The face vanished behind the trees, and then showed
itself again. It occurred to me that the native might not be
alone. There might be crowds of them hidden among the
trees, armed, and with good reason not to love English
fishermen.

I dared to take another step forward. If I were facing
implacable armed natives, I was lost anyway.

The face watched me again, and then the native slid out from among the tree trunks and came forward, a dozen yards in front of me.

We studied each other with curiosity and fear.

I saw now for certain that the native was a young man.

His garments, a long smock and trousers, were made of skins and decorated with dots and irregular lines of red and brown. The wind blew into my face, bringing me a smell of beasts which could have come either from the man's clothing or from himself. Perhaps I had offended his nose in the same way when I had been upwind.

"I am Ralph Fletcher," I told him, and pointed to myself. "Ralph Fletcher." Thus I began my ministry to the natives of Newfoundland. Well, how else could I start? Was I to begin by expounding the doctrine of the Trinity, in English, or by setting out the meaning of the Paschal Lamb, in Latin? Even Our Lord Himself began simply, by saying "Follow me."

The man made no answer, but then he astonished me by raising his left sleeve to his face and smelling it furiously. I did the same, in case this was a gesture of courtesy among these people. He barked a sound which I heard as "Aguthut," and then he said "Bettook." Was this his name? Was he telling me to go away? I had spent many years under the lash in schools, and years more in training for the priesthood, but nobody had taught me what to do in the situation in which I found myself.

The man did not seem to be carrying any weapon, although he might be hiding one in his smock. I could see both his hands, and they were empty. I noticed how brown his hands were, and how lined and wrinkled they were, even though he was not old.

I pointed to myself.

"Ralph Fletcher," and, after a pause, "English."

"Ralph Lecher," the man replied, with a surprisingly good pronunciation, even if he had given only one letter 'f' to my name. I am guilty of many sins, but Ralph the Lecher I am not.

"Aguthut," I said, hoping that was his name.

"Aguthut," he agreed, and I decided to assume it was his name although I knew that it might really be an observation on the windiness of the weather that day, or an unfavourable comment upon the morals of my relatives.

I held out my hand to him.

"Well met, Aguthut."

Aguthut, if that was indeed his name, seemed not to know why I had stretched out my hand to him. He stared at it.

I dared to come forward so as to be close enough to touch him. He swayed back, cautious and fearful, but remained standing on the same spot. I was still holding out my empty hand, and he looked down at it, seeming baffled, and angry at something. Why? I was not threatening him with a weapon.

I dropped my hand, and slowly put it into my tunic, where the little silver bell was hidden like a fugitive animal. I grasped the bell, made warm by the touch of my body, and withdrew it, slowly again, so that Aguthut would not fear that I was taking out a weapon.

"Here, Aguthut," I said. "I will present you with a gift. Take this bell."

I offered him the bell in my open hand. He looked down at it, and then looked up into my eyes, before looking down at my hand again.

He reached out for the bell. Before he could take it, I turned it with my fingers so that I could take it by the handle. I shook it gently, and the bell gave a merry little tinkle. I have always loved Mass bells; they bring such a welcome shock of joy and lightness into the proper solemnity of the service.

Aguthut swayed again. I wondered if he were afraid, but determined to stand his ground to show that he had no fear of me.

"Take it," I said. "Take it simply as a beautiful thing which makes a sweet sound. One day I hope that you will understand what it is and what it was made for."

Aguthut took the bell with a stiff hand. He moved his arm to left and right, making the bell tinkle faintly, and then he turned the bell over and over in his brown hands.

All at once he wrapped his hand around the bell, turned away from me, and shot into the trees. He vanished so quickly that I could not even tell which direction he had taken, and I could hear no sound of someone moving into the forest. He had gone as instantly as a vision, but I knew that Aguthut Bettook had been real, because I no longer had the Mass bell. In the same way, he knew that Ralph Fletcher, now perhaps doomed to be known unjustly as Ralph Lecher, was real because he held the bell as a token of me.

I was left alone in the wind, and a splash of unbearably cold rain caught me in the face. It was a sign that the incident was over, and I began walking back to our hut.

I was completely wet when I opened the door and came into the firelit warmth of the hut. Horsfall was bent over the fire, and he had been shouting something at the terrified Holy Gilbert, but the shouting stopped as soon as Horsfall noticed that I had come in. I know that I am seeing little of the life and interactions of the winter crew, in spite of hearing their confessions.

As I was shaking out my wet clothes, Tom Rudge spoke to me out of the corner.

"Where have you been, Sir Ralph?"

"Out into the forest."

"What were you doing there?"

His manner was so peremptory that I became angry. Who was he to question me? I might have no practical skills, and I would certainly die on the coast of New-foundland if these lowborn men did not look after me, but I was Tom Rudge's priest and entitled to respect for my office if not for myself.

"I went to meet a friend."

"A friend? We have no friends here in this land."

"Perhaps you don't, but I have found one. I have gained something and I have lost something," I added for the pleasure of mystifying him.

"What do you mean by that?" Horsfall demanded.

"Let me do my writing first," I said. I took out a pen and sat down by the fire to sharpen it, letting the tiny frag-ments of the quill drop into the fire, each discarded speck achieving an exquisitely short moment of glory as the glow of the flames turned it into a golden-red falling point of starlight.

I spent an hour writing out the events of the day. When at last I put away my pen, my book, and my inkhorn, I realised that the winter crew had all sat watch-ing me, as though a man writing in a book were some great entertainment or a fascinating mystery.

Tom Rudge still wanted to pursue me.

"Tell us where you have been, Father."

"Out into the forest. I told you that."

"Why?"

"Before I went, I could not have explained it, but now I know that I was sent there by God. I went among the trees and met my friend there."

Horsfall, who is less intelligent than Tom Rudge, and also less subtle and less patient, could not wait any longer.

"Who is this friend? Why are you playing with us, Father? You are meant to be our guide, the man who explains things to us, but you are casting more darkness than light upon us."

"I believe that his name is Aguthut, perhaps Aguthut Bettook, but then his people may be called the Bettook as we are called the English."

Tom Rudge now forgot his cunning approach, and attacked me as bluntly as Horsfall had done.

"A native? There are no natives near out settlement. You have met an Englishman, and there is a plot against us."

"As far as I know, we are the only Englishmen in Newfoundland," I said. "I met a native, and I have been trying to befriend him."

Horsfall cried out when he heard that.

"If there are natives here, we must hunt them down, or we will never be safe. They're all thieves and savages."

"That's true," Young Martin agreed from the shadows.

"How do you know?" I asked him. "This is your first winter in Newfoundland. You know no more about the natives than I do. Indeed, I know more, because I have met one and you have not."

Young Martin set his face in a sneer.

"What do you know of the life of men, Father?"

I had never known Young Martin to show disrespect to me before, at least not to my face. I ignored his question, and began sharpening my pen again.

Peter Slade our ship's carpenter, a man who normally has few words except curses for Holy Gilbert when he is clumsy at some task he has been set, surprised us by adding something to our uncomfortable conversation.

"I have been told to keep a close watch on all our possessions and the fishing gear. That's why we're spending the winter here in Newfoundland. The natives will pick up anything and take it away, because they are too lazy to make it for themselves. Many men from the fishery have warned me about it."

"Perhaps they see us as picking up and taking away their fish," I suggested.

Tom Rudge took command of the discussion, as he usually does.

"There is plenty of fish here for everyone. There will never be a   shortage of fish in the seas around this land. I have only one question. Are you sure that the man you met was a native?"

"Of course," I answered in astonishment. "He was a brown man, with long shiny black hair, and clothes made of skins. He did not even smell like an Englishman."

Tom Rudge slipped in another question at once.

"Did he support the House of Tudor or the House of York?"

"If he ever finds out about them, I will be sure to ask his allegiance," I replied. "You will have to question me more cleverly than that to catch me out, Master Rudge. I have been trained in philosophy and logic, and the arts of disputation."

Horsfall sneered at me.

"You despise us poor fishermen who have never been to school. We practise disputation with weapons or fists."

"And how often do you establish the truth that way? I have been equipped with weapons more powerful than swords or muscles. Tom, I am not a Yorkist conspirator, as you continue to believe. If I were, and I wanted to restore the line of Richard of York, I cannot think of a less likely place from which to do it than a hut on the barren coast of Newfoundland."

Tom Rudge said nothing to that, and neither did Horsfall. I looked at Horsfall expectantly, but he remained silent, and I noticed that he was sitting next to Young Martin. Those two always seemed to be together.

None of us knew what to say, but Holy Gilbert solved the problem by bringing in some salt fish and cabbage, our usual meal, and he began to prepare our supper.

I made a point of saying a long and elaborate Grace, in English. I did not explain why the Grace was in English. The men were all startled and worried, fearing that a Grace in English rather than Latin was not valid, or was perhaps even sinful. I committed a sin myself in doing it only for the amusement of shocking and worrying them. I worry that as the winter progresses, with little variety of food, it will become more and more difficult to give thanks to God yet again for more cabbage and salt cod.

After supper, I busied myself cleaning my portable altar, and all the items of my trade. It was odd not have my little silver Mass bell, and I felt pain at the loss, but it is up to God whether I ever see the bell again. That is how I will know whether I am really serving some greater purpose here in Newfoundland than simply ministering to the spiritual needs of the winter crew, although God knows (and that is not an impious oath, but the truth), He certainly knows, that their spirits need Him more than most men do.

People think of priests as unworldly, but we are taught a great deal about sin during our training, so that we can recognise it and advise the poor repentant sinner. In spite of what Aguthut says, I am not Ralph Lecher, but I know about lechery even though I have no experience of it.

I know about other sins which is it would be unseemly to name here in this journal, some of which I could not have imagined. Priests like myself who are innocent (that is, with little knowledge of the world, not innocent in the sense of unsinful) know sin as we know the night sky. We know that the Sun, Moon, and planets orbit around the Earth, and that all of them (except the Sun and Moon) also turn in a circle as they travel, but we have never visited the planets or the stars which are fixed on the inside of the blue celestial sphere which surrounds us. In the same way, we know of terrible crimes and perversions which men commit, without having to commit them ourselves.

Lord, help me among these men. I know so much from books, and so little of life. I understand many languages, but I do not understand men.

Chapter Four

In the last few days I have almost forgotten Aguthut the Bettook. My thoughts have all been upon England, and how the affairs of England impose themselves upon our rude life here far away in Newfoundland.

The first sign was an increase in the amount of muttering and whispering, of secretive conclaves at the edge of the forest. The unrelenting wind blew men's words away so that I could not hear them from where I stood.

The second sign was when I came upon Peter Slade the ship's carpenter with all the other men gathered around Tom Rudge and himself as though they were two Masters of a university surrounded by their students.

Peter Slade held a wooden board upright with his left hand, while his right hand gestured and danced across the board as he explained something that was written or drawn upon it. While he was pointing to one spot on the board and then to another, Tom Rudge was speaking.

The other men wore the faces of schoolboys desperate to master some new piece of learning from a strict master who they know will whip them if they do not grasp it.

All the winter crew were concentrating so fiercely on the great mystery being expounded to them that they did not notice me coming round the corner of the hut.

As I peered at the puzzling array of lines and words scratched upon the board, Peter Slade saw me and turned the board away from me with a lightning turn of the wrist like a conjuror performing a trick in the streets. Perhaps that was what he had been doing.

I challenged him in the spirit of curiosity rather than belligerence.

"May I see, too, Peter?"

"This is nothing to do with you, Father," he replied, making me even more curious, a mistake which Tom Rudge would not have made.

Tom himself now intervened, while the other men looked as guilty as if I had caught them committing a shameful sin.

"Peter was explaining a point of carpentry, that's all. He is our carpenter. You are our priest."

"Why are you so aggressive about hiding a carpentry lesson from me? Well, you will tell me that it is none of my business, which is true, unless it involves a sin or something else unChristian."

"Some might say that your interest in other men's affairs is unChristian," Horsfall said, and Young Martin giggled in approval.

"Well, well," I replied, "I have read much in books and heard much in lectures at university, but I have never heard of so much touchiness and dispute over a question of carpentry before. I have heard learned men dispute ancient questions of philosophy and theology with less passion."

Because they were clearly going to tell me nothing, I turned and left them.

As I walked round the corner of the nearest hut, I heard a clack as Peter Slade turned the mysterious board round again. Whatever is scratched on it is not some instructions for fitting pieces of wood together. Perhaps I will hear about it in confession, but if so I shall neither be able to speak nor to write about it.

The men are still all outside while I write this. When I have finished with bringing my notes up to date, I shall have to mend my black gown, which has a hole in it where a burning piece of wood fell upon it from the fire. Perhaps it is some kind of omen, although we are forbidden to believe in omens.

It may only be another symptom of the harshness of our life. One hole in a gown is of no account, but if I survive until the spring all my clothes may be patched and torn, and myself thin and even paler than a bookish priest usually is. When our captain Harry Chard returns, he may find me the ragged chaplain of a band of ragged Christians; but perhaps it was always so in the apostles' time. Were they not, too, fishermen and carpenters? Would Jesus have chosen me?

My words are written, my gown is mended, and the snow is falling. There is a new wonder, which I discovered when I opened the door to look: the wind has stopped.

I closed the door again quickly, because the snowflakes were trying to force their way inside like the angry wasps of summer. The men have not come back, in spite of the snow. They must be sheltering with the upturned boats which Peter Slade is repairing, when he is not drawing strange signs upon wooden boards.

I want to go out in the snow, but there is nobody for me to tell that I am going out. If I am lost and never heard of again, let these writings so far be my testament and my last confession, a few thousand words of black ink whereby I can be judged by God and men and my old Latin teacher from Winchester College, if he is still alive, and if he can still wield a birch upon boys' bare bottoms.

Well, now I can declare that I am not lost or dead; I live on. My cloak is drying by the fire, and I am sitting so close to the flames that I can write by firelight.

Horsfall and Young Martin were in the hut when I came back. Tom Rudge must have continued his mysterious lesson, because Horsfall looks thoughtful, a rare mood for him, and Young Martin is wearing that expression of rapt understanding which means that he is baffled by something.

When I emerged from the hut, the softness of the deep snow had made it seem that I was in a great room hung with thick tapestries. It was not so much an absence of sound as an absence of echoes. I glanced over my shoulder to make sure that I could see my own tracks to be able to find the way back, and struggled through the heavy snow that snatched at my legs.

When I tried to look up at the trees, my eyes filled with snowflakes. All my life in England, I had never known that snowflakes were so heavy. Perhaps there is a different kind of snow here in Newfoundland. Truly this is a New World.

It was such hard work pushing against the snow for every step that I had to pause to catch my breath every fifty yards.

I stopped when I judged myself to be close to the place where I had met Aguthut the Bettook.

"Aguthut!" I called. "It's me, Ralph Fletcher, the man who gave you the silver bell."

As I shouted, my breath rose in clouds like smoke, the words made visible in grey swirling mist, no clearer than the Word of God sometimes is to us.

I peered through the clouds made by my own words, and saw another cloud, or rather a thin column of black smoke, lying across the blue heavens as like a rip torn in the fabric of the sky.

That was no English fire. I began to shuffle towards it, leaning to the left and then to the right so that I should not lose it when it was masked by the trees. The waters of my nose began to freeze, and the icy air hurt my lungs as though I were drowning in cold water.

I saw a strange tree that was not a tree. It was a bundle of sticks tied together, and it stuck up out of the snow. As I came closer, I saw that it was supporting a wrapping of cloth which was the same dirty brownish-grey colour as Aguthut's clothes.

I stopped for more cold painful breath. I had never realised before what a tedious and uncomfortable business it is to breathe. When I had stopped panting, I noticed again the rich silence, so profound that I leapt in surprise when it was broken by the sound of a bell.

The bell did not tinkle; it tore the forest silence with an instant sharp ring, as though it had been struck by a weapon rather than shaken by a reverent hand.

At once the silence fell again. I wondered whether I had imagined the bell. It was like awakening from a momentous dream, to find that in spite of all the events and catastrophes one had dreamt, the world has not changed, and is impossibly indifferent to the tumbling incidents of one's dream.

Yet the forest was not unchanged. From behind the structure of sticks and cloth I saw a black head emerge and then disappear, and then two more heads, and then four.

I struggled through the snow, trying to reach them, holding out my hands as if to embrace or to restrain.

"Aguthut! Don't you know me? It's Ralph Fletcher!"

By the time I had kicked and clawed my way through the cold wet snow, the people I had seen had vanished into the numberless trees. I stood gasping by their tent, which was what I now recognised the structure of cloth and sticks to be.

The material was not cloth at all, but animal skin like Aguthut's clothes. The skin stank quietly in the cold air, and the smell was a memory of summer.

I ventured to pull aside the opening of the tent and to look within. There was only a tiny fire which elves might have built, and a few bones with old grey meat on them. There were no clothes, no tools, and no sign that men had been there only a few moments before.

I squatted down beside the little fire, grateful for any heat in this cold forest. The emptiness of the tent and the strange miniature fire made me feel that I was not among the works of men, or not of men as I knew them.

The animal skin of the tent kept in the heat and stopped out the wind, but it also blocked out much more light than cloth would have done, and the flames lit up the mittens on my hand from below. Had anyone been in the tent to see me, my face would have been the face of a demon.

The snowflakes on my face melted. I risked pulling off my mittens and warmed my hands over the speck of heat which was a perfect miracle in frozen Newfoundland.

The fire must have warmed my mind as well, for I began to think. The Bettooks would certainly return to the tent, so if I could wait long enough, I would be sure to meet them. It was obvious that they feared the English, or at least the English fishermen, or they would not have run away from the precious fire into the angry snow.

I put my mittens back on, and had another thought. Perhaps it was only me that they had been fleeing from. What a strange notion; no one in my whole life had ever been afraid of me before.

I abandoned the fire in the same combination of excitement and reluctance as a hermit abandoning the human world.

Outside, I called again.

"Aguthut! Please come back! I'm alone. You know I always come alone."

Among the trees, I had glimpses of black hair covered by hoods, and then a high hoarse voice flung an unmerited insult at me.

"Lecher!"

It was an answer! I shouted back my reply. "Yes, yes, it's me, Ralph Fletcher! Please come out!"

I waved with both my arms, even though I knew they could see me.

Slowly, three yellow-grey hoods slid out from between the trees. I could see the black hair of the people, but their brown faces were downcast. They looked like penitent monks. Why would they not look up at me?

I scrambled forward through the clammy snow.

"Here, please look at me! I don't want anything from you. I have nothing to give you. I just want—"

Well, indeed what did I want from them? I was sure that they wanted nothing from me. Neither of us had any goods to buy or sell, or any useful trade to barter for another's skill in a different one. They were hunters, and I was a priest. Perhaps one of them was a priest too.

First one face turned upwards to look at me, and then the other two, slowly and in unison, as though in a ritual. I wondered if I were not unwittingly participating in some heathen rite, and once again I became conscious of the great cold and the still silence.

All at once they ran towards me, and suddenly they had seized me, and I was helpless in the strength of their arms, and gasping in the stink of their animal-hide cloth-ing.

"What?" I cried stupidly. "What?"

They wrenched me around and around, so that I slipped in the snow and would have fallen if they had not been gripping me so tightly. They lifted me up so that I was floating in the soft new snow like an angel, and one of them thrust his face into mine.

It was not Aguthut, but it might have been his broth-er. I could not judge the age of the Bettook people. They were the first people of another race that I had ever seen, except for the black folk who live in London, and who are nothing like them.

I felt hands running over me and into the folds of my clothing. The fingers were hard and strong like weapons.

I struggled to see the face. It was so close that I could see only the deep black eyes, which held both cruelty and wisdom within them. I had not known that such a combi-nation could be, and I had not known that I could feel such fear. I may be a sinner, but truly I am an innocent.

I had blundered into their encampment, roaring and calling for the Bettooks to come to me. Well, now they had.

The strong hands pulled back and rejected me. The face moved back as well, until the man stood an arm's length away. He looked around at his companions. I realised for the first time that none of them had spoken, or made any sound at all.

"I am Ralph Fletcher," I told them. "I met Aguthut, one of your race."

"*Bettook!*" a voice roared in my ear. The sound was accompanied by a puff of misty breath which billowed past my eyes like the smoke from a cannon. I saw a can-non fired once, at the Tower of London. Is London a real place, or is there only this alien world of rock and trees and snow?

"Yes, Aguthut the Bettook!" I replied, addressing myself to the man in front of me rather than to the owner of the voice behind me. If a bear could speak, it would speak like him.

The man who seemed to be first among them pointed his dirty grey mitten at me. The patterned decorations of crimson thread on it looked like veins on a monstrous deformed hand.

"*Harree*!"

"Harree? Oh, Harry, Henry! Yes, I am a subject of King Henry, English from England, across—"

I wanted to point towards the sea, but I did not know in which direction it lay. I listened for the sound of the waves breaking on the granite rocks, but all I could hear was my own breathing and the breathing of the Bettooks who surrounded me in the stillness of the snow.

"*Inglis*," the voice behind me declared, "*fissmain*."

The hands grasped me again, and I understood how I had told them the worst possible thing I could have said. They took me for an English fisherman, a class of men for whom I was sure they would bear no love. Now they thought they had an English fisherman unarmed, alone, and helpless in their power.

"No, no," I cried. "English, yes, but not a fisherman, no." I gabbled on, not reasoning whether they could understand me. "I'm a priest, a servant of King Henry, but a servant of Pope Julius, too."

My outburst must have puzzled them, but at least they took those terrifying iron hands off me.

I tried the only way I could see.

"Bring Aguthut, here, Aguthut. He knows me. I gave him a bell."

"Aguthut," the man in front of me repeated, and then he brought both his fists together and struck his own chest. "Timaskatek. Timaskatek."

"Your name is Timaskatek? I told you, I am Ralph Fletcher."

"Ralph Lecher."

I resigned myself to the fact that if these people ever remembered me in their tales and stories it would be as the strange Englishman who blundered again and again into their woods, announcing himself to all who would listen as Ralph the Lecher.

Timaskatek growled and coughed some words in their language, and the hands seized me and began pushing and dragging me towards their little tent. They flung me into it, made me sit down on the cold floor of skins and grass, and sat down in a circle around me.

I wondered if they expected me to perform a ritual. Perhaps Pope Julius could tell me whether there is a special office called a Mass for the Unconverted Heathen, but he is not here for me to ask.

They had at least had the goodness to place me next to the tiny fire. I pulled off my mittens, and held my hands over it so that my fingers were at last warm even though the rest of my body was still cold. I felt that I would never be warm again. I do not know how the Bettooks endure it, for not one of them showed any sign of discomfort.

Suddenly another hood thrust its way into the tent, and when it was pulled down it revealed the face of Aguthut.

"Aguthut, thank God you're here!" I exclaimed. "Tell them that I mean no harm. You understand that, I'm sure."

Aguthut did not even look at me. All the other men began talking to him at once in their throaty and yet musical language, like a cross between coughing and singing, rising and falling in pitch. I could not be sure whether I found it ugly or beautiful, but I knew that the conversation was about me.

Aguthut said something short in reply, and grasped my shoulder. He was so strong that he actually lifted me off the floor.

I struggled to stand up with dignity, and tried to thank him, but Aguthut still would not look at me. He hauled me out of the tent, while I clumsily put my mittens back on for fear of freezing my hands and making them useless for ever. Such things have happened in Newfoundland winters.

Aguthut forced me through the deep piled snow, and then pulled me round so that I was facing him. In my panic and confusion I speculated that this must be how Bettook men deal with each other, so I did my best to stare back at him implacably even though my eyes were smarting and my nose was running in the mercilessly freezing air.

"*Inglis!*" he spat like an insult. "*Fissman!*"

"You know our language!"

"*Inglis Fissman!*"

"English priest, Aguthut. I gave you my Mass bell."

"*Fissman, Fissman!*"

He pushed me harder, and I understood that he wanted me to come away from the tent. He drove me through the snow like a beast, and I stumbled and slipped, but Aguthut strode through the snow with ease and perfect balance.

I had thought that he would let me go as soon as we were a little way distant from the encampment, but when we reached clearer ground where the winds of the days before had blown away a path for us he came up beside me, still grasping my arm, staring forward into the trees, not once looking down to the snow or up to the sky.

Aguthut kept pushing me through the snow, until my lungs were burning with pain as I panted in the icy air. I had to keep my eyes down so as not to stumble over a rock or a tree root, and when Aguthut halted I was too exhausted and short of breath to stand straight again.

Aguthut pulled my hood up so that the winter sun struck me in the face like a blow.

"Inglis Fissman!"

I could not have been more amazed to have found that he had brought me to the gates of the Tower of London. We were no more than twenty yards from our huts, and the icicles on the fish flakes flashed and sparkled as the sunlight shone through them. Such beautiful ornaments could not have been bought at any price, for no man could have made them.

With a grunt Aguthut released me and was gone. When I turned, I saw his yellowish-grey tunic disappear towards the trees. Our clumsy progress through the snow had left tracks enough for a dozen men.

Well, the message was clear. Aguthut and the other Bettooks wanted me to remain with the English fishermen in their huts, and not to search after the Bettooks in the forest.

I could understand the Bettooks fearing the fishermen after what   fishermen had done to others of their people before in Newfoundland, but why should they be afraid of me? Did they believe that I was some sort of scout for a fishermen's hunting party, which would come hunting for Bettooks, just as Tom Rudge and Peter Slade believed that I was a Yorkist spy?

There was none of our winter crew in sight. I could do nothing but go back into our hut, hoping that I would find that most wonderful of things (or so it seemed at that moment), a warm fire.

As if to answer to my wish, as soon as I opened the door a breath of heat wiped over me, and a crown of flames danced before my eyes.

A chorus of voices called "Close the door!", I was doing it already with all possible speed and will.

I found two empty nails protruding from the walls on which I could hang my clothes and mittens to dry. All the nails placed closer to the fire had already been taken and were festooned with garments even more rude than those of the Bettooks, and smelling little better.

I stood behind the semi-circle of fishermen's backs which surrounded the fire, and held my hands out over the men's shoulders to try to make them feel and move properly again.

Peter Slade looked up at me.

"That was a short walk, Father."

"It was cold," I replied. It was not a lie, only part of the truth, and Peter had made a statement, not asked a question.

"Few men go out in such cold and in the deep snow," Peter continued, as solemnly as if the words were a scriptural text upon which he would base a homily.

"It is certainly wise to consider that before venturing away from a warm fire," I said, as pompously as he, and still holding out my poor cold hands, palms facing forward, as if I were fending off an attack.

Whatever his game might be, I intended to force him to make the first move. I was in no hurry; one may face many shortages and privations in a Newfoundland winter, but one is rarely short of time, which is in generous oversupply. A foolish verbal game of contesting wills and verbal puzzles is a good a way to use up the surplus as any other.

Peter and I might have been exchanging meaningless sentences until the spring, if Tom Rudge had not blundered in.

"Why did you go out, Father?"

The repeated mention of my title shamed William Durdle and Holy Gilbert into shuffling about on the floor, making enough room for me to sit cross-legged on the floor between them. I could almost have expected someone to pass me a garment to stitch, my own ragged black gown perhaps.

"The wind had stopped," I replied. "It struck me as a remarkable novelty in this country. I had thought that it would blow forever until we were all frozen. I simply wanted to go for a walk."

Horsfall had lost his momentary fit of respect for me, now that we were sitting together at the same level on the same rough floor. Perhaps I was not the only man sitting on that floor who was wondering whether it would be wise or polite to complain that splinters were trying to insinuate themselves into his posterior.

When Horsfall made to speak, I thought for a moment that he was going to talk about the splinters.

"We all wondered where you had gone."

"I don't concern myself with where you all are," I replied. "I had no idea that you were interested. If it had not been a clear sunny day I would never have risked it."

Holy Gilbert sprang up and knelt before the fire, pointing a shuddering finger at me.

"God was watching over you."

"God cares no more for me than He does for you," I said, "and God will not protect me from freezing or starving if I become lost in the snows because of my own folly."

"Then who will minister to us?"

"Nobody. You must save up your sins and tell them to the next priest you meet."

I noticed that a pool of water was forming on the floor and hoped that everyone would understand that it was no more than ice melting from my clothes and hair.

Now a most prodigious thing happened, unexpected by everyone including the victim: Holy Gilbert had a thought.

"Who will hear your sins, Father Ralph?"

"Another priest, unless I believe that I am dying here, when I will confess to one of you instead."

Peter Slade intervened before Holy Gilbert could bring up another uncomfortable question.

"We don't even know why you are here, Father."

"Nor do I. Harry Chard abandoned me here when the fleet sailed away. I had thought that I would go with them. My presence with the winter crew is as much of a puzzle to me as it is to you, and perhaps just as unwelcome."

"We've never told you that you weren't welcome," Horsfall protested.

"We've shared everything we have with you," his obedient companion, Young Martin, added.

"Ah, there I can correct you," I said, "because you have all kept a secret from me. You know what I mean, the mysterious board and the writing on it."

Young Martin and Tom Rudge were about to reply to that, but Peter Slade raised his pointing finger to order silence.

Once again I felt that he was treating the men like schoolboys, and for the first time I wondered whether he actually was a schoolmaster who had abandoned the classroom or been forced out of it. All at once a chill inside me balanced the winter cold from outside: was Peter Slade another priest?

I sat back and waited for his words. They might prove not to be the truth, but at least they would provide entertainment to pass the time.

"You are an educated man, Father, and the board doesn't record anything that you do not know."

"Tom Rudge said that it was a point of carpentry, and of carpentry I know nothing. I could learn something if you would instruct me in it."

"Tom is a faithful man, and I must take the blame for what he said. My lesson was not in carpentry but in history and statecraft."

"What use is history and statecraft to a crew of fishermen and carpenters on the shore of Newfoundland?"

"Father, your class of men think that history and statecraft are of no use to fishermen and carpenters in England or anywhere else. Are you not the servant of a carpenter yourself?"

"Yes, I am. I should not have said that."

Tom Rudge burst into the conversation.

"No, you should not!"

I made no reply, and Peter Slade said nothing, so Tom fell silent again in shame and confusion. The ruddy light of the flames on his face made it impossible to tell whether he had gone red or not, but he wore the uncomfortable expression of one who has thrust his head into a window and bellowed a joke or an insult only to discover that he has used the wrong window.

Peter Slade resumed his quiet battle of words with me.

"We must all remain here together until the spring. It is not right that there should be quarrels or factions between us. We are like a ship's crew—and they do call us the winter crew—and we must work together or all be lost."

"This is not in dispute," I said. "What is your point?"

"Will you make a bargain with me; or rather, with us?"

"Who are 'we'?" I asked.

"Everyone else but you."

"What is the bargain that you are offering me?"

"I will tell you everything. I will show you the board from which I teach, and I will explain the lesson to you and tell you what I have been doing here since we were first left behind by Harry Chard and the fleet."

"What am I supposed to pay you in return, assuming that I would place any value at all on what you would give me?"

"Oh, you will value it, Father. In exchange, I want you to tell us one of your stories."

"Another story? A classical one of ancient times?"

"No, Father, I want a true story, a story of today. I will reveal dangerous secrets to you. You must pay for them by revealing secrets to us. I want to know why you came to Newfoundland as our priest. There are much easier ways by which a man can earn forty shillings."

Chapter Five

"I have nothing to hide, and you would find my tale a dull one," I replied.

"Will you make the bargain?" Peter Slade persisted.

"I will."

"Young Martin! Bring me the board."

Young Martin crawled across the floor as if he could not walk, and reached under one of the crude platforms that we use as beds. He reached under it, and pulled out, not a chamber pot (for we have no such luxuries here in Newfoundland), but the mysterious board which had so intrigued me.

He handed it to Peter Slade, who turned it round so that the inscribed side faced the fire.

"Now, Father, let me show you what this is."

I shifted my position so as to be able to see the side of the board which was lit by the flames, and I collected more splinters in my nether parts in the process.

Now I saw that the board was covered by a network of lines, completely black in the heaving firelight which makes all dark things blacker than by day.

Peter Slade angled the board towards me. Tom Rudge knelt beside him, scowling at me.

"Now, Father," Peter Slade began, "do you see this one line that runs from one side to the other?"

"The one with scribbles of writing along its length?"

"Yes. Now this line represents the children of King Edward III, and the writings, if you look closely, are the names of his sons and daughters in the order of their birth."

"I have seen all this before."

"These men have not, and you demanded to see what this was. You made a bargain, and now we shall carry it on to its completion. Now, in the next part of the board, going down, are more names."

"These are the next generation," I said, "and so on in the next part down, and so on. I don't need to be able to read the names. I know where all this is leading. This diagram has led men to the scaffold, the gallows, and the battlefield."

"Yes, and it has led me here to the snowbound coast of Newfoundland."

I wanted to take the lead in the conversation away from Peter, before the men came to regard me as being an ignorant schoolboy whose place was to be silent and receive instruction from his betters. I held Peter Slade to be my equal as a man in the eyes of God, but I did not consider him to be my better or to have any right of authority over me. If either of us held authority, it was myself as his priest.

"Let me finish the story for you," I said. "The purpose of this board is to demonstrate that King Henry VII has a weaker claim by descent to the throne of England than do the descendants of the late Duke of York, because they are descended from the third son of Edward III while the present king is descended only from the fourth son."

"You have learnt your lessons well, Father. You are a good scholar."

"You, though, Peter, are not, or you would recall that the Queen is the daughter of Edward IV of the House of York, and so both claims are united. We have a Lancastrian King and a Yorkist Queen, so all men should be satisfied and these disputes can be at an end."

Tom Rudge could no longer contain his desire to speak.

"We thought you were a spy, Father."

"That was Harry Chard's belief, but I was never sure who I was supposed to be spying for. He believed that I am a Yorkist, when in truth I have never thought about such things. Anyway, who would I be spying upon? What use is a conspiracy here on the faraway coast of Newfoundland?"

"There is no conspiracy here," William Durdle said, "but there is a loyal brotherhood."

"So I should hope," I said, contriving to say nothing in order to make the men tell me more before Peter Slade would silence them again. "I am loyal to the king and to my church, and indeed to my duty to you all. I try to show my loyalty by carrying out my duties."

Tom Rudge interrupted again.

"So you support Henry Tudor?"

"Yes, I do, as I would support any lawful king. My bishop prays for him, as does the Archbishop of Canterbury."

"Do you support him because his face is on your forty shilling coins?"

"Our Lord said that we should give to Caesar what is due to Caesar."

"But what if Caesar is not really Caesar?" Tom Rudge shouted, and then he sat back on the floor again, as if he had just made some triumphant declaration which settled a contentious question once and for all.

It reminded me of a student sitting for his Master's examination, answering one last question so well that his examiner declares *"Quod erat demonstrandum,"* and awards him the degree.

Well, he is not the only man who can play the fool, but I played the part deliberately.

"Harry Chard thought I was a Yorkist spy, and left me here all winter. Now I find that I am the only man here who is not a Yorkist."

Peter Slade sighed, probably out of impatience with Tom Rudge's blurtings and blunders.

"That's true. Harry Chard left you because he thought you were one of our party, although I told him over and over again that you were not."

"Well, then, why did you not kill me? When the fleet came back in the spring, you could easily have said that I had died from cold or illness during the winter."

Peter Slade made no answer to that, and nor did anyone else, not even blustering Tom Rudge.

An uncomfortable quiet fell inside the hut, and I became aware of the crackling of the logs on the fire, the men's rough breathing, and a sudden wailing of wind outside. The calm outside was ending just as all became silent within, as though discord and conflict had been swept out of the door like bad luck on New Year's Eve. (That is a pagan superstition, which of course I do not believe myself.)

Finally it was the quietest of our company, William Durdle, who broke the painful silence. I had been surprised several times that day, but what he said was more unexpected and astonishing than anything else which had happened.

"You see, Father, we came to like you, and so we could not kill you."

Holy Gilbert swiftly muttered a prayer to himself, or rather he said it so quietly that the words of his prayer were a secret between him and God, and there is nothing wrong with that. I was beginning to feel that I would rather that more secrets were kept among us than that unwelcome truths should be uncovered and proclaimed to all.

I felt the mantle of my priesthood falling upon me, as heavy as when I had first experienced my vocation.

"I am honoured that you like me, but it would have been as wrong for you to kill a man you hated as to kill a man you liked."

"We were trying to save ourselves from being betrayed and killed," William Durdle said. "So many of us have died, in nearly twenty years."

"You have not told me the whole secret," I said to Peter Slade. "Why have a band of Yorkists volunteered to come to Newfoundland for the winter?"

"It is to create a sanctuary, somewhere safe where loyal men can keep their king until the true royal line is restored."

"Here, in Newfoundland? You will have to find a hardy pretender who will agree to live his life here, through winters such as these. You could not have persuaded Perkin Warbeck to have lived in this hut."

"He was a false claimant."

"Many did not believe so," I said, remembering how many people had rashly hailed him as the lost second son of King Edward IV. Perkin Warbeck died on the scaffold five years ago for his presumption and imposture, and he took others across the river of death with him, both fools and wise men among them.

"They were wrong," Peter Slade said. "There is a true son of the House of York, and he cannot be safe in England or even in Flanders."

"So this is what the winter crew is for?" I asked. "You are going to build a palace for a pretended king, a palace built of wood here in Newfoundland. I haven't seen any sign of this palace rising from the forests yet."

Tom Rudge boiled over again.

"That is because you have not looked for it!"

Young Martin leaned forward and pointed to my chest.

"What will you do with this knowledge, Father?"

"Nothing. Who is there here in Newfoundland that I could pass it on to?"

Peter Slade stood up and took the inscribed board with the diagram of English royalty and its descendants. He snapped it across his knee, and then took each of the two halves and broke them in half in the same way.

He put two of the four fragments into the fire, which passed exploratory fingers of flame over them before pouncing upon them with its full force.

I was surprised at how fiercely the pieces of the board burned, in spite of having apparently spent so much time outside in the damp coastal air.

Horsfall spoke.

"Why did you do that, Peter?"

"There is no more need for this board. It can serve us usefully in the fire."

He gazed down at me where I still sat on the floor.

"Well, now, Father Fletcher. We have told you our dangerous secret. You must pay for it as you promised, with a secret of your own."

"I need time to consider and to write it down," I said. "I have been trained to prepare for public speaking by writing my words and shaping them first."

Horsfall was alarmed.

"Will you write down what we have told you? Anybody could read it."

"What I write in my book is in Latin, and is only to help my own memories. Nobody else will read it. I will keep it as faithfully as I keep what I am told in confession."

"Then write, Father," Peter Slade said. "Meanwhile, we have work to do."

I did not know what work he meant, or whether that was a coded signal, but the men all took down their smocks and began dressing for the cold outside. He led them out in a file through the door, through which I could see a picture of sparkling snow. Only Holy Gilbert was left with me.

He said a strange thing.

"I wish we had more glass here, Father."

"Why glass, of all things, Gilbert, when we are having to live without so many other things that we think essential at home in England?"

"Because then we could have big windows that we could see through, and still keep the heat of the fire inside. It's always so dark in here."

"If the price of heat is darkness, I'm willing to pay it," I told him, "but certainly I would like big windows, too."

Holy Gilbert persisted in his hopeless wish.

"I always feel that we're locked in, Father. Oh, I know I can go outside and walk around the fish flakes, or stand by the sea, or go up to the edge of the woods, but it's so cold. It's always cold. The only way to keep warm is to stay in here, and it's so gloomy. There's nothing to do but to look at each other and listen to stories."

I tried to imagine the hut with grand broad windows, looking out over the grey restless ocean on one side, on the dark green woods on another, and on yet another a view of the fish flakes, the only work of Englishmen's hands to be seen on the coast of Newfoundland. We might truly be cast away on a new world.

"Well, Gilbert, I cannot give you great windows with costly leading and beautiful stained glass, but I'll try to remember some good stories to tell you."

"I have to go, Father. I know Horsfall will have some work for me to do."

He scuttled out of the door, and then closed it gently and quietly, as though not to disturb someone who was sleeping within.

Does Gilbert think that I fall asleep while nobody is watching me, like the tree which falls noiselessly in the forest when there is no man to hear it? How the forests of Newfoundland must witness the silent fall of innumerable trees through the unvarying years of this nearly empty country.

I was left alone, not asleep, nor yet inactive. Perhaps the men thought of me at first as so many people think of priests: that we do not exist when we are not in church, that we are animated dolls who spring out of tight-closed boxes a few minutes before our presence is required to make God out of bread and wine.

I knew I still existed, even if nobody else did, and I too had work to do, although, unlike Holy Gilbert, I did not face kicks and blows if I did not do it to someone else's liking.

Unholy Ralph took out his pen and ink and sat down by the fire. I set my book across my knees, and began to write by firelight. Holy Gilbert is quite right; it is far too dark in here, but if we made the windows any wider we would certainly freeze, enjoying for a short time an abundance of light at the cost of a killing shortage of heat.

I wrote up my journal and brought it up to the events of today, up to this very moment, writing by the light given by the burning board with the diagrams of the descent of Lancaster, York, and Tudor. Is this a sign?

I will stop writing now. How odd the moment of 'now' is. That special instant when life is actually happening is so real and yet so impossible to grasp as it is transformed at once into memory.

Memory, yes, that reminds me. I have to tell my story to the men in order to fulfill my bargain with Peter Slade. Well, then, let me stretch by the fire, put away the clothes which it has dried for me, wait for our supper, and then I will take out my pen and ink to write it out.

Let me begin it with bold proud capital letters as though it were an important text which men might be set to study.

THE HISTORY OF FATHER RALPH FLETCHER:
OR,
THE FISHERMEN'S PRIEST'S TALE

This tale begins, as all good stories do, at the beginning, but only God knows where and how it will end; and that is true of all good stories as well.

I was born in the year 1479, in the reign of King Edward IV. My father Dominic Fletcher is a gentleman of the county of Surrey. He hates both his names; Fletcher, because, as I have written before, it proclaims our origins as mere tradesmen, and Dominic because he thinks it unsuitable for a gentleman, although he reveres the church.

My mother died when I was six years old, and if it were not for my scant memories of her she might never have lived, because none of her possessions are left in either of our houses.

We have two houses. One is in the country in Surrey, and one is in London. My father to stays in our town house when he comes up to London for the lawsuits, that pastime which has supplanted archery as the Englishman's national sport.

My father must have thrown away everything which reminded him of my mother, but he ensures that her tomb is well tended although he never visits it.

My sister lives only in the house on our estates in Surrey, and never comes to London, because she must be in the care of her nurse at all times even though she has the body of a grown woman.

My father has accepted God's action in depriving him of my mother and in making his daughter a little child for life, but he knows that he cannot blame God for me.

If my father had let me play with the tenants' boys on our estates I might be more at ease with men today. When I was old enough, a couple of years after my mother died, I was separated from father, sister, and country home, and sent away to school at Winchester College.

Whatever else I may be, I am a good scholar. I do not boast of it, but the masters told me so, and my school-masters were men who dispensed strokes of the birch far more willingly and often than they dispensed words of praise.

My skill at letters, Latin, and mathematics did not make me popular with the other boys, who considered me a weak and arrogant creature. I had few friends, but in truth I would have been happy to join in their rough play if I had only known how.

Denied the company of many other boys, of girls completely, and of my only parent almost completely, I had no companion other than God.

I prayed to Him nearly as often and as assiduously as Holy Gilbert does. I cannot speak for Holy Gilbert, who has also spoken to God day after day for years on end, but I can say that God finally responded and spoke to me.

He told me what I feared He would say. I was studying my *Donat*, my ancient Latin textbook so called because it was written by Donatus, may his memory expire in infamy, when a sudden certainty filled my heart in the same way that one becomes aware of a physical pain. I knew in that moment that God was calling me to the priesthood.

I cannot be the only man who has answered inwardly in the way that I did: "No, Lord, I don't want to be a priest!" I wanted a free life, which in my innocence as a schoolboy I could think of only as freedom from the scowlings and beatings of my masters at Winchester College.

I wanted to experience life, to enjoy wealth, to travel, to do as I wanted and not be at the bidding of others. Yet, like what happened to St. Paul, and there is a sign from God for you who would not believe, I had to submit to the unwelcome knowledge because I had been struck by the very presence of Christ seizing my life.

I told my schoolmasters, and they cautioned me that it was not for me to judge my vocation, and that I was too young to enter the Church yet. I knew that I could not escape. I told my father when I came home to our country house for the school holidays, and I believe he would have shown less grief if I had announced my conversion to Islam or that I had taken a vow of sodomy.

"My son, my son!" he cried like King David after the death of his son Absalom, but with this difference, that my father's grief was real. We were standing in the Great Hall, from which the servants had prudently withdrawn to leave us on our own.

My father had never remarried, and he knew that my sister would never be a grown woman and give him grandsons. Now he raged because his only son would never grow into his image.

He turned away from me, and then spun round to face me again, with his fists tight. For the first time in my life I noticed how strong they were, and I feared that he might strike me.

"I always feared this," he said. "You have never shown any interest in the manly life. I took you hunting, and you were afraid to see the quarry killed. I showed you how to manage the estate, and you asked the peasants questions about the best way to grow different crops. I offered to buy you swords and longbows, and you asked for books instead."

"I don't want to be a priest," I told him. "I feel it as a calling, just in the way that it is supposed to be felt."

"Sit, sirrah!" he commanded me as if I were a dog, and I sat at the table while he prowled around it.

"Yes, that is the place for you, sitting at a table," he declared. "You would like always to be sitting at tables, with books to read, English books, French books, Latin books! I wanted a son who would be beaten by his schoolmasters every day because he would rather be on horseback and drawing a bow than studying at his books."

"They do beat me nearly every day," I protested, "and verily I could show you the marks to prove that it is so."

Though my father raged at me for days, I knew that in the end he would accept my fate, because I knew that I had no choice but to accept it myself. It was a sort of predestination. I have known better men than myself who desperately wanted to be priests, and who were rejected. God chooses us strangely, and His purpose does not necessarily require that it is the best men who join the clergy.

My father could not understand it at all.

"I would not have been surprised if you wanted to be a monk," he said. "I can imagine you in the cloister, reading, praying and singing—though you have always sung abominably badly. I could not even see you as a friar, going about in the world preaching. How can you ever make a priest? How will you preach to all manner and condition of people? Who will listen to you?"

"I do not need to be skilled in preaching. My homilies may be boring and hard to endure. All I need is to be granted the laying-on of hands, and then I can celebrate Mass as validly as the Pope himself. I may be a fool and I may make a dreary preacher, but I will be able to give the Body and Blood of Christ."

My father seemed to be considering that, but when he spoke I realised that his mind had been on another subject, and that he had not even been listening to me.

"What will become of our family? My daughter is a half-wit—"

"Father!" I protested.

"Well, it is so, my daughter is a half-wit, and the only kind of man who would marry her is the kind of man that I would whip out of my house. Now I have a son who will never give me grandsons. When I die the estate will be sold and broken up."

"Someone will get the money," I pointed out. "You could leave it to a good cause."

"Oh, I will see that your sister is provided for to the end of her life. God will have to provide for you. I know that secular priests take no vow of poverty, but I shall impose one upon you."

"That is only fair, but how am I hurting you?"

"You see, Ralph, it is not only you and I who are concerned. We might both die tomorrow and the sun would still rise upon the world, but the Fletcher family will come to an end if you do not carry it on. We began as Fletchers, makers of arrows, and before that we must have been plain labourers, working the soil, bound to a lord's service."

"I will be bound to the service of a greater Lord," I said. "Being a servant and a worker is nothing to be ashamed of."

"Work! What do you know of work? You have never worked and never known hardship. Our ancestors first became craftsmen, and then merchants, and then landowners, so that the men of our family need never work again. If you have never worked in your life it is because others have toiled to set you free from work."

"I will know work when I become a priest," I said. "I will have to serve where I am sent."

"Hmph," my father said, which was often all that he ever contributed to a conversation, and it brought that particular conversation to an end, and properly so, because there was nothing more for either of us to say. My father had accepted that I would offer to become a priest, and I knew that there was no doubt that I would be accepted.

So indeed I was, and my schoolboy studies seemed like a merry holiday in my memory after I had begun my course of learning for the priesthood.

It was not only the books which were hard, although they were difficult enough. Theology is a fearfully complex subject. It is easy to know God as a simple Christian parishioner, but priests have to know how God works in this world and the next.

It is like myself compared to Harry Chard's sailors. I came safely across the ocean knowing no more than to step onto a ship in England and to step off it in Newfoundland, but the sailors and the ships' masters know about winds and tides and currents and navigation, how to steer the ship, which sails to set, and what each rope does when it is pulled on.

Thus is it for priests. We apprentices to the trade had to read and understand complex philosophical works and the writings of the ancient Fathers of the Church, as well as having to read the Bible and see the four levels of allegory in every story.

We also had to learn to use our memories. When I was a small boy I used to marvel that the priest could recite the words of a complete Mass and never make a mistake (although how would I have known if he had?). I marvelled even more when I had to learn the words of all the services myself. It is just as hard to find out which are the correct readings and special words to be said on every day of the year.

I might make a poor fisherman but I was a good student, so I passed my tests well enough, but another difficulty arose when I began to approach the age at which I could be ordained. Before I even became a deacon, the problem was explained to me by the dour Father Brighthelm, who had charge of me.

"The Church does not ordain men who have no income, because she cannot support her priests. You must either live at your own expense, or be given a post of some kind, either in a parish or in some other institution. Have you or your father made any plans?"

"My father will not support me," I replied at once.

"Nor should he. I wondered if he had some influence whereby he could secure you a parish, or a post in a household, or as a chantry priest."

"I would rather not be a chantry priest," I said.

Since few fishermen can ever have endowed a chantry, I had better explain that it is a chapel to say prayers in perpetuity for the soul of the person who endowed the chantry, or for someone whom they have nominated.

A living in a chantry might be considered an easy life for a priest, but I thought that it would be too easy for me, and I had felt that strange certainty again. This time it was telling me that God did not want me to serve a chantry.

"You do not need to find a permanent place immediately," Father Brighthelm reassured me. "There are situations where a priest is needed only for a few months."

"I would be willing to start in such a way," I replied. "Do you know of any household which needs a priest for only a short while?"

"Posts as household chaplains are eagerly sought after by the idle and the corrupt," Father Brighthelm rightly warned me. "You should look for something more rigorous, perhaps out of England."

"Out of England? But I have never been out of England myself, and I have never thought of doing so. Of course," I added hastily, "I know that I must go where the Church sends me."

"Well, I am sad to say that we have no Crusades or missions to offer you, but there is one opportunity which nobody seems to want. Perhaps it is for you. It is to spend the summer with the Newfoundland fishing fleet."

"Newfoundland? Across the ocean?"

"That is what every other young man has said. Are you like every other young man, or are you different?

Furthermore, the king himself is offering payment of forty shillings to the priest who will go."

"What would I do when I came home?" I asked.

"Remember that you would be noticed. Even the king himself would know your name. It may be a good way to gain preferment."

"I might be lost at sea, going out or coming home."

"You may be lost on land if you stay in England. It has happened to many priests before now."

Once again I felt that powerful presence of something in the room, like an invisible third person in the room with us. I am not arrogant enough to believe that God selects me for special signs, but I do believe that God speaks to all of us if we will only listen.

That is the story of my life up to this frozen winter afternoon, and the explanation of why I came to Newfoundland for a spring and summer, never imagining that I would be left behind with the winter crew.

Chapter Six

After supper yesterday evening I read out the unimpressive tale of my life. The winter crew were surprisingly interested, especially Holy Gilbert.

"How can I become a priest, Father?"

"You're too young, Gilbert, and besides the priesthood is not like a trade which you choose. The choice is made for us by God, and many of us sometimes wish that He had picked someone else."

I did not tell him that as the unschooled son of a poor widow, Gilbert probably had no chance of ever being selected. It has been known for boys from poor families to enter the priesthood and even to rise to the summits of the hierarchy, but the fact that such men are so famous shows how rare it is.

More important than Gilbert's lack of education is the fact that he has a religious temperament. His piety probably makes him unfit for the priesthood. So many priests are hardbitten men, as they need to be to minister to a hard world. I think the king wanted a man like that to come to Newfoundland, and had to settle for Ralph Fletcher instead.

Gilbert would probably not be accepted as a monk, either, because for him the life would tend to encourage his eccentricities and eventually drive him to a strangeness beyond the toleration of his abbot.

Perhaps he might make a friar, preaching in the world, but I believe that deeply religious people like him are meant to live the life of the laity as an example to their neighbours.

I still had the book open on my knees at the page where I had stopped writing, and which I am covering with writing now.

William Durdle came over and looked over my shoulder at the page. The firelight illuminated his expression. It is the way the illiterate always look at a page of writing, with a mixture of wonder, jealousy, and anger.

For a moment William's face looked like that of an apostle, striving to accept the teaching of Christ, with its unwelcome hard lumps upon which one unexpectedly bites while enjoying the sweetness of the message.

What he said was unexpected.

"Were you trained as a teacher, Father?"

"No, I was chosen to be a simple priest in a parish, or a chaplain in some special place like this. I have never taught anyone in my life."

"Well, this will be a long winter and I am an old man, past fifty. I wondered if you could find the time to teach me to read."

I just stopped myself in time from asking what chance he would ever have to read anything in his manner of life. God made me realised that it would be a cruel question. I have had pains in my life, but I have also been given many advantages which have been denied to these men, except, perhaps, (I suspect) to the mysterious Peter Slade.

"I can try, William, although I learnt my letters when I was small and I can't remember what methods were used, apart from the stick, of course."

All the men laughed, and urged me to use the same means of instruction upon William, frequently and with vigour, assuring me that it was the only aid to learning which would suit his meagre understanding.

"Let us try, then, Father," William replied when the laughter died down. "I've always wished I could read."

"I'm willing to teach you as best I can," I said, "but books are expensive, and the writings I have with me here are nearly all in Latin."

"Teach me Latin, then, so I can understand the Mass."

"Latin is complicated and takes many years to learn," I replied, quite astonished. "I can explain the words of the Mass to you, if you like. There is nothing secret about them. We use Latin only so that the Mass is the same everywhere in Christendom, and so that we all agree on what the words mean."

"Teach me English, then, even if there is hardly anything to read. Teach me to write. At least teach me all the letters. How many are there?"

"Why, there are twenty-six," I replied, and then I silently rebuked myself for answering him as if I were astonished at his ignorance. How would an illiterate know how many letters there were? There are not even the same number of letters in English as in Latin.

Young Martin now took an interest, which really was astonishing to me.

"Are all words made up from only twenty-six letters, then? It seems so small a number."

"The mathematicians at the universities could prove to you, though neither you nor I would understand the proof, that such a small number of letters is enough to construct millions of words in all the languages of the world."

I thought of the Bettooks, and the strange sounds of their language. How many letters would they use, if they were ever to write their language down?

Young Martin thought about that.

"Only twenty-six letters."

"Well, everything in the world is made up of a combination of only four elements," I told him, "Earth, air, fire, and water. In the same way, every man's temperament is made up of only four humours: the sanguine, the choleric, the melancholic, and the phlegmatic."

In the harsh light of the fire I noticed for the first time that Young Martin's face has begun to show wrinkles and lines, and yet he still bears the appearance of youth which goes with that strange nature which has given him his nickname.

William Durdle came and knelt beside me. He looked over my shoulder at this book.

"Show me one letter, Father. Let me learn one letter, and then there will be only twenty-five more to learn, and I will be able to read and write anything."

"Here is an 'A', then, William," I said, pointing to a capital 'A'. "It looks like two sticks standing upright, with another stick lying between them, bracing them and keeping them from falling. The letter 'A' stands for the sound in—well, *stand*: 'a'. You find 'A' in sat, and fat, and bat, and apple. When it is at the beginning of a word it is written like this, and when it is anywhere else in a word it is written like this."

William studied the two forms of the letter, moving his eyes back and forth like a cat watching a spider. He closed his eyes and muttered "A: sat, bad, apple," and then he opened his eyes again, and pointed at a word in my writing.

"Is that an 'A', Father?"

"Why, yes, it is. You have learnt your first letter."

"May I try to write it?"

I took out my pen and my inkhorn. I gave William the pen, and opened the inkhorn and held it out to him.

"You can write in this blank space on the page, William. Dip the pen into the ink, and then make the letter 'A' here."

William fumbled the pen around in the fingers of his right hand, and then looked to me for guidance.

"I have never held a pen before, Father."

I yielded to a wicked temptation at that moment.

"I need to hold the book and the inkhorn. Here, Peter, show William how to hold a pen."

Peter Slade took the pen out of William's hand, which made William look frightened and sad, as though he had been allowed to hold a pen only once and would now have that precious gift withdrawn for ever.

"Hold it between your forefinger and thumb, like this," Peter told him, "and steady it with your next finger."

William grasped the pen gingerly.

"Here," I said, offering him the inkhorn. "Dip the pen into the ink, and then withdraw it. A little of the ink will cling to the nib, enough to write a few words with."

William stabbed the surface of the ink with the nib, and then snatched the pen out again. I pointed to the right blank place of the page, and William slowly lowered the nib towards it. Then he halted.

"Do I make the sides of the letter first, or the bar which lies across it?"

"Whichever you please, William. There are no rules, but I always make the left-hand side of the letter A first, then the right-hand side, and then the crossbar."

William placed the point of the nib on the paper, slowly drew it down to make his sloping line, and lifted the pen up again, leaving a tiny spherical blot.

"Must I dip the pen into the ink again?"

"No, William, I told you, enough remains for a few words. You can finish the letter with the ink which you already have."

William brought the pen down to the paper again, and after shifting it about so that his second downward line would begin from the first one, he drew his second downstroke, which wandered a little more on its journey than the first one had done.

"Well done, William," I said. "Now you can finish it."

William brought the pen down again like an executioner swinging down the axe, and cut the crossbar across the letter in one sharp, perfectly straight line.

"There you are, William!" I congratulated him.

"So," William said. "My first letter, and I am already an old man."

"You are not learning like a child," I told him. "They have to copy their letters from a hornbook, with a transparent sheet of horn over the page with the model letters on. You have gone straight to writing your letters in good black ink with a goose-quill pen on the best paper."

"May I learn a letter a day, Father?"

"Certainly, and in before a month is out you will know them all. Even before then, you will be able to read and write words with the letters which you will already know."

William handed me back my pen, and I put it away with my inkhorn. I closed this book and put it away safely too. I wish I had brought a book with a leather strap and a brass lock on it. I do not know who may be reading my words. I am less sure than ever than nobody else here understands Latin.

We all fell silent for a little while. It was one of those silences by mutual consent, when everybody knows that there is nothing to be said and all are at ease with the silence. Even Young Martin and Holy Gilbert observed it.

Outside, the night was unusually quiet, with no wind. I could see the pale blur of light which was the moon shining through the window, distorted and softened like the letters seen through the horn of a boy's hornbook.

I knew that if I were to open the door and venture outside I would find the heaps of snow outside the doorway sparkling in the moonlight and the firelight from within our hut.

I cannot know what the other men were thinking of, but I was planning my liturgical duties for the next day, when the comfortable silence was broken, not by one of us, but from outside in the unfathomable cold night.

From somewhere out in the trees, I heard the Mass bell ring. It rang harshly, for several moments, not at all in the way that it was meant to be rung at Mass. It was as if the bell itself had become strengthened and harder in the roughness of Newfoundland.

The men looked at each other in alarm, and it was the boisterous Young Martin, not the pious Holy Gilbert, who frantically crossed himself.

The bell rang again, from a slightly different quarter, and then once more. Whoever was ringing it, presumably Aguthut the Bettook, was moving about close to our hut.

"I know what that is," I said. For once I was the calmest man in our company. "It is only the bell that Gilbert used to ring at Mass."

"What is it doing outside?" Horsfall demanded. "And who in the name of God is ringing it?"

"I fear that it is not being rung in the name of God, but not in the name of Satan either," I replied. "I gave it away."

"Gave it away?" Peter Slade shouted. I did not think he was angry with me, but he was angry that the other men had seen him afraid. "Given it away to whom?"

"You should all listen to me more, even when I am not preaching to you. Did I not tell you that I had met a friend in the forest? Well, I gave him the silver Mass bell as a gift to prove our goodwill, and I assume that it is he who is ringing it out there."

The bell rang again, closer to the hut. Tom Rudge could endure no more.

"This is unclean and unholy! We have no friends here. This is Newfoundland, not England."

"So it is, and that is a man of Newfoundland. I believe that it is my friend Aguthut of the Bettooks. I wonder what he wants?"

All the men wanted to speak then, but Peter Slade held up his hand to silence them.

"Is this true, Father Fletcher? Have you been trafficking with the natives?"

"Trafficking? Why, no, because we have not traded with each other. I have given Aguthut the silver Mass bell which was given to me by my father, but he has given me nothing."

The bell rang again, this time from the direction of the sea. I had always thought of the Bettooks as people of the forest, and I had not imagined that they ever came to the seashore.

Peter Slade sighed like a priest who has heard a particularly bad or persistent sin in confession, and is wondering what penance to impose.

"This is worrying, Father. You should have told us."

"Why? I am your servant as your pastor, but not in any other respect. I came upon Aguthut by chance. I have met other Bettooks, but they seem to have no desire for more meetings with me. Indeed, they drove me back here after I had sought out their encampment."

I wished then that I had not said that, for fear that the men would go out and hunt the Bettooks like dangerous beasts.

The bell rang again, and then immediately we heard a sudden howl of wind, as if the ringing of the bell had raised the very wind itself. Most of the men crossed themselves in superstitious terror. Sailors fear the wind as much as they fear its absence, for they are truly at its mercy in the open ocean, and they believe that witches and wizards have the power to control it.

Tom Rudge now thought of another danger.

"They know the way here."

"This fishing settlement is not concealed," I pointed out. "Nobody has tried to hide it. It sits on bare rock beside the seashore. They must have known about it all along, and I know that they often come to within half a mile of here."

William Durdle had an idea.

"Perhaps it's you that they want, Father. They want you to come outside and speak to them."

"Or to be killed or carried off by them," I retorted. "It may be so, but I must take the risk. I have to preach Christianity to them, now that I have made contact with them. I'll go."

The men all looked relieved that it would be me who went out to face the Bettooks and not one of them. William Durdle, ever practical, made a torch for me out of rags wound around a stick, and then dipped it in pitch.

Holy Gilbert opened the door. Outside, the snow glowed faintly in the escaping firelight. William Durdle lit the torch from the fire, which is a terrible thing to do according to superstition.

"William, either you or I are condemned to be very poor, because you lit this torch from the fire."

"No, Father, it is a candle which you must never light from the fire. I suppose your candles have always been lit by servants."

That was true, and anyway the poor never have candles. They must make do with rushlights, those useless items which light only themselves and sit mockingly in the darkness, illuminating nothing of the room.

William looked determined as he handed me the torch, and I tried to look serious as I took it from him. It was like a scene from a great myth, but I was no hero going out into danger, but only poor Ralph Fletcher.

Even the open doorway, showing the empty snowy forest, seemed to give onto another world. Our hut might as well have been in England.

I stepped out into the cold. Someone banged the door shut behind me, only, I think, to keep in the heat of the fire rather than to signal that my departure was welcome.

"Aguthut?" I called. "Ring the bell again, if that's you."

I listened, but I heard no bell. I heard nothing at all. The strange soft silence had come back, and there had been no more wind after that one gust which we had heard.

I wondered if it had been really the sound of a man imitating the wind, a Bettook standing next to the window, unseen.

I also wondered if the Bettooks were afraid to approach the hut knowing that all the winter crew were inside.

They had driven me off when I had tried to approach them in their encampment; they could not have been afraid of me, but they might well fear the other men if they knew what had happened to other natives who had encountered English fishermen and sailors.

As I felt my body begin to slow down and ache in the cold, a sensation that was now familiar to me after so many weeks in Newfoundland, I tried to think of a way in which I could communicate to the Bettooks that I was different from the other men in the winter crew; not superior, but different, because I was a priest.

I stood in the snow and contemplated my own clumsy tracks leading back to the door of our hut. Behind that door was a fire, and heat. The rough door looked to me like the very gate of Paradise itself. Had I been expelled from the warm hut because of my sins?

"Aguthut!" I called again into the indifferent night. I listened, but I could hear only the tireless sea murmuring in the darkness.

If this went on, I began to think, I would cease to believe in Aguthut or the Bettooks. My stay with the winter crew was beginning to seem more and more like a romance or a moral tale, but it was a story with no plot or moral that I had yet discovered.

I had thought that I was as cold as any man could ever be and live, but my skin froze even more deeply when a voice spoke to me whispering, "Ralph!"

I swayed with terror in the snow, too cold to run away.

"Ralph Lecher! Ingliss Fissman!"

"Is that you, Aguthut?"

"Aguthut Bettook."

There was still only a voice, coming from somewhere and yet nowhere. The snow prevented it from echoing, so that Aguthut's voice seemed to be coming from within my own skull, like the disembodied voices of demons which endlessly torment the mad.

I glanced fearfully to the left and right, my ears burning in the cold, but I could still see nobody. At the next moment I nearly leapt up among the sharp stars of the winter sky in mindless terror as both my arms were seized from behind and I was dragged away from the hut. I could not turn my head, but even in my fear I was able to see how funny it was that the last time the Bettooks had attacked me it had been to carry me away from their encampment and back towards the settlement of the winter crew beside the sea. Now they were hauling me away from the fish flakes and the huts where the fire burned within. Oh, how sweet and unbearably distant a dream it was to think of that fire and its warmth.

"Let me go!" I begged the Bettooks. "I'll come with you."

To my surprise, they did let me go, and stood back for a moment while I flung my arms about to untwist them.

We were almost into the trees. There was just enough light from the window of our hut and from the brilliant night sky for me to see the two men, but that told me nothing that I did not already know.

One of them pushed me in the back to make me start walking again, and the other one stepped in front of me to guide me through the darkness. How he could see better than I could I cannot imagine.

The man behind me tugged at my cloak to pull me to the left and right so that I did not bump into the trees. At last I made out ahead a kind of triangle of deeper darkness amid the gloom. It waited for me like the entrance to the underworld, and I feared that so it might prove to be as far as I was concerned. I had certainly heard no sound of any of the winter crew coming out and following to see what had happened to their priest.

When I was thrust into the Bettooks' tent I nearly choked from the foul smell and the smoke of the fire within. I was flung down so that I sprawled on the ground that smelt even worse than the trapped air.

I managed to writhe myself into a sitting position. I panted and coughed, and my nose and ears began to sting as the warmth of the fire began to heat my face.

Aguthut had gone into the tent before me, and when I looked round I saw that there were four Bettooks in all with me, all looking dark and murderous in the sinister light of the fire. I wondered whether they knew that they were subjects of King Henry VII of England, and could not stop myself from letting out a mad burst of laughter.

The Bettooks showed no reaction at all, neither mirth or their own nor anger. They simply stared like gargoyles, which to my eye they much resembled.

Aguthut spoke to me, in only a slightly louder tone than when he had used the voice which had seemed to come from within my own terrified mind.

"Ingliss fissman. Ralph Lecher. See."

See what, I wondered? All I could see was the fire and the four graven faces around it.

Then I heard the sound of someone shuffling through the snow around the tent. I expected the Bettooks to look towards the sound, but none of them moved.

Another man pushed his way into the crowded tent. He was dressed in the yellowish-grey Bettook smock and hood, which he flung back over his head.

He was more communicative towards me than the other men had been.

"Good evening, Father Fletcher," said Harry Chard the Fishing Admiral. "You are giving me more than I bargained for when I put you with the winter crew, and more than the king bargained for when he paid you his forty testoons."

Harry Chard squatted beside the fire to melt the water out of his frozen beard while he kept on talking to me.

"Come now, Father, is it not your calling to preach? Preach to me. Bid me to confess my sins. At the very least, bid me good evening, for I did that much for you."

I tried to answer him, but I could not. I had tried to speak but I had not yet framed any words to utter, so I sat gasping instead.

All at once I became aware of the smoke from the fire, which had almost no means of escape from the tent, which was sealed against the cold that was even sharper outside than within.

The smell of the Bettooks, the smell of the unwashed Harry Chard, and no doubt my own smell into the bargain, made the air so thick and stinking that it was nearly as uncomfortable to breathe it as it would have been not to breathe at all.

Harry Chard smiled wickedly at me. His smile was split by the thin column of smoke which was rising from the fire, so that his face was divided into two, inhuman and evil. The Bettooks still remained silent and impassive. Even if I could not speak, Harry Chard still could.

"Come now, Father Fletcher, it is your trade to speak."

I managed to breathe in enough air to be able to reply.

"As you have just reminded me, it is also my trade to listen, in particular to listen to confessions, Fishing Admiral. Are you still the Fishing Admiral?"

"Why, no, Sir Ralph, the title lapses when the fishing fleet leaves Newfoundland to return in the spring."

"Then the title will be yours when the fleet returns, because you are plainly the first fishing captain on the shores of Newfoundland for the season, never having left."

"Yes, I think much upon titles, Sir Ralph, and about who should hold them."

I held my fingers out to the fire to warm them. They began to ache sharply as the heat returned to them. Pain is the price of warmth in this climate, as it is in Hell.

I decided to lay everything out in the open, so that Harry Chard's would have to explain his appearance here in a Bettook tent in the Newfoundland forest.

"This is all about the House of York and the House of Tudor, isn't that so, Harry? You were a supporter of the Duke of Gloucester, and you have upheld his cause these last nineteen years since he was killed at the battle of Bosworth. The winter crew seem all to be of the same party as well."

"Yes, they are, except for Young Martin and Holy Gilbert, who cannot think about these things. Yet the winter crew are here mainly to do their job, maintaining the fish flakes and the dories and the buildings until the fleet comes back."

"So what is this all about, then? I can understand you plotting against the king in England, but why are you all here in England's dominion on the other side of the ocean in this endless snow and cold?"

"Ah, but you have answered your own question without knowing it. When you go back to the hut and write out your account of this meeting for yourself, study your own writing as if you were studying a holy or a classical text. You will then see meaning where at first there seemed to be none."

I stared into the fire as the superstitious gaze into the flames of the hearth, hoping to see pictures. I remembered that I had asked him why these Yorkists had gathered on the coast of Newfoundland, far away from England. I could not interpret my own question, so I asked him another one.

"Why have you hidden yourself away all this time? Why did you deceive me that you had sailed back to England?"

"Who ever told you that I had gone back to England, Father Fletcher? If you think upon it, nobody told you that. Horsfall showed you the fleet sailing away, but he did not say that I was with it. Now consider whether I have been hiding myself away since then. I have not done so."

"Then where have you been?"

"With the Bettooks, of course."

"So that is the name of the people! I guessed right!"

"So you did. You are a clever man, Ralph Fletcher. That is why God called you to become a priest, or perhaps why He made you a clever man rather than a stupid one in the first place, but you have not guessed all."

I replied to him angrily.

"Since you wish to play a game with you, I will play willingly. You have forced me to spend the long winter here, and I will accept your challenge as a way to pass the cold dark hours in this cruel land."

"Cruel? No. Harsh, yes, but there is beauty here as well as cold and snow. Well, you have guessed some things. Yes, we are all loyal to the House of York."

"This would be called treason in London."

"So it would. That is why we are in Newfoundland."

The Bettooks still said nothing.

I decided to take the initiative away from Harry Chard, and blessed the Bettooks one by one with my hand as one does in the Mass.

"Why did you do that?" he asked. "They are all pagans, even Timaskatek."

I looked at Timaskatek, who had driven me away from this tent before. He astonished me by smiling at me, and then by the two words that he spoke.

"Dominic. Fry."

"Who? St. Dominic? Yes, but Fry —oh, friar."

"I," Timasketek barked, pointing at me, "you. Wessmisster, checker, I see you, vindoo."

Harry Chard smiled too.

"Timaskatek saw you through the window when you visited the Exchequer, and spoke to my dear young friend the Dominican friar. My friend was paying you out forty testoons at the time."

"—and Timaskatek—"

"was one of the three Bettooks who were taken captive three years ago and brought to England. He came back with me last spring."

Chapter Seven

Two days have passed since I last wrote in my book. The cold has eased, and the snow is melting into dirty slush, exactly the same yellowish-grey colour as the clothes of the Bettooks.

I must confess to a sin, which is that I hated Timaskatek as soon as I discovered that he had seen me in England. I do not know why. Perhaps it is all this distasteful knotting of secrets and lies which has been trapping me ever since I came to Newfoundland, indeed before.

Did the Dominican friar in the Exchequer know about Timaskatek, and that I would unknowingly accompany the abducted Bettook back to Newfoundland? I would not put it past a Dominican; indeed, few things are beyond a Dominican, as it delights them to boast to all who are willing to listen, and to many who are not.

There is nobody here to grant me absolution from my sin, and besides it could not be granted because I have not yet repented of it.

There will be a time for confession, repentance, and penance later. For the time being, let others be penitent for what they have done to me. That is not how I should think, but I must tell the truth. Truth is a rare and precious commodity here among the winter crew.

After Harry Chard had told me that Timaskatek had been in England, I had not known what questions to ask. I tried to frame a question which would not be what Harry Chard was expecting.

"What is the common cause which binds the winter crew and the Bettooks together? The Bettooks must care nothing about the wars of York and Lancaster. What does it matter to them, here in Newfoundland, who sits on the throne in London?"

"The king who sits on the throne in London also reigns here in Newfoundland. John Cabot claimed this land for England seven years ago. Newfoundland is as English as Calais."

"Nobody rules here but the Fishing Admiral, and you know it. Who rules the Bettooks?"

"As far as I understand it, they have no king. Each little band has its own chief. There are not many Bettooks in the world, anyway. Timaskatek has been in England and seen how many English people there are. Imagine what London and Westminster seem like, to a man who has never known anything but this empty forest!"

"Our towns must seem like heaven or hell to them," I replied. "The forest seems just as strange and as frightening to me."

"It is all part of God's Creation and great purposes, as you ought always to be aware, Father Fletcher."

"I have no doubt of that. What I doubt is that the Bettooks are interested in the dynastic wars of England."

Timaskatek surprised me by interrupting us then.

"Ingliss many. Ingliss here. Bettooks not—many."

"The English are not here," I told him. "They are far away across the sea. You know how far it is. You have made the crossing yourself."

"Ingliss here."

"Timaskatek, there are only the fishermen in the summer, and in the winter there are only the few men of the winter crew. You can see that we are only a small number."

Timaskatek scowled, and roared at me.

"Ingliss here!"

Harry Chard answered for Timaskatek.

"He has been in England. He has seen how many we are. He remembers the first coming of the fishing fleet, more than twenty years ago, long before John Cabot or Cristoforo Colombo. Now the fleet comes every spring, with more ships every time."

"No more than a few hundred men come with them, and nearly all of them leave at the end of the summer," I objected. "The fishermen never go far from the shore. There have been unworthy incidents between Englishmen and Bettooks, I admit, but there is no serious threat."

"Timaskatek saw more in England than the Palace of Westminster and the Thames. He saw that we are divided."

"I would say not. The Crown is not in dispute. England is at peace."

"The Crown is in dispute, between Henry Tudor and the rightful heirs of Richard the Third. England will not be at peace forever."

"The Bettooks cannot care about that."

"Think upon this, then, Father Fletcher. Here in Newfoundland we are in English territory. No heir of the rightful House of York is safe anywhere in Europe, where Henry Tudor's agents can find him. But, here, though? Here is a safe place. These forests could hide a million men."

"You would bring a million Englishmen, here? That would half empty the kingdom at home."

"No, Father Fletcher, not a million Englishmen. Just one or two. Enough to keep the royal blood safe."

So that is it. They plan to create a sanctuary in Newfoundland for some Yorkist claimant to the throne. I know that I will never be allowed to take this book back to England, not with these words in it, testimony to treason, and with the names of the traitors in it. I will keep writing regardless, because I doubt that the conspirators will ever allow me to go back to England either.

For an instant both Harry Chard and Timaskatek looked at me with the same expression, a mixture of triumph and contempt. They were truly well pleased with themselves. Harry Chard is pleased because he has his Yorkist sanctuary, and Timaskatek is pleased, too; but why?

There was another mystery that I did not understand.

"Why did you bring me here to Newfoundland? You did not know whether I belonged to the Yorkist party, and I do not."

Harry Chard shrugged, making shocking cold drops of water fall on us all from the sides of the tent.

"The merchants in England thought that we needed a priest. They were right. The fishing fleet is made up of rough men who sin more than most."

"But why me?"

"You will not want to know the reason."

"Why then, Harry? I must know. Why was I carried across the ocean to Newfoundland?"

"Because, Sir Ralph, no other priest would come. You said that you needed to know."

I could bear to hear no more.

"Is there to be no end to insults in my life?" I cried. "I am sent across the ocean, dragged to this foul tent, pulled and pushed around like a farm animal. I am no mute beast. I am a man, and will not hear any more. I am going back to the winter crew. I do not know where you live, Harry, and I do not care. I say only that you have failed to appear at Mass since the day the fleet left, and I suggest that you come on Sunday. Be at the hut early so that I can hear your confession."

I struggled to stand on my cramped and cold limbs. I thought that Harry Chard or the Bettooks would try to stop me, but they said and did nothing.

When I pushed my way out of the tent it suddenly occurred to me that I did not know the way back to the seashore, and that I would look foolish if I had to go back and ask for directions. I could not go wandering in the snowy forests because I would certainly die before the morning.

Luckily I could make out the glow of the window of our hut, shining like a friendly star through the palisade of trees which separated me from it. I pushed my way through the snow, and by the time I arrived at the door I had to stop and shake a heavy coat of snow off myself in spite of my desperate desire to get inside.

The men were all clustered around the fire, so I saw only a huddle of backs. They all twisted round in astonishment at the sight of me.

"Yes, here I am," I told them, my voice trembling with cold. If they thought it was fear, then so be it.

I began stripping off my snow-caked outer clothes. The winter crew all watched me in silence.

"Am I invisible to you?" I asked them. "Am I dead, as perhaps you expected, and come back as a ghost, to haunt you all through the winter, yes, and on the ship home, and in England for the rest of your lives?"

Holy Gilbert crossed himself, and Young Martin looked piteously at Horsfall, whose face was tight with concentration as though he were contemplating some great philosophical problem.

I forced my way through to the fire. I began to under-stand how pagans could have worshipped fire and the sun above all things.

"Yes, I have been into the forest," I said. "Yes, I spoke with the Bettooks, and they spoke to me. Yes, one of them is Timaskatek, who lived for three years in the Palace of Westminster. Yes, I met Harry Chard and he explained everything. Yes, I am utterly tired of all the lies and secrets and betrayals. I have been sent here to preach you the truth. Is it too much too ask that all of you, even one of you, should give me your truth in return?"

Peter Slade gave me the answer that I had expected from him. "Pontius Pilate asked: what is truth?"

"It is facts without falsehood," I said, "o my learned friend. Are you a Dominican friar too?"

I saw him start at that. Had I guessed right? I pressed him further.

"Is that it? Are you a Dominican? If you are a friar, I am sure that you are a priest, too."

"No!" Peter shouted. "I am no priest, nor am I a friar. I have never been in the clergy, not even in minor orders."

"What are you, then?" I asked. "There have been enough lies and concealments here since the spring. You are not a simple ship's carpenter."

"I am truly a ship's carpenter. I leave it to God and man to judge whether I am a simple one."

"You have not always worked in that trade," I told him. "You have been to school, which is something that only I among us share with you. Even Harry Chard has not been schooled."

"Harry Chard is an intelligent man," Horsfall protest-ed.

"So he is, but he is not a book-learned man," I continued. "That is my point. Where did you learn to read books, Peter?"

"In my father's house. I tell you again that I have never been to school. School came to me. My father paid for me to be tutored, and all the accoutrements of schooling came to me, schoolmaster, schoolbooks, hornbook, pen, and cane."

Now I began to see why Peter Slade was labouring as a carpenter on the coast of Newfoundland.

"Your father was attainted. Is that what happened?" I asked.

"It might well have gone the other way!" Peter exclaimed.

"You mean he might not have been attainted?"

"There might have been a different king! There may yet be again. Henry Tudor came to England from France. Let the next king, the true king, come from Newfoundland, the first king to come from England's dominions across the western ocean."

"Let him set himself up as King of Newfoundland," I suggested, "if the Bettooks will have him."

Peter leaned forward at that, and I realised too late that he had taken my suggestion seriously.

"King of Newfoundland!"

Young Martin intervened with misplaced eagerness.

"There has never been more than a Fishing Admiral before."

"Yes," I said, "and he behaves as if he were a king. Anyway, do the Bettooks have a king? You must know much more about them than you have told me."

I wondered whether Peter would give me a different answer than Harry Chard had done.

"Peter has told us nothing about them," Holy Gilbert said in his innocence.

"Well, Peter?" I asked. "Do the Bettooks have a king? King Aguthut the First? King Timaskatek the Third? Have there been wars between rival families claiming the crown?"

"For all I know there may be. I think that they live in small families, travelling across the land by season, hunting the animals who live in the forests. They come to the coast in the spring to fish, and to hunt the seals. Harry Chard says that there are great rivers in the middle of the land. Newfoundland is bigger than you may know. It is larger than Ireland. We know so little."

"How much does Harry Chard know about them?"

"Ask him. He's spent more time with the Bettooks than any Englishman has."

"I will certainly ask him when I see him again, which I am sure will not be a long time from now. For the moment, all I want to do is to say my prayers and go to bed."

Holy Gilbert caught my sleeve, which was still dripping with icy water.

"Father Fletcher, could you say a Mass instead?"

"Why, Gilbert? An evening prayer will be enough for God."

"I don't feel safe tonight, Father."

"Not safe? What are you afraid of Gilbert? Is there yet another thing that everyone else knows about without having told me?"

"No, Father. I just feel that there's something dangerous about."

Horsfall spat into the fire, which spat back at him.

"We have a fire against the cold, and walls against the wind. The Bettooks are our friends, and there are no other men here in Newfoundland. What have we to fear?"

"I don't know," Holy Gilbert admitted miserably, "but I know I want a Mass."

"This is dangerous thinking, Gilbert," I said. "The Mass is not a magical incantation to protect us against danger or evil. Even Jesus Himself was crucified, though He feared it and asked to be spared if it was the Father's will to spare Him."

"Will you not say Mass?" Gilbert begged.

For a moment I considered it, if only to comfort him, but then I saw again that I would only be encouraging his superstitious attitude.

"No, Gilbert, but I will pray with you if you think it would help. I believe we are safe here, safer indeed than we would be in London, where no man is safe even in his own house, because the thieves will cut through the very walls to break in. There are no thieves in Newfoundland."

Horsfall laughed at that.

"How can you be sure of that, Father?"

"Why," I asked him, "do you know of one among us?"

Horsfall laughed again, but this time it was forced.

"No, Father, for none of us has anything to steal."

Just for an instant I felt an impulse to open my chest to see whether my forty testoons were still there, but I realised that I would look foolish if they were still there, and equally foolish if they were gone.

I asked myself again why I had brought those coins across the ocean to Newfoundland in the first place. They might have gone to the bottom of the sea with me, and they may yet do so on the homeward voyage, if indeed I ever get the chance to sail home.

"This has all been enough talk for me," I declared. "It has been a long cold evening. I want to go to bed. Come here, Gilbert, kneel with me and we'll pray together."

Gilbert hurried over and knelt beside me, pressing himself against my side like a little child. I recited the prayer for the day, half a sentence at a time, so that Gilbert could repeat it. I am always amazed at his ability to say the Latin words exactly.

Young Martin can do the same. He is a grown man, but as I have written, there is something odd and unformed about him, so that he does not think and act like a grown man; yet he, too, can say his prayers accurately in words of which he has no understanding. Is this a gift of God to the simple?

There are lessons here for a priest to meditate upon, perhaps. So many of us seem to forget that we are not called to the priesthood because of any ability or goodness in us, but because in some way we are needed for God's plan. Man does not understand that plan, which may well call for stupid and corrupt priests from time to time.

As I knelt and muttered to God, to Holy Gilbert, and to the icy winter night, I remembered the story of St. Francis of Assisi.

A village priest was denounced to him for fornication and other wickedness. St. Francis publicly went to the man and kissed his hand, saying that he honoured the hand which was empowered to participate in the ritual of the Mass, even though the man himself might be unworthy of honour.

Is there a lesson for me, too, in that story for me? I am no fornicator, in spite of what Aguthut the Bettook calls me, but I am certainly not free from sin.

I felt again that sense that I had been sent to Newfoundland to carry out some little operation which is part of God's plan for the redemption of all mankind, not because of any strength or merit of mine, but because that is why I am in this world.

I finished the prayers with a special supplication for the protection of all the men of the winter crew against the dangers of this world, and I added to that a prayer for the protection of the Bettooks, which made some of the men draw their breath in, and then a prayer for Harry Chard our former Fishing Admiral, which made the men gasp their breath out again when they heard it. I suspect, from what little I know, that Harry Chard needs prayers more than do most other men on the land of Newfoundland.

That night, I found it hard to sleep, an affliction which rarely strikes me, even in the hardships and discomforts of this place. At least there are no fleas here to bite us, because any that we brought with us from England have not survived the cold when the hut has been left with its fire unlit. There are little biting insects here in the summertime, but none in the winter.

From where I lie in the hut I can see out of the window. There is almost complete darkness in the hut, but I can make out the bodies of the other men stacked in the rough bunks around me. When they are sleeping quietly, and not snoring or raving, it is disquietingly like being in a sepulchre with corpses deposited throughout unknown ages, all waiting for the Resurrection when we shall all be rewarded or punished as we deserve.

These are not the best thoughts to be thinking when a man is trying to sleep in a dangerous winter thousands of miles from home across a pitiless ocean.

Of course we leave the embers of the fire to glow feebly through the night. We are not observing the old English custom of allowing the embers to burn on so as to keep the fairies warm but to warm ourselves.

Whether there be fairies in England or not, I do not know, and I know even less of what supernatural beings live in Newfoundland, whether they be friendly or malign. No, we leave the embers glowing so that we can set the fire roaring early in the morning when we are all desperate for warmth.

We run the risk of burning our hut down, but there is plenty of wood to build another, although it would be hard work in this cold. We would all have to shelter in the storage huts in the meantime.

That thought put me in mind of Peter Slade's wild plan to keep a Yorkist claimant to the throne of England here in Newfoundland, sheltering in this land of snow and wind in the hope of one day achieving the warmth and comfort of palaces in London and Westminster.

Well, Peter knows why he is here, and so does Harry Chard. They both believe that I know why I am here, because no other priest would come.

It is not so in the Spanish colonies, where the friars are eager to come and preach Christianity to the newly-discovered souls in this New World. The Spanish friars' reports say that the natives they meet are eager to hear the Word and to be converted. Where in England could one find such eager Christians? My very presence here in this land, because no other priest would carry out this ministry, proves that most English priests would rather preach to the damned (that is, most of their English parishioners) than to the heathen (that is, the Bettooks).

Now that I think upon it, Pope Gregory had great difficulty a thousand years ago finding priests willing to go to England and convert the English.

The last picture in my mind that I remember before I fell asleep is that of St. Augustine and his companions, unwilling evangelists to the English. Did they find

England and the English as unwelcoming, mysterious, and fearsome as I find Newfoundland and the Bettooks?

I was woken by Holy Gilbert putting more wood on the fire and thrashing the flames into life, while Horsfall, still lying in his bunk, growled and swore at the boy to work harder and faster.

Although I would gladly have remained wrapped in my bed as well, where although it was not warm it was at least less cold than outside, I got up and helped Gilbert, for the fun of annoying Horsfall and undermining his threats and abuse.

I nearly wrote that I wanted to shame Horsfall, but thinking upon the matter now, I doubt that Horsfall has ever felt shame. He tells me in confession about sins of which I may neither speak nor write, and he tells me that he repents, but I do not gain the impression that he feels ashamed of his sins. Sometimes I feel ashamed to have heard them.

All of a sudden the fire roared up as though commanded to do so by a pagan god. The men all slid unwillingly out of their beds. Young Martin held the frozen night pot in front of the fire to melt the ice so that he could empty it out of the door.

William Durdle cursed Young Martin for opening the door just for those few moments, because the cold sprang inside and bit us like a beast that had been hovering outside ready to pounce upon us, but I found Young Martin's simple household act tore at my spirit. It made me think of all the homes in faraway England where thousands were carrying out that ritual in damp grey mornings with no snow or sparkling cold.

"Do you feel safer now?" I asked Holy Gilbert. "Nothing has befallen us during the night."

"Thank you, Father. I am never so frightened during the daytime. I hate the darkness, but look how bright it is this morning."

Indeed it was one of those jewelled winter mornings that we sometimes see even in England; or, let me write that again: that we sometimes saw in England, for none of us may ever see England again.

It was one of those mornings where the sun shines brilliantly on fresh snow. It must have snowed again during the night, because the tracks that we had all left in the snow were now half filled in as though they had been melted by heat. I find it as difficult to summon up the memory of heat as it is to remember pain after it has eased.

After Mass, Peter Slade called all the men together.

"I have some work to do which will warm us all up. I need some lifting and carrying, because today is a dry day and I want to do some repairs to the fish flakes."

"Can I help?" I asked him, surprising even myself when I spoke.

"No, thank you, Father. Stay here and labour at your own trade."

I sat close to the fire and wrote up my book. I studied the Scriptures, and looked over what I would need to recite in the services over the next few days. We are already well into Advent, and Christmas is approaching.

Christmas, indeed! Well, there will be no goose and no plum porridge, unless someone has been hiding them in a secret place all these months.

It does not matter. I shall celebrate the season with all the correct forms, and most of the other men in the winter crew will have known nothing but meagre Christmases all their lives. Perhaps Peter Slade is an exception, as he is in most matters, but I am sure that Holy Gilbert, and perhaps Young Martin, have yet to encounter goose and plum porridge.

It took half the morning for my hands to warm up enough to write with, and then I still had to wait for the ink to form itself back into rich blackness instead of ice stained with shapeless lumps of soot. I wonder if the cold will harm the binding of the great blank book in which I write. It will be a rare irony if I should open it on the deck of a homebound ship, and have all my pages fly loose and scatter over the waters like blessings or curses.

I still wonder whether I have been sent by God to this place as a punishment, or as a reward, or as a duty. Is Newfoundland my blessing or my curse?

I had brought my writings up to date when the men burst in, banging away the snow from their clothes. William Durdle pulled his mittens off and shook them over the fire.

"Pardon me, Father, but you know the old jest: at home it is like Hell, with the priests nearest to the fire, ha ha!"

That was truly the first time in my life that I had actually heard a man say "ha ha" when he laughed. I was reminded of my astonishment at seeing the sea actually blue when I came across the ocean.

"Sometimes the old jests still make the best laughs," I replied. "We should ask the Bettooks for some jokes. They must have some that no Englishman has ever heard, and we can make our name as wits when we get back to England with our novel jests."

"Is that what you are writing, Father, so busy with your pen and so prodigal of your ink? Father Fletcher's Book of Merry Jests?"

That made even me laugh, in spite of the cold, and in spite of the fact that I hardly ever laugh. It is a trick which I have found difficult to master.

I have almost never wept, either, but then Jesus wept only once that we know of, so I may claim to be following the example of my Lord.

The other men were crowding into the room and forcing me further from the fire, no doubt all believing with William Durdle that eventually I would be compensated by roasting in flaming heat for eternity. It may yet come to pass if I do not make something of my life, and find a use for whatever talents I may have been given.

"Well," I replied to William, "it is always a precious gift to be given a laugh."

"Harry Chard is a rare wit," Horsfall remarked.

"Perhaps so, but he has not yet given me reason for mirth, rather the opposite," I said.

The men ate their meal slowly. There was no need to hurry, and if they had done so it would have meant a quicker return to the winter outside.

I put my book away, and wrapped my inkhorn in the rags which I hoped would protect it from freezing but which rarely do so.

Peter Slade watched me.

"Will you ever tell us what is in that book, Father?"

"I can tell you now. It is an account of these days since I came here, and it is also a commonplace book of my thoughts. My account is true, and whether my thoughts are worth anything can be judged only by others."

Young Martin put on his intelligent look again.

"Who will read it in England?"

Perhaps Young Martin is not such a childlike fool, not all the time.

"Nobody but myself, I suppose. I am writing it for myself, to myself. If I live to be old, it will be a comfort to me and a prop to my memory."

Holy Gilbert thought about that.

"So you will always remember us? And Harry Chard, and the Bettooks?"

"Come and do some work, Gilbert," William Durdle growled, and the men filed reluctantly out into the brilliant snows.

I knelt and said my prayers. How could I forget any of these men, or any of these events, unless I lost my reason altogether?

Reason, yes, reason, for what reason was I in Newfoundland, where the winter crew saw me only as a wizard reciting incantations to propitiate an angry God for their many and vulgar sins, and where the Bettooks did not need me at all?

The rough floor bit into my knees, and the cold made my back ache, but that was not made me leap up, for I had realised why I had been sent to this place. First of all, I needed to find Timaskatek again.

Chapter Eight

I pulled my furs and wools and cloaks around me, and slipped out of the hut like a successful thief. I closed the door behind me, leaving the fire burning.

I blinked in the sunlight reflecting off the snow, and my eyes filled with tears which I wiped away at once with the back of my mittens in case the tears should freeze and blind me.

I hurried off towards the forest. By now I was sure I knew in which direction the Bettook encampment lay. Because the air was still and the sky empty of clouds, there was no chance of a sudden snowfall filling up my tracks to prevent me finding my way back by following my own trail.

Once I had gone half a mile I was warm and sweating with the effort of wading through the snow, although my face was still aching with cold.

I shouted "Aguthut! Timaskatek! Harry Chard!" drinking in icy air as I did so. How much of my time in Newfoundland has been spent in shouting or talking to those cannot hear, will not listen, or will not reply to me?

"Harry Chard!" I roared again, in that loud voice which all priests are taught so that their words can fill a church. It is a trick which any man could learn, but which we keep to ourselves lest the congregation learn it as well and then shout us down.

I started with surprise when a voice at my shoulder gently said, "Good morning, Father Fletcher. How may I serve you?"

After I had paused for a moment to make sure that my voice would not quaver, I replied "Good morning to you, Harry Chard. You may serve me first by giving me some shelter from this cold."

"Ah, indeed that was what I was planning to do soon, but today will serve as well as any other. My shelter is some way from here. We must visit my friends the Bettooks first. Will you come with me?"

"Gladly, because I have some questions for them."

Harry Chard strode off, clearing the snow with vigorous kicks, and I fell in behind, happy to have him plough a way through the snow for me.

He spoke to me from under his hood. Because his back was turned to me and the echoes of his voice were softened by the snow, it was like a voice coming from within my own mind.

"More questions, Sir Ralph? I thought that it was the business of a priest to give answers to the poor faithful, not to torment them with questions."

"We arrive at truth by questions and answers working together at each end of a problem," I told him, "like two men sawing a plank out of a tree trunk."

"Ah, but one of the two men is the top sawyer, in the fresh open air, while the other man is the bottom sawyer, crouched in a dirty pit with sawdust and splinters showering upon him. Which of the two is the question and which is the answer?"

I paused for a moment before replying to that.

"Now there you prove my point, Harry. You and I hand questions to each other, and we are both trying to be the top sawyer and drive the other man into the pit. It doesn't matter for the time being, because my questions are for the Bettooks and not for you."

"Perhaps I can answer them for you," said the knowing and frightening voice from nowhere.

"Answer me this, then. Timaskatek spent two years in England. Was he ever baptised?"

"Not that I know of. In fact, I'm sure that he wasn't."

"Didn't anyone preach Christ to him?"

"No, I don't think so. Most of the time he was kept in the Palace of Westminster as a curiosity to be looked at, not like a man as other men, to be listened to or preached at."

"Not even that insolent Dominican friar whom I met over the Exchequer table? He was so proud of himself. Didn't he carry out the mission that St. Dominic entrusted to his order?"

"The Dominicans were formed to bring heretics back to the Church, and to make sure that converts from Judaism and Islam didn't slide back out of Christianity once they had been received."

I was struck by Harry's correct use of the name Islam.

"So nobody has preached to the Bettooks. The Spanish would not have left this land unconverted. It would be swarming with friars today if Newfoundland had been found by the Spaniards rather than the English."

"Something may be done to correct that," Harry replied between gasps, because he was beginning to pant with the effort of struggling through the deep snow. "Remember again the Palace of Westminster, and the Abbey next to it? Think of London, and the great spire of St. Paul's Cathedral."

He stopped, and his heaving breath filled the air with smoky condensation as though he were a demon exhaling fire. He held out his arm, thick with furs and mittens, and gestured towards the trees.

"There is your new St. Paul's, your new Westminster on this side of the ocean."

I thought he was joking, or dreaming, or deranged by the cold, but I looked where he was pointing. I saw only trees and dark green evergreen branches hung with ragged blankets of snow.

"I can see nothing. Where is your great cathedral, Harry?"

"I never promised you a great cathedral. Look again, at look at the shapes of things rather than their colours. Come with me."

We began stamping through the snow again, while I squinted against the sunlight reflecting off the snow. The harsh glare painted my vision with pink and green shadows, shadows of objects that had no existence. Was Harry's cathedral the same, with no substance other than his own imagination?

Men can believe strange things after they have spent half a winter in Newfoundland; the strange fears of Holy Gilbert show that.

"There, Father! You must see it now."

Wearily I looked again as I was commanded, and saw a hut like the one in which the winter crew had been living since Harry Chard's fishing fleet had sailed away at the end of summer.

"Just another hut for an English winter crew? Why didn't you stay with us?"

"That is no fishermen's hut, Sir Ralph. Come in with me. You will be the first to come in, apart from me, since the fleet left. Come along. There is a fire burning in there.

That should entice any man who is not a native of this land."

I would have entered any building in Newfoundland for the promise of a warm fire. Once again I stepped through Harry Chard's tracks.

The hut still looked much the same as ours to me, except for a strange conical projection at one end. The branches of the trees had been cut off to allow room for the thin high cone. It resembled the high pointed hats which noble ladies used to wear in the last century, as you can see them on funerary monuments.

Harry Chard saw me looking up at the cone.

"Yes, it is a poor thing compared to what one can see in England, but it will do for a beginning, the very first one there ever was here."

That was another of his statements which told me nothing.

He opened the door, and beckoned me to go in before him. I shook as much snow off my cloak and mittens as I could, and blinked the ice off my eyes. When I opened them again the first thing I saw was the figure of Christ upon His crucifix, the human body strangely bare, for I had seen only men closely wrapped up since the onset of winter.

I spun around on the spot in astonishment. Along the tops of the walls, just below, there were handsome carvings of the Stations of the Cross. Close to the door stood a great purple rock, that same purple-grey rock of which the whole land of Newfoundland is made, with a hollow hewn out of it.

"What is this?" I said, moving by instinct to the promised fire which was indeed burning with welcome warmth, shining golden flickers upon the carved body of Christ crucified. It cast lights and shadows upon the busy little wooden figures acting out their ancient drama in the Stations of the Cross above my head.

Harry Chard laughed, and the sound was eerie and frightening because it made no echo. It was like hearing the laughter of Satan.

"You, of all the winter crew, can't recognise what this is?"

"It's some kind of coarse parody of a church, an unhallowed jest," I said. "I feel that I'm in the presence of sin."

"Sin? No. It's an honest attempt at piety, by a man who's been guilty of more than his share of sin, I admit. The man without sin may be allowed to cast the first stone at an adulteress, but he will never become the Fishing Admiral of Newfoundland."

"Why have you built this imitation of a church?" I asked. The fire was smoky, and the bitter smell made gave the heat a dark and unholy quality.

"It's no imitation, Father. It's a real church."

"Who consecrated it, then? Even I have no church here, and I am a real priest. Have you also got a bishop hidden in this forest as well?"

"No bishop yet, no priest but for you, and certainly no other holy men. This is a beginning. This will be the chapel of the rightful king."

I glanced again round the little wooden likeness of a church. If it were properly consecrated, it would, I had to admit, make a beautiful little church, but it was the kind of beauty which is frightening, like seeing a woman whose beauty is so perfect that one dares not approach her.

Harry made a plea to me.

"Can you consecrate this church? I have an altar stone under what will be the altar, there below the crucifix, there where it should be."

"No, you would need a bishop for that, or at least a bishop's permission. No English bishop will do it, because the king would hardly allow you to consecrate a church in his overseas dominions to be a chapel for a pretender to the throne."

"I will find a true bishop, just as I will find a king."

"I thought you would go on say that you would find a priest to replace me," I replied, "poor unsatisfactory Ralph Fletcher, or Ralph the Lecher, as Aguthut calls me."

"I cannot judge whether you are unsatisfactory as a priest. Only your bishop and God can assess that. You do your job well enough. You listen to the men's confessions, and say the Mass, and read the right prayers for every day."

"That reminds me of a question I should have put to you earlier, Harry. When did you last attend Mass? You cannot use the excuse of being too far away. You have been here in Newfoundland all this time, and you knew I was here, too."

"It's true. I should have come. Now that you know I'm here, I'll come on Sunday."

"So you would not have come otherwise? I may refuse you Communion."

"You have given Communion to men who have committed worse sins that I have."

"I do not discuss what I am told in confession. Where is your confessional here?"

"There, Father, look."

It was true. There was a confessional, silent and unmanned, waiting for a priest to lend his ear in this antic parody of St Paul's Cathedral.

"You have thought of everything," I said, "but it is still not a real church."

"Would you hold Mass here?"

"Not if you use the fact later to accuse me of being part of your treasonable conspiracy. You have your ambitions for your life in this land. I have my own."

"You, Sir Ralph? You plan to make something of yourself in Newfoundland?"

"You caused me to be abandoned here, so you have no right to complain if I try to make myself useful. I have a calling as a priest and a duty."

"You have carried out your duties for the winter crew well enough."

"I am pleased by your praise, but there is another crew here in Newfoundland, not a winter crew, but a winter and summer crew. Nobody has preached Christ to them in all the eight years since this land became English."

"You mean the Bettooks. Few of them know that they're subjects of the king of England."

"They're all subjects of the king of Heaven, and I will tell them so."

"They should already know. They must have their own gods."

"Don't you even know? Haven't you been living with them?"

"Among them, yes, but not with them. I live here in the cathedral, or in the palace which I am building for His Grace."

"Not His Majesty, then? A mere duke, not a king?"

"Henry Tudor wants to be called Your Majesty. No king of England has ever demanded such a title."

"What of your palace, then? Is it as small as your cathedral?"

"A little larger, but it is only a beginning."

"I have a beginning to make, too. I must speak to the Bettooks. It is a crime that nobody has ever tried to evangelise them."

"I doubt that it will be easy. The Bettooks are not fond of the English."

"What do you expect, when the only treatment they have ever received is to be shot at or abducted across the ocean?"

"Well, you must face that enmity. If you are serious, you are as likely to be remembered as the first martyred priest in Newfoundland rather than as the hero of their conversion. Hundreds of years from now the Basilica of St. Ralph may stand on this spot; who knows?"

"I do not think I can ever make a saint, and only with God's help to strengthen me could I ever become a martyr, but I was called to the priesthood, and that carries many duties."

"What do you know of duties? You have spent your life in an endless boyhood: school and church. You know nothing of a man's life."

"I know only what I have been taught. I am in this world to minister and preach, whether I am worthy to or not. As for you, what of your duties? You've built this church. Will you allow the Bettooks to worship in it?"

Harry Chard looked up at the Stations of the Cross and ran his eyes along them, as if he were seeing the story for the first time.

"What a strange question, but it is a fair one, I admit. The answer is, yes, I would allow them to worship here, but even if you convert them they will not come in."

"Why not?"

"Because they are afraid of buildings. They live only in tents. Walls and ceilings terrify them. Even this church, which you find so small, frightens them too much. For them, you see, it is like going into a box. They never know such confinement."

"Yet Timaskatek spent two years in Westminster, within the thickest walls and ceilings in England."

"For him it would be as for you or I to spend two years locked in a coffin. He cannot forgive us for it, though I have tried to make him understand that it was neither a punishment nor a torture."

I remembered something else.

"Three men were taken from Newfoundland to England. What happened to the other two?"

"They are still in the Palace of Westminster."

"Within walls and under ceilings?"

"Would you have the king build a tent of untanned hide for them, so that they would feel at home?"

"Why, yes, I would, and I would have trees of the forest installed around it, and snow piled high about their tent in the wintertime."

"Perhaps you will succeed in evangelising the Bettooks."

"You promised to take me to them."

"Come along, then. They have moved their tents."

Harry Chard led me out of the west door of the cathedral that was to be. As I felt the cold again, I regretted having asked to be taken to the Bettooks quite so soon. I wished I could have remained a little longer beside that blessed fire.

Once again Harry spoke invisibly to me, not turning round to show his face.

"They have pitched their tents near the king's palace, but they will not come into it, any more than they will come into the cathedral. You have arrived in time for a feast. They have hunted down one of the great deer that live in these woods. The Bettooks are hospitable people and will let you share the meat."

All I could think of as my nose began to burn with cold was that meat meant cooking, and cooking meant another fire, and the sweet relief of heat.

I was watching Harry Chard's tracks in the snow in front of me, so I did not look up until he called to me again.

"There is my palace, Father Fletcher. That is my Whitehall, my Westminster, my Sheen, where I have been living all this time."

I saw another wooden building like the cathedral, but without the spire. Instead, it had been whitewashed in a pattern to suggest that it was only half-timbering built up with plaster, like a merchant's town house in England. I suppose it would have been too difficult to have made it resemble a stone castle.

"Harry, surely you did not build that all by yourself?"

"Lord, no. Sorry, Father. It has been building four years now, with one winter crew after another toiling upon it. You must admit that they have done a handsome job."

"Why do you not simply have a full crew of men living here all the year round?"

"In the summer, every man must work in the fishery, and we could not support all the men through the harsh winter."

"The Bettooks live here."

"Yes, but they do not live like Englishmen."

That reminded me of another question which I had been pondering.

"There must be another settlement nearby, because I have seen only Bettook men, and no women. Where do the women live?"

"I don't know. I have never seen their women."

"I can understand why you do not send women here with the winter crew," I said, although in fact I did not understand why the fish merchants did not do so, "but I do not understand why the Bettooks live apart from their women."

"You, a priest, ask that?"

"We do not choose to live apart from women. It is part of the life we are called to, so that we have no families and can give all our attention to caring for our flock."

"Well, I do not know where the Bettook women are. Perhaps they hide them for fear of the fishermen. Our winter crews are rough men, or boys who will soon become so."

"Young Martin has never become rough, and I am sure that Holy Gilbert will never become so."

"Well, you can be sure that we are not lost in these woods, because there are the Bettooks' tents."

This time there were three tents, with smoke leaking out of all of them. The head of one of the great deer lay bleeding in the snow.

Harry Chard pointed it out to me.

"They have such animals in the north of Europe. I have been told that we had them in England, too, in the time of the Romans, but that they were all taken by hunters. Now we do not even have an English name for them."

The beast's huge eyes were fixed upon the distant forest. It was like an allegory, or a fearsome dream, and I felt that it was a sign and a mystery, and that if this had been a dream or a legend the head would have spoken, and uttered some mysterious declaration or unfathomable prophecy.

I needed no more mysteries, having been showered with an abundance of them since I had landed in Newfoundland. Harry Chard slipped into the first tent and I followed him.

As I blinked in the warmth of the tent, I saw that Aguthut and Timaskatek were sitting beside the meat roasting on the fire. Timaskatek glowered at me, but I had learnt that this was his habitual expression. Any man who has spent two years of his life imprisoned in the Palace of Westminster with Dominican friars for company has earned the right to a foul disposition.

"Father Fletcher has been seeking you," Harry Chard explained in answer to a question that neither of the silent Bettooks had asked.

The Bettooks did not answer him, but exchanged words in their rapid language.

Timaskatek spoke for them both.

"Lecher no fissman."

"No, I am not a fisherman. I am a priest. Priest, that is. No friar, no friar, no Dominican."

To my astonishment, Timaskatek howled like a wolf, and then I realised that it was a laugh. He closed his eyes and roared with mirth. I saw his rows of pointed teeth, and I wondered if this was how all men used to laugh, without restraint, before we were civilised.

When Timaskatek had collected himself, he took out an English knife and carved off a slice of meat which he handed across the fire to me.

"Thank you," I said, hoping that he had been taught the words for gratitude. What kind of time had he passed in England, being given a sharp knife and yet not one sweet word about Christ?

"Pliss, Harrichard," he said as he handed the next hissing slice of meat to Harry.

Aguthut began to laugh too. I nearly scorched my bare hands on the hot meat, and while I juggled it among my fingers the two Bettooks laughed and laughed, while Harry Chard smirked and I sat in baffled silence.

"I am glad that you can be so happy," I said to Timaskatek. "I am sorry that you were taken by force to England." Harry Chard interrupted me.

"I do not think he knows where he was."

"I was told that the three men who were living in the Palace of Westminster dressed and bore themselves like Englishmen," I replied.

"So they did, while they were in England. We dress in furs and mittens while we are in Newfoundland, but we will not do so when we get back to England."

"Oh, so we will get back? You have no plans to murder me because I know about your plot?"

"We will all get back to England, God willing and a fair wind blowing across the ocean. Much has to happen first. The fleet must return for another season's fishing, and then we can go home."

Oh, Lord, I thought to myself, even if I live through this winter I must stay through spring and summer here before I can go home.

I decided to pretend to Harry that I saw my time in Newfoundland as an opportunity, when it fact I see it as a duty, laid upon me by God or man or both.

"That gives me plenty of time to preach to the Bettooks," I said.

Aguthut interrupted me.

"Bettook!" he insisted.

I looked at Harry in puzzlement.

"Aguthut means that you are not saying the name properly."

"So that is the name of his people," I replied.

"Yes, but you are not saying it quite right. Listen again. Aguthut, *bassa beerthook iki*."

"Bettook," Aguthut repeated again, and this time I noticed that the first vowel was drawn out a little long, and the consonants in the middle were soft, almost like our "th" sound in English. The last vowel was also shorter than I had thought.

"Beothuk?" I ventured.

"Yes," Aguthut answered, "Beothuk."

Thanks be to God, I had at last exchanged meaning with a Beothuk, for now I know that is who these people are. I am sure that it was as much a sign from the Lord as it was a sign from the Beothuks.

"Aguthut," I said, pausing to bite off another lump of the delicious hot meat, "I want to talk to you about God."

Aguthut turned to Harry, just as I had done a moment before when I had been the one who did not understand.

Harry now explained to Aguthut, in phrases where I thought I caught the words *'tun'* and *'shurra'*, whatever they may be. I wished that I had brought this book with me, so that I could write down all the words that I heard, and then write the English meanings next to them when I had worked out what they were.

I could also perhaps teach the Beothuks to write their own language. For the time being I had only my own memory, but fortunately it has been well trained by my masters in all subjects since I started school.

"Since you can speak to Aguthut," I said to Harry, "tell him that I would like to learn more of his language. I know how to speak only in English, Latin and French."

"Well, I know no Latin," Harry said, "I know a little of several languages, but this Beothuk speech seems like no other that I have other met. We need a scholar to study it properly, or perhaps for some English fishermen to marry Beothuk women and breed a generation who understand both languages."

"Let the Beothuk women become Christians first before I marry them to any of our English fishermen," I said.

"Many would say that you would have a harder task to make Christians of the English fishermen."

"The king has paid me forty testoons to do so." I took some more meat, while the Beothuks did the same. The tent was filled with the sound of chewing, so that it sounded like an English common pasture on a hot silent summer day with no noise except for that of beasts peaceably munching.

Harry Chard finished first and took the opportunity to speak.

"Nobody has paid you to convert the Beothuks."

"Yes, they have. I have accepted the calling of a priest. The Church will keep me all my life, but I must give some service in exchange for that. Here is the plainest need I have ever encountered. I am the first English priest in nearly a thousand years to meet pagans in an English dominion. I would probably not succeed in making them into Englishmen, and I may not succeed in making them into Christians, but I must try."

"Good luck, then, but you will get no help from me."

"I don't ask for your help, but I do ask you not to obstruct me. If you truly believe in your strange scheme to set up the House of York in Newfoundland, I think you would find that a native population of Christians would make your colony more secure than an angry population of pagans who feared everyone and everything English, as they do now."

I took my last piece of meat, and spent a little while chewing and thinking.

My training as an English priest had not provided me with any preparation for missionary work to heathens. I must discuss that with my bishop when I get home, if I ever get home.

Even if I do not, others will come after me and will face the same task. We could ask the Spanish for advice, because their friars have shown extraordinary zeal in preaching in this New World, but whether they are seeking souls for Christ or bodies for slavery is another question. That is another danger, because there are plenty of Englishmen who would willingly enslave the Beothuks if they could.

Harry Chard took a length of bloody bone and ran it through his teeth like a dog. He spoke again, brandishing the bone in my face for rhetorical emphasis.

"There, I have brought you to the Beothuks. Your mission to them is your responsibility. As for myself, I must tend the fire in the king's palace."

He hoisted himself up, and lumbered out of the tent, closing the flap carefully behind him. It is evidently a point of good manners in this country do so in time of winter, and quite rightly so.

I chose to address Aguthut.

"Aguthut, you still have the bell which I gave you. I heard it ringing in the night around our fishery buildings. You know, the bell?"

I mimed the action of ringing the bell, and imitated the sound of it as best I could.

Aguthut reached into his smock and brought out the bell. I nearly cried out when I saw how dirty it had become. I swear I could actually smell it even across the smells of meat, smoke, and unwashed men.

The bell had turned a dull grey, streaked with damp and unidentifiable dark filth which must have come off Aguthut's own body, but when he shook it the sound was as sweet as ever, although it made Timasketek growl something at him.

"The bell," I said, knowing that he could not understand me, "is one symbol. There are other symbols. You reached into your breast to take out the bell. Watch me do the same."

I took out the crucifix which I wear around my neck. It hardly ever sees the light of day now, not since autumn and then winter set in. It is on a generous length of fine chain which I have looped and knotted. I undid the knot so that I could loosen the chain to its full length and put the crucifix into Aguthut's left hand, while he still clutched the bell in his right.

"This is the most powerful symbol of all," I told him.

Aguthut studied the tiny figure of Christ crucified, which caught the light of the flames in the same way as the figures in the Stations of the Cross in Harry Chard's little cathedral.

I spoke up again.

"To find out what it means, you must come and see me. In the hut, by the sea. You know? Among the English fishermen."

Timaskatek looked up at that, but I took back the crucifix, put it back into my clothing, and left the tent. I found my way back by following our tracks, past the empty wooden play-cathedral and through the silent trees.

Chapter Nine

I came back and wrote all these events into my book. I have set down my pen, and now I must wait. It may be that nothing will happen, but I must wait nevertheless.

Indeed, in the calendar of the Church it is the season of waiting, Advent, and perhaps that is another sign. I am halfway through this book as well. It will perhaps be another sign if I see no more events, and think no more thoughts, than will fill the stiff blank pages which remain. At least I brought enough ink, and I have learnt to husband my limited supply of goose feathers. What a strange word to use, husband, by one who will never be the husband of any woman.

I am sitting here writing by the fire. Holy Gilbert is tidying up the room. There is little to tidy, but a good sweeping is often needed, because we all make a lot of dirt in a small room. When men live communally without women, they either live in filth and disorder, or maintain a superb cleanliness, as the sailors do at sea.

The great mystery remaining to me is where the Beothuk women are. If I can learn their language well enough, I will ask them. I can understand them hiding the women from the fishermen, but not why they hide them from me. Harry Chard must have told them that I am no lecher in spite of my name.

I must also ask to see the interior of Harry's palace for the Yorkist pretender. I wonder whether that boy or youth, whoever he may be, living in some great house in Flanders or Italy, knows that a plan has been laid for him to come and live in a rough hut in the middle of the forests of Newfoundland, an land of which he may have heard, but of which he knows nothing?

Even Holy Gilbert does not like it here. I wonder if his mother knew what she was sending him to. He seems cheerful enough as he sweeps and wipes, but that may be only because none of the men is here to cuff and kick him.

I used to wonder where the men go when they are supposedly working on the fish flakes and the other structures which the winter crew are here to maintain, but now I am sure that they are working on Harry Chard's palace. Should I do something about that? If so, what? After all, I am here as a priest, not to enforce the rule of one king or another.

I had to stop for a little while because Holy Gilbert interrupted me with another of his questions.

"How shall we celebrate Christmas, Father?"

"Just as we always do, Gilbert, with all the services and observances. I fear there will be no goose or plum porridge, though."

"Will it still be Christmas, though, here where we are?"

"Well, of course it will be Christmas. It is Christmas all over the world. It has been Christmas in Newfoundland ever since it was Christmas in Bethlehem 1500 years ago. I believe I am the first English priest to celebrate Christmas in Newfoundland, which is a great honour for me, but even if I were not here you could still have celebrated it."

Gilbert thought upon that.

"Do the Bettooks have Christmas?"

"I have discovered that we should call them the Beothuks, Gilbert. Like this: Be-othuks. No, they do not have Christmas, because they have not yet heard of Christ."

"It is a sad thing that they should not have Christmas."

"Yes, but it is even sadder that they should not have Easter, which is much more important than Christmas."

"Christmas is more cheery."

"Whether it will be so in this country, we shall see. I would like this to be the year when the Beothuks have their first Christmas, but I know that it will take more time."

"Are you going to preach to them, then, Father?"

"If I can. I don't know their language, and they know very little of ours, although one of them has lived in England."

"Timaskatek," Holy Gilbert said, surprising me. "I know about him. I was on the same ship coming out, and I tried to talk to him, but he wanted to be silent, although I'm sure he understood me."

To think that Gilbert has been silent about this until now! What else have I not been told?

"Well, he had received ugly treatment from us. Carried off from Newfoundland, and then kept prisoner in Westminster for three years, in a great stone building when the Beothuks fear a roof and walls above all things."

Gilbert threw the sweepings out of the door, and the wind flung winter into the room for a few moments. I pulled the form on which I was sitting closer to the fire. I am in danger of becoming a pagan myself, worshipping fire.

I wrote no more that day. I sat by the fire, idle when others were working, and thought upon how I could communicate with the Beothuks. As always, I am sure Harry Chard is not telling me all the truth. Indeed, I wonder if he has ever told me the truth.

Lord, how can I speak to the Beothuks? Did you really send me to this place so that I could try to convert them, when one of their number has been all the way to an England overrun with priests and nobody preached to him?

If that smug Dominican at the Exchequer had meant what he said about wishing he could do pastoral work, he could have been a pastor to poor Timaskatek. Instead, he paid me forty testoons and sent me off to Newfoundland. I am sure that he will be enjoying a sumptuous Christmas this year.

I finished writing at that point, and put my book and pen away. I spent the rest of the day studying what I needed to do for Advent. I am, after all, still a very new priest although I have been rigorously trained, and I need to look up the readings and order of service for every day.

I know older priests who can do it all from memory, even knowing the readings for each day of the year, and which ones to substitute when a saint's feast day falls on a Sunday.

That evening all of us were sitting around the fire, which is how we spend every evening, for there are no taverns here to go to. Doubtless there will be drinking places in Newfoundland one day. The men were curious about my idleness.

William Durdle pretended to be friendly.

"Not writing tonight, Father?"

"No, William. I brought my writing up to date earlier today, when I came back from seeing Harry Chard's church and palace."

"Is that what it is?" William blurted out before he could stop himself, and Peter Slade looked angrily at him. Peter can glower even more effectively when his face is hellishly illuminated from below by the firelight.

"Harry Chard tells me that it is to be a palace, or the best that can be constructed in the woods of Newfoundland. Have you been working on it, William?"

William would not answer me. He looked at Peter Slade, seeking permission to speak. What hold does Peter have over these men, who are rough and strong-willed? They always do his bidding.

Peter did the answering himself.

"We all work on the buildings for the fishery. We have to do so, because they must be ready for the spring."

"Could that not be done by sending a ship full of carpenters and workmen, a few weeks before the rest of the fleet?"

"The site must also be guarded," Peter explained, "because the natives steal so much. They particularly take nails, because they have no metal of their own, and they fashion the nails into the points of spears and other hunting weapons."

"Steal? How are they to know that you have not abandoned these things?"

"They know now. Not every winter crew is as tolerant of the natives as we are."

"Cruelty to the Beothuks makes my task here much more difficult. Why should they trust me?"

Horsfall interrupted me.

"Why should you trust them, Father? They are cruel heathens."

"I have seen no evidence that they are cruel. No doubt some of them can be, but Englishmen can be cruel, too. As to their being heathens, it is our duty to convert them."

Then there came one of those silences, when everyone in a room stops talking, and there is an unexpected hush. When that happens, the common people say 'an angel flew over.' Whether an angel flew over our lost encampment on the rocks beside the ocean I cannot say, but I do know that in that silence we all started in surprise and fear when from outside there came again the tinkling of the silver Mass bell.

I know that the men did not expect me to say what I said.

"Not again!"

Holy Gilbert was shocked. That boy is too easily shocked to be a fisherman; what will become of him?

"What is the matter, Father? That is a Beothuk out there, and the sound is nothing but your own Mass bell, that you gave away yourself."

"I know very well what it is, Gilbert. Are they summoning me again? I do not want to have to go out into the cold and darkness every night. Do not rebuke me by saying that St. Francis of Assisi or St. Dominic would have done so. I am sure that they would, but I am only poor Ralph Fletcher, and I am no saint."

Peter Slade saw a chance to taunt me.

"Will you ignore him, then, for all your talk about converting the Beothuks?"

"No, I will not ignore him. I want him to come in here."

"He will not do so," Horsfall said. "They fear our buildings, and they fear us. Peter told us so."

"No," I replied, "Peter did not. Harry Chard told you so. Harry has told many things to many men, and now I do not believe anything merely because it came from Harry Chard."

I went to the window and peered out into the night. There was nothing to be seen except a patch of snow faintly lit by the window. As I looked to right and left, my own shadow swayed on the white snow like a threatening ghost. Truly I really am I man who can be frightened by his own shadow.

"Aguthut!" I shouted.

There were no tracks in the snow except for the ones that the men of the winter crew had made, all crowding towards the door.

I heard the bell again. It seemed to be coming from a point just beyond where I could see from the window. The rough cheap glass chilled my face when I pressed against it, trying to see farther.

I went to the door and opened it far enough to lean through, in spite of the groans and protests behind me.

"Sit closer to the fire if you are cold!" I told them, and then I called again.

"Aguthut! Why are you ringing the bell again? I won't come out. Come in here with us. We won't hurt you."

I listened again for the bell, disregarding all the pleas for me to shut the door and keep out the devil of the winter cold. There was silence outside as intense as the shouting and protests within.

The bell rang again, this time on the other side of the hut, where the fire was and where there was no window. I closed the door and drew the crude wooden bolt across it. For the first time it occurred to me to wonder why someone had bothered to make a bolt for it. Who were we supposed to be bolting the door against, in this empty land?

The bell rang again, but this time it was closer. All the men looked in the direction from which the tinkling had come, even though they could have seen nothing through the walls built of thick logs and caulked with earth.

There was silence again for a few moments, and I became aware of the sound of the men's breathing, fast and desperate as though they were running.

The bell rang again, so loudly that it might have been within the room itself. Holy Gilbert began to cry. I expected Horsfall or William Durdle to cuff Gilbert and tell him to be silent, but they were both transfixed by the sound. I decided that I had to break the spell.

"In the name of the Lord, it is only a poor native out there ringing an ordinary Mass bell! You all know that. What are you so afraid of?"

The fire spat, making Holy Gilbert squeal. He glanced round the room at all the flame-lit faces in turn, as if he were looking for someone to run to for comfort.

Well, his mother is far away across the sea, and he will never receive any tenderness from these harsh men, nor even from me. I am not a cruel man, but I do not know how to be kind.

I lost my temper with Aguthut.

"What does he want? He runs around the hut, ringing that bell, but he will not come in."

Young Martin had one of his brilliant insights.

"He wants you, Father."

"I know that, but what does he want me for?" I replied. I went to the wall at the point where the sound of the bell had last come from, and thumped with my fist against the wall, making flecks of earth fly out from between the logs, and splinters fall from the ceiling.

A quick, frantic series of knocks came from the other side. Holy Gilbert snivelled again.

Young Martin considered the problem of the knocking, and while he was pondering it the knocking sounded again.

William Durdle was the only man to say anything sensible.

"It would be better for him to come round and knock on the door, instead of a blind wall. Is it possible that he doesn't understand what a door is?"

For a moment I considered it.

"I doubt it. He must have seen Harry Chard go in through the door of the church and the palace, and I am sure he has seen us come in and go out through our own door here. Anyway, Timaskatek has seen real doors in London, and he must have told Aguthut about them."

"Then why knock on the wall like an angry neighbour?"

"Because he is an angry neighbour, William. He wants me to come out and talk. I do not think I will play that game again. Let him come to me now."

There was no more knocking. After a long enough period of silence, the men relaxed and I no longer noticed their breathing.

Horsfall stretched his legs out towards the fire.

"I think we should—" he began, but I shall never know what he was going to suggest, because Holy Gilbert squealed again and flung himself down at the bottom of the wall, pressing himself against the rough logs as though he were trying to burrow into them.

"Come on, Gilbert," I said, shaking him by the shoulders and trying to pick him up. "You are no safer making yourself into a ball on the floor than if you were standing up. You are no hedgehog, you know. Come on, stand up. There's nothing to fear, I'm sure of it."

Gilbert managed to stand up, still sobbing. He chose Tom Rudge, of all of us, to go to for comfort. Perhaps Tom seems like a grandfather to him.

Comfort is supposed to be my trade as a priest, but clearly Gilbert, at least, does not see me as a master of that craft.

At least somebody wanted me, for the bell rang again.

"All right!" I shouted, so that Aguthut would be able to hear me. "It is louder for bellringing here than the City of London on a Sunday morning."

I had resigned myself to going out in the snow yet again for yet another uncomfortable errand, but the bell fell silent. We all watched the same point on the wall, as though Aguthut should burst through it any moment, or words would be written upon it by an angelic hand, as on the walls of Nebuchadnezzar's palace in the ancient time.

Holy Gilbert turned and cried out, pointing over our shoulders towards the window.

A face appeared for an instant, and then withdrew, so suddenly that I wondered whether I had actually seen it.

Horsfall's voice breaking the silence was like an axe splitting wood.

"It's you he wants, Father. Go and see."

I was already scrambling towards the window. I wiped away the condensation. I peered out through the filaments of ice frozen on the outside surface of the glass, but there was nobody to be seen either to the left or right.

The face rose up from below and stopped a finger's length from my own.

It was not Aguthut. It was Timaskatek. A monstrous ornament was hanging in front of his nose, and then I recognised it as my little Mass bell, made huge and threatening by my own bafflement and fear.

"What do you want, Timaskatek?" I called through the thick dirty glass. "Do you want to come in?"

Timaskatek shook his head like an animal. He had learnt that from his captors in Westminster.

"Do you want me to come out?" I asked.

Timaskatek shook his head again, and pushed his face against the glass. The pressure distorted his features. He looked like a mask to be carried in a Mystery Play or a procession of penitents to terrify the faithful and the sinful alike.

"Gill-bert," he groaned. "Send Gill-bert. Harry say Gill-bert."

Young Martin leapt over to the window.

"Gilbert? You'll never have him, you dirty heathen!"

Gilbert rushed to Tom Rudge and clung to him again. All the men seemed to be expecting me to act. Peter Slade was silent, and even William Durdle had no stupidity to offer.

I was hoping that Timaskatek understood more English than I knew, or that he might admit. I also thought that Harry Chard himself might be lurking somewhere nearby where he could hear us. Harry seemed to do so much at night. Is he a creature of darkness, or of evil itself?

"Timaskatek, if you want Gilbert, come in here and ask him."

I beckoned to Timaskatek. The men were horrified. Young Martin made to hit me, and then stopped himself, fortunately just before I would have quailed back and made myself look weak and silly.

"Don't worry. Timaskatek won't come in here. If Harry Chard wants to send Beothuks here like servants to summon us, there is no reason why we have to go. Gilbert, you are safe. Gilbert, what are you doing?"

Gilbert was clambering into his boots and decayed fur smock. It was one of those moments of grief and crisis when one notices foolish and unimportant things, and I realised that the fur must once have been a valuable garment owned by a rich man. How had Gilbert's mother obtained it?

It was more pressing to discover why Harry wanted Gilbert, and why Gilbert was agreeing to go.

"Why are you going, Gilbert?" I demanded.

"Because the Admiral wants me."

"He's no longer the Fishing Admiral. The fleet has gone home, and he should have gone with it. Peter, stop him."

Peter shrugged while he helped Gilbert into his cap and mittens.

"I obey the Fishing Admiral too, Father. If he summons Gilbert, then Gilbert must go."

"In the middle of a freezing night, for an unknown purpose?"

"I am sure that everything will be revealed," Peter replied. "Off you go, Gilbert."

I stepped over to stand between Gilbert and the door.

"No! Too many secrets have been kept from me, and when answers have been revealed to me, I have yet to like anything that I have been told. I want to know what this is about. Wait, Gilbert. I'm coming with you."

Peter shrugged again while I struggled into my own outdoor clothes, which had not yet dried out. I flinched from the cold dampness of them, and it took even longer than usual to put them on.

I opened the door, and Gilbert skipped out in front of me, but he slowed down to an old man's pace as soon as his boots were engulfed by the snow.

I closed the door, and went after him, but Timaskatek jumped in front of me and pushed his fist into my chest.

"No," he said, "no!"

He reached behind me and opened the door with surprising skill for one who should have known little about doors. He must have learnt much as a prisoner in Westminster.

Perhaps his guards also taught him how to push a man back through a door. He must have been pushed thus into his cell many times. How he must have enjoyed doing that to an English priest.

Timaskatek flung me back into the room, so that I fell onto my back on the floor. I was neither hurt nor frightened nor angry; all I felt was puzzlement.

None of the men helped me up off the floor, and none of them offered to fight Timaskatek on my behalf, either.

They all formed a circle around me as though I were a defeated contestant in a fight for money. Well, I had lost the fight, if it had been one, but I still have my forty testoons.

By the time I had stood up again, all the men were clustered at the window. I noticed that they had not opened the door for a better view, and I do not think that fear of the cold was their reason.

Without waiting to take off my outdoor clothes, I shoved my way through the mass of shoulders and ears blocking my sight of the window.

"Has Gilbert gone?" I asked. "Did you see him?"

"He went into the woods," a hot voice spat into my ear. "All the savages followed after him."

"All? There was more than just Timaskatek?"

Peter Slade assumed his normal mastery.

"I cannot be sure, but I think there were six or seven of them. Don't worry too much, Father. I'm sure that Gilbert went willingly."

"Peter, do you once again know far more than you are telling me?"

"No, Father, I swear I know nothing of this. This is one of Harry Chard's plots, or japes, or maybe both in one."

"What are we going to do then?" I asked, not really knowing to whom I was addressing the question. "Nothing," I answered for myself. "I don't trust Harry Chard, but I see no reason why he would want to harm Gilbert."

"Nor do I," Peter Slade said, and because we had both spoken the same opinion, the other men accepted that in silence.

Because there was nothing we could do to help Gilbert, if indeed he needed help, the other men rolled themselves up in their thick rough blankets and went to sleep. I sat by the slowly fading fire, writing all these events up in my ledger. There was no sound except for men's breathing, the cracklings of the fire, and the scratching of my pen.

Although I am sitting next to the embers, I feel the cold slowly wrapping itself around me like an invisible beast. Soon my ink will begin to freeze, and so will I.

There is no point in my staying awake and waiting for Gilbert to return, and still less point in struggling against sleep while I wonder what Harry Chard wants from him. I will go to bed as well, but first I will make sure that the door is barred. Gilbert can come in but nobody else.

I was the first to wake up in the morning, so I lit the fire and when ink and hands were warm enough I began writing again.

One convenience of life here is that we sleep in the same clothes as we wear in the day, so there is no need to face putting on chilled garments.

Perhaps the others do not find that unusual; they are poor men, after all, with only one set of clothes for all days and all occasions.

I wonder what my father would think of me if he could see me now? Indeed, I wonder if anyone has told him where I am, or whether he has bothered to ask?

Some might say that I stood in the place of a father to Holy Gilbert, or perhaps Peter Slade does, but in any case someone needs to worry about the boy.

I came here to Newfoundland to be a plain priest for the summer and go home. When I found myself stranded here by Harry Chard, I thought I would spend the winter still being an ordinary priest to a parish of a few men, and then go home, but this is a strange place, much stranger than I had imagined.

I have started to wonder whether this great continent, of which Newfoundland is but a small part, and which men like to call the New World, really is a New World, one that did not exist only fifteen or twenty years ago.

As I meditate upon this idea, I wonder if this is a new Creation, where this time Man is to be tested in a harsh wilderness rather than in a Garden of Eden. Perhaps the Beothuks are a permanent Winter Crew, abandoned by God to a land with no summer.

Even the fact that we never see their women may make sense. In this re-enactment of the testing of Man, there are no women to blame if we fall, and there is no serpent in this land. It is literally true: the men tell me that there are no snakes at all on the island of Newfoundland.

Am I Adam? I am not innocent, as he was, even if I am innocent of the knowledge of woman and will always

remain so. Is Holy Gilbert Adam? He, at least, is an innocent, and now that I remember it he did appear naked last
summer, although I doubt that he will do so at this time of
year.

Am I the serpent? Is that role to be enacted by Harry
Chard? What is the Beothuks' part in all this? It is, now
that I think upon it, truly like one of those rough old
Mystery Plays that are played in the streets every year,
with roaring devils, piping angels, the greatest sinners in
town playing pious saints, and the Gate of Hell carried
around on a groaning cart with flames and fireworks for
more effect.

How I loved the Mystery Plays when I was a boy. Let
me be honest: how I love them still, and would gladly go
to see one if I could. Could we put on a Mystery Play here
in Newfoundland? Would the English fishermen play the
devils, or would the Beothuks?

If I were a better priest I would be giving answers
instead of asking questions. The question of the moment
is what Harry Chard has done with Holy Gilbert, who will
find it difficult to remain holy if Harry has mistreated him.

Just as I wrote that, the other men began rolling into
unwilling wakefulness, and I put away my pen and ink.
The winter crew took their breakfast as if it were an act of
duty rather than something to enjoy, and put on their furs
and mittens ready for work, when we were all struck
motionless by a man's voice crying out from outside.

"Peter Slade!" the voice demanded. "Come out here!"

"That is Harry Chard!" Young Martin exclaimed, as
though it could have been anyone else.

"Why does he want me to come out?" Peter wondered.
"Has he become a savage, too, unwilling to come under a
decent English roof?"

"Go out and ask him, then," I said, with testiness which surprised even myself.

Peter made no reply, but he went out through the door. The winter cold crouching outside leapt inside and struck us hard. Horsfall prodded furiously at the young fire, while the rest of us stood still and waiting.

I watched through the window as Peter trod through the snow and slipped between the trees. We all waited. The practical among us, such as Horsfall and William Durdle, knelt by the fire, while the dreamy ones such as myself and Young Martin stared out of the window.

That is why we were the first to see Holy Gilbert come out of the woods. Peter Slade followed, walking three paces behind Gilbert, whose face was hidden by the woollen cloth which he wears against the cold. All I could see of Gilbert was his eyes, blinking against the sunlight shining off the snow, but as he came closer I thought from the set of his eyes that he was smiling.

Behind Peter Slade came Harry Chard, walking three more paces after. The strange procession came towards us like three characters in a pageant.

I even looked to see if anyone else was coming three paces further back, perhaps Aguthut and Timaskatek carrying the Gate of Hell with flames and fireworks issuing from it and melting the snow, but there was nobody.

It was the unshakable Tom Rudge who opened the door. Holy Gilbert walked in as if it were a new place to him, and unwrapped his face. He truly was smiling.

Peter Slade followed, and stood to the left of Gilbert, gazing at the opposite wall, and saying nothing.

Harry Chard came in, and mercifully closed the door behind him. Harry wiped ice off his beard, and flung his mittens onto the floor by the fire. He stood on Gilbert's right, forming a pair with Peter Slade standing on Gilbert's left.

Harry grandly lifted his right arm in a salute which enfolded Holy Gilbert in an invisible mantle. Harry spoke at last.

"Men of the winter crew, kneel on this cold hard wooden floor. Kneel before this boy, whom I have brought across the sea not as his master but as his servant, because he is the true King of England."

Chapter Ten

When I sat down to write down what happened, the principal thing I remembered was how frightened Holy Gilbert looked even while he was still smiling. It takes a great and strange happening to bring fear and laughter upon a man at the same time, even to bring them together upon a boy.

Everyone knelt except me. Now that I think back upon it, I believe that I too felt fear and an impulse to laugh. I restrained my laughter, but it was harder to hold back my fear.

Gilbert, still standing among the bowed heads of the winter crew, looked at me questioningly, and, I thought, beseechingly.

I spoke to Harry Chard instead of him.

"Harry, this has gone too far," I said, afraid of what Harry Chard and his strangely-found Beothuk confederates might do.

There was also Peter Slade, who had expressed the hope that Harry's scheme would restore Peter to the wealth and high social station that he claimed to have enjoyed before the fall of Richard Duke of York who had styled himself King Richard III.

Harry made no reply. He was still mutely kneeling, a posture in which he had probably not been seen since the time of King Edward IV or perhaps even Henry VI, so I spoke again.

"Harry, you may foolishly entangle and endanger yourself with this mad plan, but I cannot allow you to force Gilbert into it. You could bring him to the execution block on Tower Hill for this."

"Who are you to allow or forbid anything?" growled Harry, still with his face to the floor. "You are only a foolish and very young priest, who only came here because we could get no better."

"Foolish I may be, which is my own fault, and very young I may be, Harry, which is not my fault, but I am still a priest, called by God and ordained by a bishop, and I have a pastoral duty to look after the spiritual welfare of every Christian here."

Harry did his best to express his anger effectively while his head was still bowed down and his face was turned away from me. His neck was turning rash-red in spite of the cold air.

"Do you presume to order the affairs of your king?"

"No, Harry, my king is in England at this moment. He has his own priests, bishops, and archbishops to minister to him. There is no bishop in Newfoundland, and no king here either."

Holy Gilbert, whom Harry had obviously told to look regal, was striving to do so. Gilbert was achieving a surprising dignity which I had never seen on him before, in spite of his unease at the quarrel.

I appealed to him to relieve the other men's discomfort at least.

"Gilbert, please ask everyone to rise. It is hard for them to kneel on the floor for a long time."

I was startled by the voice of Young Martin, rising from the floor.

"Father, you have made us kneel many times."

"Yes, but I have never made you kneel to me, only to God, and I spend much more time in prayer than any of you, except perhaps for Gilbert. Gilbert, please ask them to stand up."

Harry Chard spoke again.

"His name is not Gilbert. It is William."

"No it's not!" Gilbert exclaimed, shocked out of his royal silence. "It's Gilbert. I was baptised Gilbert."

"You were baptised, but not in the name of Gilbert. Your name is William."

Gilbert rocked, and for a moment I thought that he would fall down. Instead, he collected himself, and finally granted my request.

"Please stand up, all of you."

I am sure that it was the first time in his life that Gilbert had issued a command to anyone, and he seemed astonished and relieved that it was obeyed.

"Now, Gilbert," I told him, "no matter what Harry Chard has told you, you are not the king of England, and you must not think of yourself in that way. If you make such claims in England, you will finish on the execution block, like Perkin Warbeck five years ago."

"Lambert Simnel was not executed," said William Durdle. It was one of those foolish and pointless things that men say in moments of great tension.

"No, he was last heard of working as a scullion in the royal kitchens, but I doubt that any future pretender will receive such light punishment."

Gilbert forgot his lessons in behaviour and began to cry.

"I don't know anything about all of this! I only know what the Fishing Admiral told me."

I pounced upon that, taking my chance to question Gilbert when Harry Chard could not interrupt or contradict him without undermining his own plot by seeming to show disrespect to his supposed king. I was guilty of pride in feeling that I had made Harry's own scheme spring shut upon him like a mishandled mousetrap.

"When did he spin this story to you, Gilbert?"

"He told me in England, at my mother's house," Gilbert replied, apparently relieved at being allowed to speak for himself. "He came to see her, and they went into the back room behind the shop and talked for a long time."

"Out of your hearing?"

"Yes, and then my mother told me that I had work for the summer with the fishing fleet, and that I would see and learn many things."

"Did he tell her about this mad scheme?"

"He must have done."

I turned to confront Harry Chard.

"Did you bring his mother into this?"

"No, Father Fletcher, I did not. It was she who brought me into this."

"What do you mean?" I asked, as Gilbert gasped.

"It was his mother who told me the truth: who she was, and who he was."

"Is she truly a poor widow, then?"

"Poor yes, but she has not always been so. Like Peter Slade, she has known a better life with greater state and honour."

"The taverns of England are full of men and women who will tell you that they once knew a better life with greater state and honour," I replied. "Half the beggars in the streets of London will tell you the same thing about themselves."

"It is true that most of them are lying or mad, yet some of them are telling the truth."

"Can you tell truth from lies?"

"You are a priest. You hear confessions nearly every day. Can you tell which are true, or whether the penitent is withholding sins which they are not confessing?"

"I can guess, sometimes, but I have no right to think such thoughts. I am sworn to trust the penitents as well as to keep their confessions secret."

"I believe Gilbert's mother. I believe that Gilbert is the rightful King of England."

"Many believed that of Lambert Simnel and Perkin Warbeck. They will not be ready to accept yet a third pretender to the throne."

"This one is different. He is true and rightful."

Holy Gilbert wrung his hands, glancing around the room as though his eyes were following the flight of a trapped bird or insect.

I decided that there was no point in arguing with Harry Chard. I suspect that many people have reached the same conclusion over the years of his life.

"Very well, Harry. You plan to set up poor Gilbert as the true King of England. What is the whole plan?"

William Durdle interrupted us.

"Don't tell him, Harry! You haven't told us yet." That interested me.

"So you have not told your band of brothers, your fellow conspirators?" I said. "You're asking them to risk going to the gallows to be hanged, drawn, and quartered. I suppose you consider that you belong to the upper classes, and so you will claim the right to be beheaded on the block instead."

"It is Henry Tudor and his supporters who will go to the gallows and the block."

"Have you told Gilbert himself? Gilbert, what has he told you?"

Peter Slade tried to intervene, turning to Gilbert.

"No, listen —"

"Do you presume to say 'no' to your king, Peter? Let me ask the question. Gilbert, do you know the plan?"

"No," Gilbert replied in a tiny voice that we could hardly hear. It was like the sound of a thought, words without breath or body.

"Well, Gilbert, I can tell you this much. Harry's plan is treason, and it will fail. If rebellions made in England did not succeed, a rebellion made in faraway Newfoundland is sure to fail. You will not finish as a kitchen servant like Lambert Simnel. You will be executed on the gallows, half-hanged, gelded, with your belly ripped open by the knife. The executioner will tear out your heart with his bare hands and hold it up to your eyes while you are still alive. Has Harry told you about that?"

"He tells me I am the king," the ghostly voice answered.

"There it is, Peter," I said. "Harry has placed the whole winter crew literally in mortal danger, and yet he will not tell them the plan."

I let silence fall, and the men shuffled and coughed. Young Martin and William Durdle both lunged towards the fire, meaning to poke at it, but the fire did not need tending. They were merely seeking something to do to try to cover their embarrassment. Although he is much older, William Durdle had moved faster, and Young Martin shrank back, smiling in defeat. I wonder how many times in his life Young Martin has had to smile when other men have pushed him aside.

Harry Chard clasped his hands behind his back, and assumed the posture of command which he liked to take up when he was on the ship coming over from England.

"Very well, Father. You say that I should tell them the plan, and why not, indeed, because no word of it can get back to Henry Tudor's spies in England now. You see before you the rightful king of England, not born in wedlock, I admit—"Holy Gilbert gave a start at that, his royal holiness shocked, but Harry went on, not having noticed the Royal Pretender's hurt "—but bastardy has never been a bar to the throne."

"But only for genuine royal bastards," I said.

"Indeed. Holy Gilbert is the grandson of King Edward the Fourth."

"So are half the men in England," I objected.

"Yes, but they do not know it and cannot prove it."

The men of the winter crew looked upon Holy Gilbert in awe. What a power it is to be royal.

I decided to stir the pot with a new question.

"What part are the Beothuks to play in this conspiracy?" I asked. "Is an army of Beothuks to land in England, overthrow the king in a great battle, and carry Gilbert in triumph to the throne?"

"There is no Beothuk army," Harry Chard replied. "As far as I know they have no wars, not because they are better than us, but because they have nothing to fight over. As long as they can hunt in the interior of the land in the winter, and come to the coast in the spring for fish and seals, they have all that they need. There are so few of them that they cannot afford to waste men in war."

"A happy people," I said, "to have no enemies."

"They have an enemy now. Their enemy is England."

The other men exclaimed in astonishment at that. I put their question for them.

"How? Few Englishmen have heard of the Beothuks. Even the king hardly knows of them."

"This is a vital fishery for England," Harry Chard said. "The fleets have been coming over here for more than twenty years, before John Cabot, before even Cristoforo Colombo."

"This is nothing new for the Beothuks, then."

"No, but winter crews are new. Before long there will be more than winter crews who spend the whole year in Newfoundland. There will be fishing villages, and then towns, with women and children. What of the Beothuks then?"

"There is room in Newfoundland for all. As I understand, most of it is barren rock."

"So it is, but the sea is rich, and the fishery will bring people over from England. The Beothuks need the sea as well, for fish and seals. They hunt the herds of great deer in the winter, but in the summer usually they come to the coast and stay until the fall."

"So why do we usually never see them?" I said, suddenly understanding.

"When the English fishing fleet arrives, the Beothuks avoid the seacoast."

"But if we settle the coast—"

"Oh, it will all be peaceable and friendly at first," Harry said. "There are not many Beothuks, after all, and to begin with there will be few settlers. In a few years, though, we shall find ourselves competing against the Beothuks for the codfish and the seal furs and the whales."

Horsfall interrupted.

"Who will want to come from England to live in Newfoundland? We ourselves may yet not last out this one winter. Who would choose to live here all the year round for the rest of their lives?"

"Poor people who want to become rich from the fishery," Harry Chard told him. "Rich men who want to become richer, and who will force all their servants and their families to come with them so that they can continue to live in comfort. What will they care for the Beothuks?"

I thought Harry was probably right in his prophecies, but there was one thing which I could still not understand.

"You have told me of a plot to overthrow the King and to enthrone Gilbert in his place. You have also told me that you want to protect the Beothuks from having their land overrun by English settlers. What have these two plans got to do with each other?"

"I am disappointed, Sir Ralph. I expected that you would have seen it already."

"Put me down for a fool, then, and explain to me in the weary and patronising way that laymen always speak to priests. You all see us as being like children."

"Why so you all are, for what do you know of a man's life? Never mind that. No, my great plan is that Gilbert shall be King over the English and over the Beothuks too."

"What do the Beothuks say to this? We are told that they have no king, and have never known kings."

"They know about kings now, from Timaskatek's captivity in England. They know about palaces and castles, and about priests and soldiers."

"They did not want to know. We forced that knowledge upon them. They were innocent."

"Innocent? Oh, they have sin here, too, Sir Ralph."

"I do not mean that. I mean that they knew only of Newfoundland."

"That's true. They thought that Newfoundland was the whole world. They have no history of where they came from."

Once again I had my vision of Newfoundland as a cold Eden, unlike the first Garden of Eden, which was warm and full of birds and beasts, and of trees bearing fruit both blessed and forbidden.

Were the Beothuks God's new Creation, as I had wondered before, set here to play the drama of Man once more, to see if they would choose innocence rather than the evil of knowledge as Adam and Eve did?

I could not tell the others of that, because they would only have laughed at me again as an over-schooled man with a mind full of childish fancies.

I had to answer Harry.

"Now that the Beothuks know of England, and of religions and wars, of ships and castles, how are they to play in your plot?"

"I am plotting, as you choose to put it, for them and not against them. I want to give them a place in the new English Newfoundland which is coming to be."

"They are English subjects already. Most of them do not know it, but three of them at least know it only too well."

"They have no nobility to restrain a king."

I could make no sense of that strange remark.

"Why should they need a nobility for their simple life?"

"Because their life will soon cease to be simple. I will give them an honoured place among the nobility of England."

William Durdle could restrain himself no longer.

"Are we to make lords of these people? They are hardly better than beasts."

Harry Chard turned upon him.

"There are many in England who would say the same of men such as you!"

That quietened William because we all knew that although it was unjust, it was true. How many lords, merchants, and townspeople despise the fishermen who feed them at least once a week?

I had to rebuke William.

"Any man is better than a beast, no matter what his behaviour, because God gave us dominion over the beasts. In exchange for that, He has given us responsibility for our own behaviour because we know the difference between good and evil."

"What of the trials of animals, then?" William demanded, surprising me that he should know of such things. "Beasts have been tried and punished for all manner of crimes."

"We are not here to discuss beasts," I told him. "They, and things which are not alive, cannot be tried for not fulfilling their proper role in the scheme of the world. It is all set out in the philosophy of Aristotle, and I have no time to dispute that now. The Beothuks are men and women. I agree that they are not beasts, but Harry should tell us how he plans to make them into lords and ladies."

Harry was ready for that.

"May a king not make lords and ladies?" he asked, leering because he was setting a trap for me. I walked into it deliberately so that I could do battle with whatever evil was waiting to pounce upon us from within.

"Of course a king may do so," I said, and even Horsfall and Young Martin saw what was coming before I did.

"Gilbert—" they both cried together as if they had been drilled to do so.

"So Gilbert will make Beothuk lords and ladies," I said.

"Why not?" Harry Chard demanded. "You said that they were people as good as us."

"There is nothing against it, except that there is no king here. Well, there is, Henry the Seventh, but he is far away in England and has sent us no word to ennoble any of his subjects in Newfoundland, whether they be Englishmen or Beothuks."

Harry Chard raised his hands above his head, and stamped his boots on the floor, so that snow was knocked off the roof and fell past the window in a cascade of brilliant sparkles.

"The king will make nobles," he declared. "The king will make knights and squires. The king will make—"

He lowered his arms and grasped Gilbert by the shoulders. The boy flinched, and for an instant I was shocked by the impropriety of a subject laying hands upon a king. Is this madness spreading to me, too, now?
Harry spoke in a quiet voice to Gilbert, as though he were imparting a secret.

"The king will make a queen."

"A queen?" William Durdle exclaimed.

"A queen. A Beothuk queen. The king is to be married, here in Newfoundland, and when he goes to England to take his throne he will bring his queen with him."

"Gilbert—" I exclaimed, but Harry Chard was too exultant in his declaration to allow anyone to interrupt him.

"I have found a bride for the king, a lady highly regarded among the Beothuks. She is worthy to be noble, more, worthy to be royal, and you, Father Fletcher, will have the honour of marrying them one to the other! What of that, Father? Did you ever think that one day you would perform a royal wedding? Have you ever performed any wedding?"

"No, I have not," I answered at once before I had time to realise how foolish I sounded. I had been talking about my own experience instead of reacting to Harry Chard expounding his wicked scheme to marry the hapless Gilbert to some innocent Beothuk maiden.

I had to speak again, just to forestall more thundering announcements from Harry Chard.

"I will not marry any couple without the consent of them both. What is more, Gilbert needs the consent of his mother."

"She has given it, in writing. Would you like me to fetch the document, so you can read it? It is done in English, in good French, and in very fine Latin, and his mother has signed all three texts."

"I am sure she has," I replied, because I have no doubt that Harry was telling the truth. In observing Harry I have learnt that merely because a man never lies, it does not mean that he should be trusted.

"Nevertheless, Gilbert must also give his own consent. Gilbert, what do you say to this?"

"I, I, don't know," Gilbert said.

I was sorry for him, but I had to press further.

"You must say yes or no, of your own free will."

"I don't know," Gilbert repeated.

"Why don't you know?"

"I don't know who she is."

Harry Chard intervened.

"Kings do not meet their brides. You are not some village labourer. You must make a royal marriage, for the benefit of your kingdom."

"Gilbert has said that he is uncertain, and for me that means that he refuses his consent," I said. "What is more, even if he agrees, his bride must agree, too. As well as that, she must be a Christian, or I cannot marry her. Where is this Christian Beothuk princess, Harry?"

Harry restrained his rage, but I noticed that he took care to make sure that we noticed he was holding back his anger. It must be a trick that he has long employed to intimidate people, by implying that it is only his own good grace which keeps him from bursting into violence.

"You want to see a princess, Sir Ralph? Well, I shall bring you a princess, the first one that you have ever seen. Peter, set the men to work. I will come back this evening."

Harry shot out of the door with astonishing speed, and puffed away into the woods, leaving a trail of ploughed snow.

Peter Slade shook his head, and beckoned the men to follow him. The Pretender to the throne of England did not know what to do, so I had to help him.

"Follow them, Gilbert. I am sure that there is work to be done. No matter what Harry may say to you, you are not the king, and I promise you that I will never marry you to any woman against your will."

Gilbert nodded silently, and went out to join the others.

I found myself alone again, as I so often am, as I so often have been in my life.

It is not an unpleasant state. I sometimes wonder whether I might not have made a monk in some contemplative order, but then I remember that God called me to be a priest in the world, not a monk in the cloister, and God has reasons for His choices no matter how odd and surprising they may seem to us.

I, too, had work to do. I had prayers to recite and scriptures to read. When I had finished, I sat down, checked that my ink was unfrozen, and wrote up my journal up to this moment.

Now I must wait for Harry Chard to return. I have nothing to do, so I sit by the fire, an idle luxury which the working men must envy.

I have time to think. As I often do in idle moments, I wonder at the special quality of the present instant, with its sense of 'this is actually happening' which lasts for only an instant before it rushes by and joins the great ocean of the past, which can bear storms which rush in upon the present and the future.

The men came in silently to their midday meal. Only Gilbert would speak to me.

"Peter set us to a task which we have never done before," he said. "We are building a fire in one of the other huts."

"Why? Nobody lives in them. I understood that they are used only to store equipment for next season's fishery."

"So they are, but Peter insists that we must build a fire in one of them all the same."

I have no idea of what this means or whether I should care. Perhaps it is something to do with the maintenance of the fishing gear.

I have never tried to learn more about the men's work. I am here to minister to the winter crew, not to join in their tasks.

They would not allow me to work with them, in any case. They see me as a pale bookish youth incapable of practical work, good only to recite prayers and to hear confessions. The men confess astonishing sins to me, but they tell me nothing of the honest work which they do every day.

I was left alone to do nothing all afternoon, while the sky clouded over with those flat dull grey clouds which mean that more snow is coming. We shall have neither goose nor plum porridge for Christmas, but we shall have snow.

When the day began to darken, the men came back. Usually they shake snow all over the floor, to melt into dirty puddles, but this time their clothes were dry.

"Have you flown to the hot lands of the south and east," I asked them, "to Africa or Araby?"

"Nowhere further than the fish flakes," William Durdle replied. "We have a warm place there now."

Before the men could finish throwing off their smocks and caps, Harry Chard burst in through the door as though a violent wind was behind him.

"Peter, take all the men to the other hut. I'll come with you. No, not you, Father Fletcher. Your place is here."

I turned on the bench and sat facing him as the other men all filed out.

"Well, Harry, I am in my place," I said. "What am I to do?"

"Preach, damn you! You're a priest, the only English priest on this side of the ocean. I've got nobody but you, or I would not be calling upon you to do this."

"I will not marry Gilbert against his will."

"I am not asking you to. All I want you to do is to sit here until I come back. The other men will not disturb you. Fetch them back from the other hut, the one with the fire, when you have finished."

"When I have finished what?" I asked.

"Preaching to the heathen!"

"I believe I've been doing that ever since we left England," I said, although I was already beginning to realise what it was that he wanted from me.

"I do not want to hear jokes, Father Fletcher. Be silent and sit still like the schoolboy you are, and wait for me to come back."

I sat immobile on the bench, truly, as Harry had said, feeling like a schoolboy waiting for a beating, while he snorted out of the door. At least he remembered to close it against the cruel cold.

I was startled when he knocked on the door, a thing I had never known him to do before. I could not see him, of course, but no other man on the land of Newfoundland could have communicated who he was simply by the force and sharpness of the sound of his fist upon wood.

I opened the door, and found his face thrust against mine. I drew back, but the face remained locked in a fierce stare as he came round the door.

"Here, Father Fletcher," Harry said, reaching behind him. "Here is a princess for you. Make her into a Christian if you can."

In one movement he leapt out of sight behind the door, and pushed a Beothuk into the room.

As I recovered my balance, the door slammed shut, and as I heard Harry tramping away through the snow I found myself staring at the Beothuk.

I had not seen a woman since the previous spring when we had left England, and I had never seen a Beothuk woman at all.

She was young, younger even than Gilbert himself. I could see only her face because she was so wrapped up against the cold.

"Here," I said, drawing her towards the fire. "You can take your furs off and sit here in the warm."

She seemed to press towards the fire and struggle against my grasp in the same movement. It was like a cat or dog which is not sure whether to trust you.

To try to put her at ease, I sat down myself, and gestured that she should remove her smock and hood.

The girl took them off slowly, and laid them on the rough splintered floor with surprising neatness and delicacy.

We were sitting next to each other on the bench, and neither of us had any idea what to do next.

I do not know what the Beothuk elders had told her of what she was supposed to do. I, at least, had a clear mission, laid upon me by Christ Himself fifteen hundred years ago. I had to preach Christianity to her and convert her; but how was I to do that?

Chapter Eleven

I must be the first English priest in a thousand years who has been called upon to preach to a heathen who knew nothing of Christianity. God had given me an opportunity that others have perhaps dreamed of, but I did not know what to do.

The Beothuk girl kept looking nervously up at the ceiling. I glanced up at it myself, to see if I could tell what was making her uncomfortable, but to me the ceiling looked as it always has done: a dark jumble of roughly-shaped pieces of wood, even more uneven and splintered than the floor, but with pieces of clothing hanging from it like trophies.

In one corner, so that we shall not accidentally bump into it and be showered with its contents, hangs the bucket of ease.

"What's troubling you up there?" I asked, not knowing how much English Timaskatek might have taught her. The girl pointed up at the ceiling, and then covered her head with her hands. I noticed how beautiful and dainty her hands were.

"Oh," I said, "you're not used to ceilings!" To one who has known only Beothuk tents or the open sky, a solid ceiling must be frightening, seeming to threaten always to fall and crush you. She must not have visited Harry Chard's church yet.

I took her hands away from her head. Her hair was startlingly cold from the winter air.

"I suppose the best thing is to start with names. I," I said, pointing to myself, "am Ralph Fletcher. Ralph—Fletcher."

The girl placed her right hand over her left breast, in the pose of a modest Venus in an Italian painting.

"Anasaquit," she said. "Anasaquit."

"Anasaquit," I repeated, and she smiled.

I noticed that the fire needed tending, so I sprang off the bench and piled on more wood. The flames rose up again like a curtain, as though they would be lowered again with the same grace, to reveal some wondrous scene or great mystery.

I sat down on the bench again with Anasaquit. It was passing strange to be in the company of a woman again, after spending more than half a year only with men.

The best place to begin was to find out what she knew of English, if anything.

"Do you know any English, Anasaquit?" I asked.

"I, want, to, be, battised. *Baptised*," she answered. She must have been made to rehearse that sentence over and over.

"That is good, Anasaquit, but I must be sure that you know what it is that you are asking for, and that you know what it means. Can you tell me anything more?"

Anasaquit smiled at me, glanced up in fear at the ceiling once more, composed herself in an instant, and then smiled at me again.

"You Ingliss priest. Fissman, no."

"That's right, I am a priest, not a fisherman. Someone has taught you well. Was it Timaskatek?"

The smile vanished, and she showed the same expression of fear that she did when she was thinking of the solid, heavy ceiling over her head. What was Timaskatek to her? Father, brother, friend, enemy?

"Was it Aguthut, then?" I asked.

Anasaquit looked down at the floor and wrung her brown hands together.

"Never mind, Anasaquit. I only want to find out if you understand me. How much English do you know?"

"Ingliss, yes. You Ralph Fletcher."

At last I had met a Beothuk who could pronounce my name without imputing lechery to me.

"Yes, that's right."

"I'm Anasaquit."

"Yes, you are. Do you know Gilbert?"

"Yes. I seen Gil-bert."

That was a matter to be raised later.

"You know that I am a priest. Do you know what a priest is, Anasaquit?"

I wondered what priests the Beothuks might have, and of what strange faith.

The Spanish have told dark and frightening tales of what the native priests do in the hot lands to the south. Perhaps Newfoundland makes up for its cold winds and harsh rock by having a gentler religion.

I wonder whether pagans with a kind religion are easier to lead to Christ than those with a cruel religion?

Anasaquit smiled and nodded. She reached down into her smock, and drew out my own sweet-voiced little silver Mass bell.

She placed it into my hand. The metal was warm, with the heat of her very breast.

I gazed upon the bell as if I had never seen it before, and when I could finally bring myself to look up I found that Anasaquit's eyes were staring into mine, only a hand's breadth away from my face.

I held the bell up to her. I was no St. Patrick, and in this icy land no shamrocks grow. He used the shamrock, three leaves growing on one stalk, to expound the mystery of the Trinity.

Had I been given this bell by my father, so long ago, so far away in England, for a purpose here in Newfoundland of which he can have had no vision?

I remembered how the bell kept coming back to me. Gilbert, simple Holy Gilbert, had asked me about it. I had given it to Aguthut, and then Timaskatek had rung it around the walls of our hut like a warning; or perhaps, like a proclamation of good news.

"Anasaquit, do you know what this is?" I asked.

"Mass bell."

"You have been taught well. Tell me more."

I desperately needed to know whether Harry or Timaskatek had simply coached her in a few phrases, or whether she had been taught more English by them or by someone else.

Someone else? There was no someone else; and yet so many unexpected faces have emerged out of these cold silent forests that I am afraid to wonder what more men and women may be out there.

"I, Anasaquit, Beothuk. Marry Gilbert. I, Anasaquit, Ingliss queen."

Lord, why are you allowing Harry Chard to try to lead yet another innocent to death and damnation?

"I'm still not sure how much English you know, Anasaquit. Tell me more. Tell me where you live."

"Snow time, by river big beasts. Sum time, by ocean."

That was no rehearsed speech. The Beothuks moved with the seasons, as I already knew, and in Newfoundland there are only two seasons: a summer, which is short, and a winter, which is long.

Indeed, as I write, the winter seems endless. If I ever get back to England I think that I shall always imagine Hell as being a place of perpetual snow and ice and flesh-freezing wind.

Because we are in winter, most of the Beothuks are inland. They follow the great deer into the interior of the land, and hunt them for their meat and hides.

All of this had been told to me by Harry Chard, but I am so distrustful of him that hearing it from Anasaquit was like hearing it for the first time.

"How old are you, Anasaquit?" I asked.

She looked at me, not understanding.

"How many times have you come from the river to the sea?" I held up my fingers. "One, two, three, four—" I held up all my fingers, and then started again "—eleven, twelve?"

Anasaquit laughed. I had an idea and placed this book in her lap. I dipped my pen into the ink, and put it in her hand. She gripped its shaft in her fist.

I pointed at the page.

"Mark it with the number of times you have moved to the sea."

I took her hand to show her.

With surprising grace Anasaquit quickly drew ten or eleven straight vertical lines, and then she paused and laughed. She put the pen to the paper again and drew five more lines.

"You are sixteen, perhaps only fifteen," I said. "You are the same age as Gilbert."

"Ingliss queen."

"So Harry Chard has told you. I wonder what Timaskatek has told you about England."

Anasaquit shook her head vigorously. I thought at first she intended to signify that Timaskatek had told her nothing of England, but then I saw that the gesture meant only that the subject of England held strong feelings for her.

She stood up, raised her arms, and lifted her eyes up to the ceiling. She waved both her arms slowly from side to side, while she still stared at the hanging clothing and the smoke-stained logs. Was it a dance?

"England," she said mysteriously. "Timaskatek, England," she repeated, still waving at the ceiling.

She sat down on the bench again and embraced herself in her arms.

"Timaskatek, England," she repeated, more quietly, and she gestured all around the room.

Now I understood, or I believe that I did. She had let me know how she feared the simple wooden walls and ceiling of our little hut.

Timaskatek must have told her over and over about his captivity in the Palace of Westminster, all stone, stone walls, stone above and below, stone confining him except for some iron-barred window giving him a view of towers and more stone.

Perhaps he could see the roofs of London at the other end of the Strand, and perhaps he could see the river, whose grey water would be the one familiar thing that he could understand.

I wish he could speak better English to me, or that I could question him in Beothuk, so that I could know more of what he saw in England and what he made of it. He could tell me so much about Newfoundland as well. I wonder what the Beothuks call it? This land is not newly found for them.

"You would find it hard to live in the palace that Harry has built for Gilbert, and hard to attend services in his church. Although they are built of wood and not stone, you will find them nearly as frightening. All of our buildings must seem like dark prisons to your people."

Anasaquit will see far greater buildings if she ever sails to England, which I pray that she never will, because all she will find there will be the axe, or worse yet, the rope.

I realised that I was holding the Mass bell. Surely someone had preached Christianity to Timaskatek? If that arrogant Dominican had meant what he had said in the Exchequer about wishing he could do pastoral work, he had had a lost sheep greatly in need of help and comfort somewhere within the very walls of that same palace in which he sat counting coins.

He knew that Timaskatek was there, and that he could have taken my place here in Newfoundland if he had wanted to. I believe Harry Chard when he says that he would never have brought me if he could have found another priest, any other priest in England, rather than me.

For all my sins, which I know of better than anyone except God Himself, I believe that I have been treating Anasaquit with more goodwill than she would ever have received from that clever, haughty Dominican.

I rang the Mass bell gently in my hands, while I looked into Anasaquit's dark eyes, so that the sound seemed to come from nowhere, or from within my own imagination.

"When this bell rings, if I have carried out the ceremony correctly, Christ becomes present on the altar," I said, more to remind myself of my duties than to inform Anasaquit, who would have understood nothing of my words.

Perhaps she would understand my actions. My spirit leapt. Is this what the mystics mean by ecstasy?

I would perform a private Mass before Anasaquit. I motioned to her to stay on the bench while I prepared the tools of my trade. It is no impiety to speak of the bread, the wine, and the candles in such a way. Priests have no higher calling than men who earn their living in rough and common trades.

We are no more than a voice and a pair of hands, which may belong to a corrupt and unworthy man. Such has often been the case, and will be so again.

My idea was that the ceremony would make Anasaquit curious. I let her stay sitting and watching me, rather than trying to make her stand. After all, the elderly and infirm are allowed to sit on the benches which run around the walls of our churches in England, while the rest of the congregation stand.

We always excuse them by saying that 'the weakest go to the wall,' but Anasaquit is not weak. I am sure that weak Beothuks never survive to grow up.

I muttered to God in Latin, a language which she must never have heard before. I knelt down and stood up, I whispered and chanted, I prayed for Anasaquit and begged the Lord for help in converting her and for help in knowing what to do for Holy Gilbert, in recompense for the simple piety which he has always shown. One does not have to be a wise Dominican, learned in philosophy and Latin, to be pleasing to God.

At last there came the moment when I was about to elevate the simple things, simple as Holy Gilbert, which were to become the Body and Blood of Christ. I placed the bell in Anasaquit's coarse and yet beautiful brown hands.

"When I raise my arms, like this," I said, acting it out for her, "ring the bell," I continued, acting that out as well.

Anasaquit gripped the bell as if it might fly away. I was afraid that she might crush it, but then what it is the cost of a deformed handbell compared to the prize of a soul won for Christ?

I lifted up the bread and wine towards Heaven. Anasaquit rang the bell with a crashing clang which might have announced the end of the world, and it perhaps it will indeed prove to be the end of one world for her and her entry to another one.

She rang the bell again, while I held God in my hands, and then laid Him reverently upon my precious little altar, made of English wood and containing an English altar-stone.

Anasaquit watched me eat the Body of Christ and drink His Blood. I knew that she would see it only as a meal, which of course it is, and that she would probably not recognise the bread. What she would make of the wine I could not imagine.

I laid my hands upon her head, and recited a blessing upon her. Her hair was thick and oily, and although it was like no hair I had ever seen on an Englishwoman I found it beautiful to look upon and pleasing to touch.

I withdrew my hands before Anasaquit could misinterpret my action, and recited the prayers which close the Mass.

Anasaquit held out the little Mass bell to me, and then clutched it back to her.

"Yes," I told her, putting her hands back on her breast, "keep it with you, Anasaquit. This bell shall be my shamrock. It will be the tool, I hope, by which I can begin to try to make you understand."

I was speaking to her so gently that we were both startled when the door was opened and the icy wind blew in.

The wind threw a shower of icy sparkling snowflakes before it like flowers to be strewn for Harry Chard to walk upon. He is the kind of man who would like to walk upon flowers, I think.

"Well, have you made her a Christian yet, Father Fletcher?" he demanded.

"I believe that it will be less challenging than trying to make a Christian out of you, Harry," I replied.

"Because I am a rough and harsh man it does not mean that I am a bad man, Sir Ralph."

"There are men who do bad things, and men who are bad," I replied. "I have not yet decided which of the two you are."

"What makes you think you can talk to me like that?"

"Because I am your priest, not one of your fishermen or servants."

"You are no better than they are."

"That's true, but they have to take orders from you, and I do not."

"By God, I will make you obey me," Harry roared.

"How will you make God obey you, Harry? In any case, I choose to do your bidding in this matter of Anasaquit. I am going to try to make a Christian of her."

"Aye, and a wife and a queen, too."

"I have promised you nothing in those questions, Harry. I could make her a wife, but neither you nor I can make her a queen, any more than you can make poor Gilbert into a king."

Harry and I had been arguing across the bowed head of Anasaquit, who was still sitting on the bench.

As if by mutual agreement, Harry and I both fell silent, except for the sound of our rough breathing. A puddle of water was collecting around Harry's boots.

Harry spoke first.

"Ah, enough of this. I have no time to waste disputing with a foolish schoolboy. I will bring this lady to you again tomorrow for further instruction."

Harry seized Anasaquit's arm and forced her to stand up.

The Mass bell fell from her hands and dropped onto the floor, and the sound was exactly the same one that it makes at the climax of the Mass. I cannot forget that.

Harry bent down and picked up the bell while he still held Anasaquit's arm. Only a short man could have done that. He roughly thrust the bell back into Anasaquit's smock.

She fought against him as he tried to drag her to the door.

"No, no!" she cried.

"Harry, let her go. She doesn't want to come with you."

"I don't care what she wants, Father Fletcher, or what you want. She is coming back with me to her own people."

I seized Anasaquit's other arm and held her to me. The sight of two men fighting to pull a woman in opposite directions would have been comical in other circumstances, but there was no humour in our struggle.

I may be a bookish and unworldly man, but I was winning possession of the Beothuk woman, even though she seemed to be struggling against me as much as against Harry. I suppose she could not understand that I was trying to defend her.

All of a sudden my ears were struck as though by a thunderclap, as Harry bellowed in that voice which he has used on ships in the middle of an ocean storm.

"Peter! William! Here, to me!"

Had it been one of those usual Newfoundland days with the wind whipping and roaring, the rest of the winter crew would never have heard him, but his voice carried to the other hut because all was calm and peace outside even while it was all tumult and rage within.

I head the distant sound of voices, and then a swishing in the snow as the men ran over, as fast as men can run in this deep snow.

They tumbled in through the door, while Harry, Anasaquit, and I all stood motionless, still linked together.

It made the scene seem more than ever like something out of a Mystery Play, some sort of still tableau illustrating a moral point. The struggle between Good and Evil for the soul of an innocent young girl, perhaps? Have I the right to cast myself as the representative of Good?

Harry has more experience of fights than I have, so he was the first to give an order to the baffled men of the winter crew.

"Get the priest away from this girl!"

Not 'this queen,' nor 'this lady,' but 'this girl.' In the fierce heat of our dispute Harry had forgotten his own part in this sinister play which he had written.

Harry had cast himself as the Kingmaker, like the Earl of Warwick who cast down King Henry VI to replace him with King Edward IV, grew displeased with Edward IV in turn, and brought him down as well. Warwick brought back King Henry VI, baffled and blinking, from the cell in the Tower of London where he had lain prisoner for ten years.

Perhaps that was where Harry got the idea. Is Harry, perhaps, named in honour of King Henry VI?

The men hesitated as they moved towards me on Harry's command, so I took the chance to answer.

"Will you lay hands upon your priest?" I demanded.

It was the only weapon which I could employ against Harry, playing upon the superstitious regard in which the common people hold priests, even priests whom they despise or fear.

The men all stopped moving, so that it was once more like a tableau. I leapt into the silence as though into a pool of warm water.

"This woman does not want to go with Harry. I do not know why, but she seems to want to stay with me."

Anasaquit must have been able to understand some of that, because she shrank against me. We were both wearing such thick clothing that we could not feel each others' bodies through the cloths and furs, and it seemed that she was bodiless within her clothing, like a spirit.

"She cannot stay with you," Peter Slade said, "and not with all these other men here as well."

"I know that," I replied, since I would not have let Anasaquit stay with us. "She has to go back to her people, but I am trying to persuade her to go willingly. Harry is frightening her. Have you promised the Beothuks that she will be back within a certain time, Harry? I think they will come looking for her if she is late, so you had better not cause any more delay. Let her go."

Harry, puffing with rage, released Anasaquit.

She flung herself against me, and I tried to calm her.

"Now, Anasaquit," I said, "you must go, but you heard Harry promise that he will bring you back tomorrow. You will keep coming back so that I can teach you Christianity. Isn't that true, Harry?"

"Yes," he growled. I hoped that Anasaquit also knew that although Harry may hold back part of the truth, he never lies.

"There, now," I said. "Go with Harry, and he will bring you back tomorrow."

I led her gently to the door, which Horsfall flung open with a flourish. I could not tell whether his gesture was meant to be courteous to Anasaquit or insulting to her, or perhaps he was just being Horsfall.

Anasaquit stepped forward and backward as in a dance, looking fearfully at me. I pushed gently at her elbow, feeling again only those thick clothes as though there were no human body within.

I was surprised that Peter Slade came over, and feared that he was about to shout at Anasaquit or force her out into the snow, but instead he spoke to her calmly.

"Go along, Anasaquit. Nobody will hurt you. Go along quietly, and Harry will bring you back to see Father Fletcher again. Harry, stand aside. You're frightening her."

Harry did step out of the way, puffing again. I let go of Anasaquit's arm, and she twisted away from me and leapt out of the door. We all watched as she ran across the snow and vanished into the woods like something wild.

Only when she had disappeared did I realise that the whole scene, from when she had broken away from me until she had slipped between the trees, had passed in complete silence. I actually looked to see that she had made tracks in the snow as she had run, or I might have believed that she was a spirit of some kind after all. Who knows what spirits may live in this strange vast land?

"There is only one thing to be done now," I said, as we all stared at the snow and the trees.

"What?" Young Martin asked.

"Close the door," I replied, and for once in my life I issued a command and it was obeyed.

Gilbert spoke next, a simple ordinary boy once more, seeming to have forgotten all about being the next king.

"What will you do now, Father?"

"I shall do as I have promised," I said, "which is that I shall instruct her in the Faith as best I can, and I shall prepare for Christmas."

William Durdle simpered, an odd thing indeed in such a grim and practical man.

"It will be a strange Christmas, Father."

"There have been many strange Christmases in fifteen hundred years," I replied, "and some of them in stranger times and stranger places even than those in which we find ourselves. There will be no goose and no plum porridge, but we will do what we can."

"It will be a good way to pass twelve long days," Peter Slade said sagely.

Harry Chard had been staring at the floor, and suddenly he spoke out savagely, in an unexpected anger which was as eerie as William Durdle's sniggering had been a moment before.

"Who is to be the Lord of Misrule, then?"

"It cannot be you, Harry," I told him, "for you have been engaging in misrule since the fishing fleet went back to England, if not before."

Horsfall stated what we all knew, as is his annoying custom.

"It should be a servant, or a boy," he said.

"We have no servants," William Durdle said, "and Gilbert is the only boy."

That made Harry Chard even more angry.

"I will not have the King of England set up as the Lord of Misrule. It is not seemly."

I tried to calm everyone with the best suggestion I could think of.

"We cannot have a true English Christmas," I pointed out. "We have no goose and no plum porridge. Oh, I can carry out the Christian rituals as well here as anywhere else, but if we cannot have all the traditions of Christmas in England, we can surely drop this one custom as well. We can go through one Christmas of our lives without a Lord of Misrule."

"I rule here," Harry Chard replied. "I am the Fishing Admiral, and so I am in the place of a Lord of the Manor in England. I rule all the rest of the year, and I say we shall have a Lord of Misrule."

"Very well," I said, "then let it be Young Martin."

At last I succeeded if bringing about, if not the peace I had sought, at least quiet. Every man turned to stare at the discomfited Young Martin, and, as always when we fall still and silent, we all became aware again of the cold and of the great silence outside in the trees and snow.

Young Martin, the boy-man, shuffled like a boy, not knowing whether he was honoured or insulted, and not knowing what to say to me.

Harry Chard rescued him.

"I am the Fishing Admiral," he repeated, "and it is my right to choose a Lord of Misrule. I say it will be Timaskatek."

"Timaskatek?" I exclaimed, while the younger men asked "Who?" and the older men looked alarmed.

"Timaskatek is a Beothuk. He is no Christian."

"Who says the Lord of Misrule has to be a Christian? Who says that only Christians may feast and celebrate at Christmas?"

I have heard stories that many of our Christmas traditions come from pagan times, but that was not something I would say to unlearned men who would be frightened by it, worrying that some innocent game or custom might bring them to damnation.

I fear that sometimes we spend too much time telling our flocks about the punishment of the damned and not enough time describing the joy of redemption.

"Even if Timaskatek may celebrate at Christmas, although I will not give him Communion unless he is baptised, what does he know of Christmas?"

I had not even finished saying those words before I realised that I had fallen straight into Harry's trap. Indeed, I had dug the hole myself.

"Timaskatek knows all about Christmas, Father Fletcher. He has seen three Christmases in England. He has seen how we mark and celebrate it."

I tried to imagine what Timaskatek must have seen while he was imprisoned in the Palace of Westminster. What songs had he heard? What dances had he seen? Had he seen any religious services, and what could he have understood of them?

I could make only a feeble answer.

"I hope he did not see anything unseemly."

All the men roared with laughter at that, and of course Young Martin went on laughing just a few moments too long.

Even Harry Chard was forced to laugh in spite of his black mood.

"Unseemly! Father Fletcher, I know you are a priest and have spent all your life in schools for boys and men. I know that you know nothing of a grown man's life. You are innocent of women, have never fought a man, and would have no idea how to dig a hole or row a boat. Yet even you must have seen unseemly things during the Twelve Days of Christmas! By God, it would have been a good joke to have made you the Lord of Misrule, just to say that we had seen the worst Lord of Misrule there ever was in all the fifteen hundred years of Christmases!"

"I am indeed a priest, and have heard many confessions," I said. "I know far more about unseemly things than you believe."

"We must take your word for that," Horsfall said, "because you are forbidden to speak of what you hear."

"There are those among you who are glad of that," I said, which I should not have done, but at least it stopped them laughing.

"Very well," I said, "I have no authority in these things. I will celebrate this faraway Christmas as best I can. You can make Timaskatek the Lord of Misrule, while I try to make Anasaquit into a Christian."

Chapter Twelve

How could I explain Christmas to Anasaquit, when I had not yet explained Christ to her?

As Christmas approached, I thought more and more about this, while Harry Chard brought Anasaquit to me every day for instruction.

I remembered reading accounts of missions to the pagans of Europe a thousand years ago, and tried to recall the techniques which those missionaries had used.

I had found no pagan idols which I could dramatically throw down, and no receptive pagan kings to whom I could preach the Word. For the future, this meant that I could not anticipate that painters would represent me in such scenes, or carvers cut my achievements into the sides of stone sarcophagi.

I am still unsure that I wish to appear as the central character in 'The Martyrdom of St. Ralph at the Hands of the Beothuks,' whatever merit such an end might gain me.

I did manage to recall that the old missionary priests had found that the pagans were impressed by beautiful things. I already knew that Anasaquit had been fascinated by the beauty of the little silver Mass bell, so I brought out the gold chalice and the embroidered altar-cloth, and let her handle them.

She could make nothing of their meaning, of course, but I could tell that she knew that these things were connected with the religion which I was trying to expound to her.

She exclaimed long throaty words in her own language as she rotated the gold chalice in her brown hands, holding it up to catch the light from the window.

When the winter sun is shining and reflecting off the snow, the chalice sparkles with astonishing beauty while she turns it this way and that. If it makes her associate Christianity with beauty, that is no bad start.

As Christmas approaches, so does the reappearance of Timaskatek, of whom I have seen and heard nothing, although of course he is still out there in the snows and woods.

Harry Chard is lurking somewhere among the trees as well. It is like finding myself in a frightening old folk tale, in a lonely house in a strange country, with evil half-human monsters prowling through sinister forests.

What a comfort the liturgy is, and the daily readings of prayers and Biblical passages. Some of these Latin texts have been recited and read for hundreds of years, even a thousand years in some cases, by many voices in many accents, but all of them saying the same Latin words in places all over Christendom and beyond.

Whenever I begin to think of myself as being in a plight because I was forced to overwinter in Newfoundland, I remember all of those who have been priests before me, and recited the same words in far more cruel circumstances, in places which were even more foreign and strange than Newfoundland.

I now have a purpose, which is to instruct Anasaquit. It has made me confront Christianity myself as though it were something new.

I looked at the crucifix in a new way when I saw how horrified Anasaquit was when she examined it and saw a tortured man nailed there. All my life it has been only an image to me, but now I too see a suffering man hanging there, as human as myself even though He is God as well.

Anasaquit seems to understand that the image is of a god. I wonder if she will ever be able to explain to me what gods the Beothuks have worshipped up to now. She also understands that I want to convert her to the worship of this god.

This morning I was woken up by a voice crying that a miracle had taken place. I thrust my frozen beard out of my foul blankets, instantly awake in my excitement to see the miracle, without knowing what it was or who it was that had announced it.

The voice proved to be that of Young Martin, who had got up before anyone else. He was standing at the window, pointing outside at the wonder which he had been the first to see.

"Look," he squeaked, "the snow is melting!"

By the way we all shuffled eagerly to the window, dragging the blankets that were still wrapped around us. Anyone would have believed that we had never seen snow melting before.

Young Martin opened the door. A strange mild wind burst in, casting to left and right, exploring the room and sniffing about us like a great invisible beast.

I suppose that in England we would have found it a wicked cold wind and wrapped ourselves against it, but in Newfoundland it came as a sweet zephyr such as we had not known for four months.

I put on my boots and went out into this new world. I shuffled forward still wrapped in my blankets, so that I must have looked like a man newly resurrected who had just climbed out of his tomb.

The snow was dripping away into grey puddles, falling from the branches of the trees. The grey clouds which covered the sky seemed like a vast warm blanket thrown over our freezing world.

While I stood entranced, there was a sudden crash behind me. One of the enormous icicles which were hanging from the roof of our hut had fallen to the ground. It is a good thing that nobody had been standing underneath it at the time. I have been told that such icicles can cut through a man like a thrown spear.

I unwrapped my stinking blanket and snapped it in the wind, flinging out dust and ashes. The wind caught the tumbling specks of dirt and bore them away like a sponge cleaning old words off a page of vellum, making it ready to be written upon with a new message.

Peter Slade came out of the hut and stood beside me, glancing up around himself, looking approvingly upon the world as though he had made it himself. I wondered if Peter would speak the magical new words for which everything seemed to be waiting.

"Well," he said, "it is like a sign. A gentle day in the middle of this harsh winter."

"We have the right to enjoy it," I said. "Why don't we leave the door open and take the window out so that there can be some new air in the hut?"

Peter shouted over his shoulder.

"William! Horsfall! Take the window out!"

William Durdle and Horsfall did not answer, but I heard creaks and rattles as the window was loosened. It was as if the window were breaking free of its own will, eager for the fresh air. Fresh air; how often have I heard those words without really understanding what they mean.

I walked through the slush and hung my blanket over the branch of a tree. The gentle wind would blow the foulness out of it, I hoped.

For once there was no howling westerly gale as there usually is, which would have snatched my poor filthy blanket off the tree and blown it across the foreshore to the sea, and then perhaps across the sea to England, to baffle whoever found it washed up on the shore of Devon or Somerset.

William Durdle came over to stand beside me.

"I don't feel so old today," he said.

"I feel it, too," I replied, "even though I'm still young. It seems as though there is a newness in the whole world this morning."

"It's like a sign," he said, "but of what?"

"Not a sign of spring," I said, "because it's not even Christmas yet. In any case, they say that there is no spring in Newfoundland, only a sudden leap from winter to summer."

We walked over a little way to the left, and realised that the wind was blowing from the south.

"It's a gift from the warm seas where the Spanish and Portuguese go," I said. "I would like to visit the hot lands where the sun is bright and winter never comes."

"Trust old England to take the cold and wet part of this New World," William Durdle commented. "It is God's curse upon us."

"Now, then, William," I rebuked him, "God does not curse men lightly."

"No?" he said. "You are indeed still young, Father."

He strolled away from me towards the fish flakes, while I tried to understand what he could have meant.

I forgot his words when I saw Anasaquit floating out of the woods. She had cast off her heavy deerskin smock, and her black hair shone in the kind winter sunlight.

"Anasaquit!" I called. "You are welcome today. I did not know your country could give us such a day in the middle of winter."

Anasaquit looked as though she had not known it either, and that this was the first mild day she had ever seen. She looked left, towards the sea, and gave an open smile. For that instant I forgot the foreignness which I always saw in her. Her smile and gaiety were just like those of an English woman, and although they cheered me I was reminded again how very far from home I was.

I held out my hand to her and she took it.

"Will you share our rough breakfast?" I asked her.

She followed me back into the hut. The clean air made me notice more than usual the unpleasant smells within, but I suppose that if Anasaquit has spent her whole life in small tents in the company of men such as Aguthut and Timaskatek, then the smells of the winter crew will not offend her.

Horsfall, with surprising politeness, offered her a mug of our elderly beer and our hard bread. He indicated to her that it would help if she dipped the bread into the beer to soften it.

I observed her graceful hands as she followed Horsfall's suggestion. Such hands would be in an Italian painting if they were milk-white instead of country brown.

Her beauty is not an English beauty, but it is beauty nevertheless. Perhaps English women would favour Aguthut, and even Timaskatek. I shall never know whether they would favour me.

Peter Slade drove the other men out to work, continuing the work of securing the fish flakes against the storms so that they will still be standing and serviceable when the fishing fleet returns. That is why the men are here.

I was left alone with Anasaquit, to instruct her in the Faith. That is why I am here.

Anasaquit finished the bread, biting and chewing it roughly. I suppose that is how the Beothuks eat their food, and so they must, if their only meat is the tough flesh of the great deer.

She drank half the mug of beer with no evident pleasure or distaste, and then she dipped her finger into the mug and with her wet fingertip she drew the sign of the cross upon the table.

I stared down at the wet cross as though I were looking for a message. I remembered the story of how when Cristoforo Colombo returned from his first voyage with men and women he had brought back, he brought the Indians before the King and Queen of Spain and had them make the sign of the Cross to impress his royal patrons.

I fear that Columbus had taught his prisoners that holy sign with beatings and kicks, but I had only shown it to Anasaquit by my own example whenever I performed Masses and blessings.

On an impulse I took her hands into mine. Her finger was still wet from the beer. Her hands felt strangely light. I had never touched a woman's hand before.

"Anasaquit, I wish I knew how much you understand," I said. "Why did you make the sign of the Cross?"

She smiled at me, as if that explained it. I should have been prepared for what she said to me.

"Timaskatek," she said. "Ingliss. London."

So that was it. Timaskatek had told her about the Cross, although what he thinks it signifies I fear to think. Had someone tried to instruct him? I doubt if that arrogant young Dominican friar would have done so. He would much prefer to count coins and add numbers, rather than to fight for a man's soul.

"Yes, Timaskatek saw the sign of the Cross in London. I hope he told you that it is a religious symbol."

I tried to remember what the purple designs on Anasaquit's smock looked like. Were they a pattern? Were they pictures, figured with rough bone needles? Were they symbols of the Beothuk religion, gods and saints and heroes whose names we shall probably never know?

Anasaquit withdrew her hands from mine and sat back. I was at a loss, so I took my own bread and beer, remembering how in the first years of Christianity the Eucharist had actually been a full meal rather than only a scrap of bread for the faithful and a draught of wine for the priest, who should be one of the faithful too.

I wondered whether Anasaquit understood what a book was, so I took out my breviary and opened it on the table in front of her. Following the words with my finger, I read out a passage.

Anasaquit watched my finger intently as though it were moving of its own will.

I moved back two sentences, and read them again. Anasaquit looked interested, so I took out my pen and ink and this book, opening it at the last page on which I had written.

When I had thawed out my ink in front of the fire, and shaken it up to mix the colour back with the water, I took my pen and wrote out Anasaquit's name, reciting the sounds as I did so.

"A-na-sa-quit," I said. "Do you see? That is your name written down in these black symbols. I'll do it again. Here: A-na-sa-quit."

"Anasaquit," she repeated.

"Now, here's my name. Ralph F-l-et-cher."

"Ralph Fletcher," she repeated.

She seemed to have grasped the idea of writing. Probably Timaskatek had made the same discovery during his captivity and told her about it.

I took out my Bible. My father gave it to me, newly printed in Germany. I cannot imagine what he paid for it, but even though printed books are much cheaper than real handwritten books, it must have cost him a great amount. I wondered whether Anasaquit could recognise it as being a valuable object.

I opened the pages, and showed Anasaquit the wood-cut illustrations. She examined them, but seemed not to understand. She is a Beothuk who has never left Newfoundland, so why would she understand anything of drawings of angels and demons, saints and wicked kings, harpists and trumpeters? Kings and harps and trumpets have never been seen in Newfoundland, although I am sure that they will appear here in the years to come. Newfoundland may have to wait longer for the appearance of a saint.

The spiky Latin words marched before Anasaquit's eyes. I read some of them out to her, and then translated them into English, in the hope that she would grasp that they had the same meaning. I did not want to confuse her too much with Latin, when she still knew almost nothing of English.

Anasaquit looked up from the book.

"Ingliss?" she asked.

"No, Latin," I replied. "I wish I had an English book to show you, but there are hardly any books in English, and I have brought none with me."

Now that more men like my father can read, and now that printing has made books cheaper, perhaps more books will be printed. One day books will be printed in the Beothuk language, and what tales and histories will they tell?

Anasaquit interrupted my prophetic thoughts.

"Book?" she asked, holding the Bible up to catch the light from the window on its open pages.

"Yes, Anasaquit, that is a book."

I took the book from her, and pointed to one of the verses, from the Gospel according to St. Mark.

"But they did not understand the word, and were afraid to ask him." How had the Bible fallen open at that point? Was this another sign, like the eerie warmth and calmness of the weather?

I gave the open book back to Anasaquit. Her brown finger wandered among the black words, seeking the verses which I had read to her.

"Ah!" she cried, and rubbed at the verse with her finger. She looked up at me, her eyes bright with triumph.

I looked to where she was pointing. I read the words out to her.

"But they did not understand the word, and were afraid to ask him."

Anasaquit had not understood the words, but she had not been afraid to ask me. It had been neither a sign nor a prophecy.

I gazed at her in a mixture of joy, fear, and astonishment, as though I had just been a witness at a miracle.

"Surely you cannot make out the words, Anasaquit."

"Buh—butt—day. Day," she blurted.

She had remembered the first two words.

"Let me teach you one word," I said, tearing a sheet out of this book. "Look: WORD."

I pointed to the letters.

"W—or—d."

In the beginning was the Word. I do not know what had moved me to choose that example. I knew I could not teach Anasaquit to read, any more than I could teach her English. I wanted only to make her grasp the idea that words could be represented by signs, and that what someone had said fifteen hundred years ago could be received by someone in our own time as though they had heard those words spoken aloud.

Anasaquit looked at me questioningly.

"Gilbert?" she asked.

I decided that it was time to bring her together with him.

I went to the door and shouted, "Peter Slade! Peter Slade!"

Peter came from the direction of the fish flakes.

"You have a loud voice, Father Fletcher."

"No, Peter, I have a trained voice. We priests have to sing and to make ourselves heard all throughout a church or cathedral. It's the same as for Harry Chard, who had to learn to make his orders heard all over a ship during a storm at sea."

"Well, your priestly voice has summoned me, like the voice of God summoning Samuel. Now what do you want from me?"

"Nothing. I want you to send over Gilbert."

"He is working."

"There are five months left until the fleet returns, Peter. Your work cannot be so urgent that he cannot be spared for an hour or two."

Peter seemed about to say something to me, but instead he scowled, kicked at the melting snow like a boy, and went off to fetch Gilbert.

Gilbert entered as though I were a schoolmaster and he were expecting a beating from me.

"Please join us, Gilbert," I told him. "I was showing Anasaquit the Bible."

"But she cannot read!" Gilbert exclaimed.

"Well, of course not, but she may learn one day. If she learns English, as I hope she will, she ought to learn to read and write as well. I think the Beothuks should learn English."

Anasaquit interrupted me.

"Timaskatek," she said. "English."

"Yes, Timaskatek knows some English," I acknowledged. "I wish he had not had to learn it as a prisoner. The English language must always mean imprisonment and injustice to him. Nevertheless, the Beothuks should learn English to prepare them for contact with our people. Many more English men will come here soon, and English women, too, and I am sure that few of them will trouble to learn Beothuk."

"I will," Gilbert said.

"But, Gilbert, do you know any other languages?" I said. "You know only English."

Gilbert took a deep breath, and seemed to turn into a different person, breaking forth into elegant Latin.

"*Linguam Latinam loqui, Patre*," Gilbert said. "*Mater mea magistrem apud nos apportavit.*"

Anasaquit looked from Gilbert to me. She seemed to be unsure whether she was hearing a different language to English or not.

I was just about to tell Gilbert to speak in English so as not to puzzle Anasaquit even more, but then I thought of the question which I should have asked long before, and I put it in Latin in case there was any chance of Anasaquit understanding.

"*Qui erat magister tuus?*" I asked. I needed to know who the schoolmaster who had been who had taught him Latin, but I feared that I already knew the answer. I was right.

"*Petrus erat,*" Gilbert replied. "*Petrus senex qui est cum nobis in insula Terrae Novae.*"

"I was beginning to guess that already, Gilbert," I said, wondering whether Peter Slade knew that his pupil Gilbert thought of him as an 'old man.' "Anasaquit, do not be troubled. What we were saying is safer for you not to know."

After all these announcements I half feared that Anasaquit would answer me in Latin, too, and reveal herself to be a nun of Bermondsey.

At least there was some limit upon the shocks of the day. Anasaquit still looked baffled.

It was time to turn the conversation in another direction. I could confront Peter Slade afterwards. Had Horsfall, Young Martin, and William Durdle, and Tom Rudge all been part of Harry Chard's conspiracy even before they had left England?

I was beginning to wonder again what this conspiracy would mean for me in the end, and then, with a rush of shame, I remembered that I ought to be thinking about what it might mean for Anasaquit and Gilbert.

Had they ever met before? I observed them for a moment. Anasaquit was looking at me, still baffled, and Gilbert was studying the floor.

I took Anasaquit's hand and drew her over to sit beside me.

"Gilbert," I said, startling him, "come and sit at the table with us. You should be helping me to entertain our guest. Or is she your guest?"

"What do you mean, Father?" Gilbert asked.

"I mean that I am only a simple priest, almost the lowest rank in the Church, while you are the King of England, so I am told. Well?"

"So I have been told."

"Did the other men know of this before we left England?"

"No. They found out at the same time you did, when Harry Chard told you all."

That explained why all the men of the winter crew had treated Gilbert so roughly. I wondered why Peter Slade had not shown more respect to his sovereign, and then I realised that Peter had simply been carrying on the authority of the schoolmaster which he had been.

"What will this all lead to, Gilbert?" I asked.

"I don't know," Gilbert admitted. "I know only what my mother and Harry Chard have told me."

"I wonder what Harry Chard has told Anasaquit," I said.

She responded to that.

"Harry."

She struck her breast with her fist like a penitent at the Mass.

"Anasaquit. English kveen."

"She knows," I told Gilbert unnecessarily. "He must have shown her that foolish wooden palace. Yet I am surprised that she should want to become English, after what Timaskatek must have recounted to her about his imprisonment at Westminster."

I wished I could have questioned Timaskatek more about what he and the other two Beothuk men had done and seen in England.

If we of the winter crew could be so struck and puzzled by Newfoundland, a bare and harsh land with apparently no human habitation other than rough tents, and indeed hardly any humans, what could the Beothuks have made of the crowds and towns of England?

There is so much I do not know, here in Newfoundland where everybody seems to want either to withhold truth from me, or to be unable to tell it to me.

"This has never happened to the Beothuks before, Gilbert," I remarked. "We are the first other nation ever to come to Newfoundland."

Anasaquit stood up and grasped one of my hands and one of Gilbert's, pulling us towards her.

"What do you want, Anasaquit?" I asked as she pulled us to the door. "Oh! You want us to come with you. Another mysterious visit to the forest."

I reached for the door to open it, but Anasaquit opened it herself with surprising facility for one who can never have handled doors before.

We followed her out into the magical mildness of the open air, and splashed through the slush behind her as she led us towards the dark line of trees. That line marks the frontier between the English settlement on the rocks by the sea and the secret interior of this great land, which is still known only to the Beothuks.

It occurred to me that Gilbert might never have gone into the forest before.

"Have you been away from the shore yet, Gilbert?" I puffed as I strained to keep up with the lithe figure of Anasaquit, striding gracefully ahead of us, as proud and perfect as Diana the Huntress. No doubt Anasaquit is a huntress. What else could she be in this country?

"Only with Harry Chard," Gilbert replied, startling me because I had forgotten the question which I had just put to him. "He takes me to the cathedral or the palace to instruct me in what I must do."

"And what must you do, Gilbert?"

"Harry says that Gilbert is not a suitable name for a king of England, though it is the name with which I was christened. Harry says I must be William."

"God's hands!" I swore. "Why does he not simply set up a block outside his fatuous timber palace, have you place your neck on it, and make Horsfall or Tom Rudge behead you here, instead of sending you all the way back to England to be executed at the Tower? At least that would spare Anasaquit. How terrible, that her voyage to England should end in a shameful death for her."

"Harry says that there will be death only for Henry Tudor."

"I am sure that His Majesty King Henry the Seventh is in no danger. He overcame so much opposition to come to the throne that I do not believe that any power could be raised in England strong enough to depose him from it. God knows, enough rebellions have been started, and there have already been two boy pretenders. Perhaps you will be lucky, and not be executed like Perkin Warbeck. You may spend the rest of your life as a kitchen servant, like Lambert Simnel. What will become of Anasaquit, though?"

"You should not question me about these things, Father. If I am truly king, I could punish you for them one day."

"And if you are not, which you are not, then I am trying to save both you and this girl from dying in your youth."

Our conversation was stopped when we saw the Beothuk tents ahead of us among the tree-trunks. I expected that Anasaquit was going to take us into one of the tents for another one of those uncomfortable visits with unfriendly and inscrutable Beothuk men, but instead she led us to one side, away through the trees, and stopped beside what looked like a fresh grave.

"Who has been buried here, Anasaquit?" I asked, wondering for a moment whether Harry Chard had died among the Beothuks, or been murdered by them.

Anasaquit ignored me, and to my horror she began rifling through the piled earth with her bare hands. I feared that she would lift a pale dead hand or a yellow face out of the soil, but instead she took out a small brownish object and handed it to me proudly.

It felt warm in my hands. It was a small conical thing, light and covered in dirt. I wiped the ingrained soil away, and held the strange treasure up close to my eyes.

At first I could still not make out what it was, but all at once I realised that it was made out of ivory, and that it was a carved figurine.

I had no idea whether the Beothuks have ever made carved or sculptured figures or not, but I do know that no elephants roam the forests of Newfoundland. There are great seals in the ocean whose tusks could be used for ivory, but whoever had carved this object had been no Beothuk.

It was a little pagan warrior, with a conical helmet, and a tiny sword and shield held close to his body. The ivory was yellowed and cracked, and the cracks were filled with old soil. The little warrior had lain in this earth for many years, and Newfoundland has only been known to Europeans in my own short lifetime.

Gilbert was looking at the figurine as intently as I was. "What is it, Father?"

"It is some kind of warrior. I have seen similar figures carved on the walls of very old churches in England. It is many hundreds of years old."

"Then what is it doing here? Did some fishing crew bring it with them from England?"

"No, it has been lying here too long for that," I told him. "Anasaquit is using this to tell us that Europeans have been to Newfoundland before, long ago, and that the Beothuks know about it. Perhaps the Beothuks remember them. Who knows yet what the Beothuks have recorded in their history and folktales?"

"I wonder if Harry Chard knows about this," I said.

"Harry!" Anasaquit exclaimed, and she shook her head from side to side, in an exaggerated way, trying to mimic the gesture of denial that she had seen Englishmen use.

"So Harry doesn't know about the earlier visitors, and we do," I remarked to Gilbert.

"He thinks that he is enlisting the Beothuks in his plan, but perhaps it is they who have drawn him into some plan of theirs instead."

Chapter Thirteen

Anasaquit mimed the action of putting something into her bosom. I obeyed her and hid the little figurine away in my smock.

Anasaquit knelt and pushed away more of the soil. Gilbert and I knelt beside her.

The soil in Newfoundland is extraordinarily shallow, only a thin covering over the bare rock. I wonder how the trees grow. Certainly it is no wonder that the Beothuks live upon meat and fish, for there can be few crops on this land.

Gilbert and I soon found what Anasaquit had wanted to show us. There were flat slabs of stone, surely the floor of some lost building, yet the Beothuks are said never to build with the stone that lies all around them. It is because they have no metal tools.

"What is it, Father Fletcher?" Gilbert asked.

"It is the remains of some kind of structure. Anasaquit wants us to see it because it is very old and was built by men from Europe."

Anasaquit swept more soil away from the stones, and uncovered what at first I took to be random scratches like the marks and indentations on the ivory figurine.

When I examined the scratches I saw that they were some kind of writing, based on upright and angled marks. I felt that if I studied them hard enough I would recognise them as letters such as we know, but I could make no sense of them. Later I will try to go back and copy them out to take back to England in case some scholar of the universities or the Vatican knows this writing and who might have written it.

"Who were these people, Anasaquit?" I asked. Anasaquit shook her head.

"Are they still here?" I then asked her, waving my arm around to try to convey to her that I wanted to know whether the mysterious people yet lived here, somewhere on this great land.

Anasaquit blinked in puzzlement, and then understood, shaking her head again.

"What did she mean?" Gilbert asked.

"Whoever these people may have been, they are no longer here, Gilbert," I told him. "They will not be numbered among your subjects."

"I wish you would not taunt me over this matter of the Crown of England, Father."

"I am sorry, Gilbert. I should not have done so," I replied, truly regretful for having pained him with a foolish remark, the sort that would be made by an unpleasant over-clever schoolboy. Indeed, that is what the winter crew think I am, and perhaps they are right.

I studied the dug-up ground, wondering what Anasaquit had been trying to tell us.

We now knew that other Europeans had come to Newfoundland, that they left writings which none of us now here can read, and that these previous fishermen or colonists are here no more.

Is it a warning against our presumption in claiming Newfoundland as an English possession, a warning that others have tried the same before and been driven back into the sea, or been lost in the vast forests of the interior?

While I pondered this question within my mind I was suddenly brought back to the outer world by a chilly gust of wind around my ears. All at once the cold of winter fell upon us as if it had been hurled down by an enraged classical god.

"Come on, Gilbert," I said, "we must get back to the shore."

Gilbert turned to come with me, but Anasaquit seized his arm, and then took mine.

"No," she shouted, "no!"

Anasaquit pulled us towards the enveloping forest. I tried to resist.

"No, Anasaquit, we cannot come with you. We must go back. We cannot risk being lost here."

Even as I said it, I realised how foolish it was. The Beothuks live in the wilderness of Newfoundland all their lives without any sense of being lost.

As an Englishman, I feel that I am at the edge of the world, here in Newfoundland, but Timaskatek and his two companions must have felt the same during their captivity in England, longing for Newfoundland with its snows and forests.

Gilbert was not frightened, only puzzled, and he looked to me to tell him what we should do.

"Anasaquit means us no harm, I'm certain of that," I told him. "Let's go with her, but make sure to remember the direction we take so that we can find our way back."

We left the mysterious grave, or whatever it may be, behind us, and let Anasaquit lead us into the woods. I tried to remember the direction of Harry Chard's fantastic church and palace, but I could not tell whether we were going that way.

I feared that we would have to sit in one of those dismal stinking tents again, being glared at by unfriendly Beothuk men; but then, why should they feel friendly toward us?

I noticed that we were farther into the forest than I had ever been before, and I began to worry that I would not be able to retrace our route back to the sea.

What an astonishing shock it must have been for the Beothuks when men came from the sea. I do not mean the English fishermen; I mean those people who left the decaying treasures which Anasaquit had uncovered for Gilbert and myself to worry over.

We were not wandering aimlessly among rocks and pine needles. There was a clear track which Anasaquit was following. I doubt that it was actually cut and cleared by anybody. It is simply the smooth straight record of many years of Beothuk migrations from the interior of Newfoundland to the sea and back again, season by season.

The sight of the track comforted me. For as long as no new snow fell, I could follow it in the way we had come, and bring both Gilbert and myself safely back to the seashore.

I nevertheless began to feel frightened when we had gone more than two miles into the forest, with Gilbert loping beside me with the faithfulness of a dog as we followed Anasaquit, who never once looked round to see whether we were following her.

I was starting to remember more classical stories of spirits in the shape of young women leading men to spectacular dooms in evilly-enchanted forests, and old English folk stories of wicked half-human creatures who lurked in dark woods. I was almost relieved to see a Beothuk encampment in front of us.

"Look!" Gilbert cried unnecessarily. "Look how many tents there are!"

The bright light of the wonderful warm morning had already turned into the habitual winter gloom, so that I had not seen how many tents there were among the trees. There were six or seven.

Anasaquit turned round and beckoned to us, although we were still following close behind.

I could not understand why so many Beothuks should be here.

As far as we know anything of their lives, it is believed that usually they come to the coast only for the short Newfoundland summer, to fish and hunt the seals and other oceanic beasts, and retire inland in the autumn to follow the great herds of deer.

The English fishing fleet have truly burst into the Beothuks' lives with a shock. If the great continent of which Newfoundland is a part is a New World to us, then Europe is a New World to them.

We have never intended to disturb the Beothuks' own lives. The fleet want only to catch the fish and take them home for the pious to eat on days when meat is forbidden.

This avoidance of contact is not due to goodwill any more than it is due to hostility. The English visitors are simply indifferent to the Beothuks, not wanting to take anything from them.

It is proved by what happened to the three Beothuk men who were abducted and taken to England. Nothing was done with them. As far as I know, they were not presented to the King, and if they were then he seems to have given no orders concerning them. The three Beothuks were simply left to idle away their baffling captivity, until Timaskatek was taken home by Harry Chard for his own purposes, not out of any tenderness towards the poor prisoner.

Because we had not otherwise harmed the Beothuks, I was not as afraid of them as I had been in the past.

I expected Anasaquit to lead us into one of the tents, but instead she stopped at the entrance and made a half-bow, sweeping her hand across her lap to gesture us inside. Who taught her that?

The smells of roasting meat, wet garments, smoky wood, and dirty humans greeted me like a word of welcome. I blinked in the smoke as Gilbert entered behind me, and then I did hear some words of welcome.

"Ralph Lecher," a man said, and I recognised Aguthut, but only after I had peered at him in the dimness to make sure that it was he.

There were about a dozen Beothuks sitting about, and I sat down too because that seemed to be what was expected of us. Gilbert did the same.

"What do they want, Father?" he asked me.

"I have no idea, Gilbert, but they want something from us, or perhaps they want to give something to us."

Aguthut stood up and took Anasaquit's arm. With his other hand he grasped Gilbert's arm. He pulled both the boy and the girl down to the floor so that they were sitting on either side of him, with Anasaquit smiling and Gilbert looking uncomfortable and puzzled. I suppose that was how I looked, too.

One of the Beothuks was a woman who appeared old. I write that because I cannot be sure that we can judge the Beothuks' age properly. She might not be an old woman at all, but she had the kind and confident expression of old people who have always been happy.

She went to the entrance of the tent and peered out, looking both ways. She did not seem really to be seeking for anything. It looked more like an act or a ritual of some kind.

The old woman withdrew her head back into the tent, and addressed me.

"Harry Chard, no," she announced.

"I am glad he is not here," I said. "Harry Chard is a man to be trusted neither by Englishmen nor by Beothuks."

I hoped that Timaskatek would understand that. He was the next to speak.

"Harry Chard, *Ingliss*, friend, no. Friend, Beothuk, no."

"At least we agree on that, Timaskatek," I replied.

"Anasaquit, Ralph Lecher, friend, yes."

"I am honoured that she thinks of me as a friend," I said.

"Anasaquit, Gilbert, friend no," he continued, surprising me. Why should Anasaquit be an enemy of Gilbert, the most innocent among us? Not even the light-headed Young Martin deserves the title of innocence as much as Gilbert.

"Why is Gilbert not your friend, Timaskatek?" I asked.

Timaskatek made an exclamation of anger in his own language. I was baffled why he should feel such rage against Gilbert, but it turned out that I had misunderstood. Timaskatek was angry because he had not made himself understood. The problem was his lack of knowledge of English.

"Timaskatek, friend, Gilbert!" he said. "Gilbert, Anasaquit, friend, no."

Gilbert stared like a schoolboy who cannot understand his lesson. Anasaquit's eyes were cast down as if she were ashamed of something.

I began to believe that I understood Timaskatek at last.

"Do you mean that Anasaquit and Gilbert are not friends?" I asked. "Anasaquit, Gilbert, friend, no?"

Timaskatek let out a sigh of relief and for the first time since I had met him his face broke out into a smile, which I believe to be quite the most evil sight I have ever seen.

Gilbert appealed to me for an explanation.

"What does all this talk about friends, yes and no, mean, Father?"

"Timaskatek means that you and Anasaquit are not friends."

"Why should she be my enemy? She doesn't know me!" Gilbert objected.

"Timaskatek is doing his best to express himself in a language which he has not been taught," I told Gilbert. "What he is trying to say is that you and Anasaquit do not know each other, and so they are opposed to Harry's plans for you."

While Gilbert thought about that, and Anasaquit slowly raised her eyes from the floor, I pondered this new factor in our affairs in this place. Harry Chard thinks that the Beothuks are working with him. Since I first agreed to come to Newfoundland to be pastor of the fishermen (what a grand title, now that I consider it), Harry Chard has kept secrets from me.

Now I know something that Harry does not: the Beothuks are not his accomplices, although he believes that they are. His palace and cathedral were built for Beothuks to assemble in. Harry expects them to swear allegiance to his pretender king in the palace, and to attend that king's coronation in the cathedral.

When I was a schoolboy, the masters all said that I was good at studying. They always said it grudgingly as though studiousness were something which was shameful or of little account.

If I do have the gift of quick learning, then perhaps I learn more quickly than Harry. I have learnt that the Beothuks have their own wishes for the future of Newfoundland. After all, they have lived on this land probably for at least as long as the thousand years that we have lived in England.

I faced Timaskatek again.

"What do you want me to do?" I asked him, but it was Anasaquit who answered me.

"Harry, no," she said quietly.

"I will do my best to stop him," I replied.

I knew that Gilbert would finally understand that I was Harry's opponent, so I turned to the boy to reassure him.

"I'm not against you, Gilbert," I told him. "I'm trying to protect you."

"I don't know who's for me, who's against me, who's trying to protect me, or who's trying to hurt me!" Gilbert cried. "I don't know what to do!"

"I don't know what to do, either, Gilbert," I said. "I can only pray to God for help."

"God will help you, because you're a priest."

"God will not help me any more than He helps you, Gilbert," I replied, "and before He will help me He will expect me to use the power of reason to try to find a solution myself."

Gilbert looked around at all the Beothuks.

For the first time, they did not stare back belligerently. They cast their eyes down in the same way as Anasaquit had done, as though they were ashamed of something, or as if they were afraid.

Afraid of Harry? Afraid of me? Surely not. Afraid of Gilbert?

I looked at Gilbert again. Did he really have some regal quality that Harry Chard had detected? Was I so used to thinking of Gilbert as the ill-used serving-boy that I had failed to see some natural nobility in him?

Without straying into blasphemy, I could not help remembering that many people who had actually seen Jesus on Earth were not at all impressed or overawed by Him. I was not being asked to worship Gilbert as a god, but only to swear allegiance to him as a king.

In the dim light within the tent, Gilbert still looked like an ordinary young boy to me. In spite of the Beothuks' fire, I shivered. It still seems wrong to me that a dim enclosed place like that tent should be cold. The consolation of being confined in a stinking atmosphere with too many people is that you should at least be warm.

I announced my plan to everyone, Gilbert, Anasaquit, Timaskatek, and the other Beothuks. I had begun to suspect that more of them had some knowledge of English than I had previously thought. I know that English fishermen have been coming to Newfoundland for many years, certainly from long before its official discovery by John Cabot seven and a half years ago.

"I have one power that no other Englishman on this land has," I told everyone in the smoky tent. "I have the power to marry Gilbert to Anasaquit, if she becomes a Christian, and I also have the power to refuse to do so. Harry Chard cannot find anyone else to do that, and he has no way of forcing me."

Timaskatek replied to that.

"Anasaquit, Gilbert, friend, no."

"Friends, perhaps, when they know each other," I answered, "but they will never be married against their will."

The Beothuk men glowered at me while Anasaquit looked down at the floor again.

"What else can I do for you?" I asked, meaning it as a rhetorical question which should receive no answer, but I did receive an astonishing answer from an unexpected source: Timaskatek again.

"Christmas," he barked.

I thought I must have misheard him, or that he had mispronounced some English word or phrase.

"What was that?" I asked Timaskatek rudely.

"Christmas," he repeated, and this time there was no doubt about what he had said.

"Yes," I replied, baffled. "It is nearly Christmas, but what do you know of Christmas?"

"England, Westminster. Christmas."

I remembered that Timaskatek had lain a prisoner in Westminster Palace for two years. He must have seen two or three Christmases. Yet what would he have seen of them, kept in some dark dirty cell with only a view of stone walls inside and more stone walls outside?

Now Aguthut spoke.

"Christmas. Food. Fire."

There was a low mutter of 'Christmas' among all the Beothuks. It reminded me of a congregation giving the responses in the Mass. I supposed that the other Beothuks understood no more of what Christmas was than our parishioners understand of the noble Latin words which we recite to them. I tried to make out what the Beothuks wanted of me.

"If you want the goose and plum porridge, we have none to give you. We do not even have a supply of Christmas food for ourselves. You probably have more food of all kinds than we do, and you can light greater fires."

Gilbert surprised me by offering a suggestion.

"Perhaps Timaskatek saw the Twelve Days of Christmas, and he wants to be able to join in the fun."

"He should be heartily glad that he is missing them," I said. "I have always hated the celebrations of Christmas. What some call fun is an ordeal to me."

Gilbert was astonished, and he even laughed, which I have rarely seen him do.

"You don't like the games, Father? The songs? The Twelfth Night cake? The Lord of Misrule?"

"No, I hate them all," I told him. "I had hoped that one consolation of spending the Christmas season in Newfoundland was that I would be spared all that."

"Harry Chard wants Timaskatek to be the Lord of Misrule over the Twelve Days of Christmas," Gilbert reminded me.

I began to think, which is something which I should have done earlier. If Harry Chard had promised the Beothuks a traditional English Christmas, complete with goose, plum porridge, bad tempers, and aching heads, he would not be able to provide it. Perhaps this would set the Beothuks even more against him.

I did not know what moves were planned in this game of chess, but I decided that it would be best if I allowed Harry and Timaskatek to keep moving their pieces around the board until I understood how the game was to end.

I knew that Gilbert was meant to be the king, Anasaquit the queen, myself the bishop, and the winter crew the knights.

The wooden cathedral and the palace were to be the rooks, or castles as some call them. Harry saw the Beothuks as the pawns, but perhaps they were playing at the opposite side of the board instead of on his side as he thought.

I suddenly remembered the black and white squares of the accounting table in the Exchequer, where I was paid the forty testoons as my wages for coming here.

Had that been a sign? We priests are taught how to interpret allegory and how the events of the Old Testament foreshadow the events of the New. I remembered those black and white squares in the Exchequer and the sinister hands of the Dominican friar wandering across them like spiders.

"Christmas is for Christians," I said, but Gilbert interrupted me.

"Some who have seen an English Christmas would not say so, Father! There is some very unChristian behaviour."

"Gilbert, if we were all judged by whether we showed Christian behaviour all the time, few of us would escape damnation," I told him.

In my case, if I am to be damned, it will not be for revelry, drunkenness, and the singing of lewd songs, because I have no liking for such pastimes. I shall not be damned for fornication, either. It must mean that I am guilty of equally bad things which I do not recognise in myself.

"There are four days until Christmas," I said to Timaskatek. "I presume that you will come and join us."

Gilbert was horrified.

"But Father, what will the other men say?"

"Harry Chard said that he wanted Timaskatek to be the Lord of Misrule through the Twelve Days of Christmas. So be it, then. Harry cannot complain if I carry out his wishes. If the rest of the winter crew do not like it, let them dispute with Harry themselves. Perhaps he is right, after all. This is a strange land to us, so let us by all means have a strange Christmas."

I shifted to ease the cramps which I had begun to feel, and the little figurine which I had tucked away in my shirt bumped against my chest.

Anasaquit had given it to me because it should carry some meaning. I had given Aguthut the silver Mass bell for the same reason. Was either of us close to understanding why our gift had been presented to us? The wicked-looking old Beothuk woman handed me some strips of meat, draped like worms across her fascinatingly wrinkled hand.

I passed half of the meat to Gilbert, who studied it in alarm.

"Gilbert, we must it eat it. It would be discourteous of us not to," I admonished him, although I had no more enthusiasm for it than he did.

I suppose that it is the flesh of the great deer which the Beothuks hunt. Sometimes the English fishermen go inland in the summertime and hunt them too.

If there comes to be heavy English settlement in Newfoundland I foresee many disputes about hunting rights, especially if the king creates royal forests where only he may hunt.

There was an interval of silence. That is, there was no speech, although there was plenty of noise while we all chewed the meat, which seemed to retain some of the proud spirit of the animal, resentfully resisting our teeth.

The meat was so tough that I could hardly think. The sound of my own jaws working rumbled in the inner caverns of my ears.

I pondered upon what I had learnt, and upon how little I understood. I know what Harry Chard wants. I know what I want for myself, which is a safe return to England in the spring. I know that Timaskatek wants Christmas, of all things that he might have asked for from a band of Englishmen on the shores of his great land.

I looked at all the busily-chewing faces around me. What does Gilbert want? Does he want to be a pretender to the throne, and to marry Anasaquit? Anasaquit, who appears so serene and beautiful most of the time, looks frighteningly savage as she angrily tears and chews at the smoked meat.

What does Aguthut want? What do the old Beothuk women want?

The English merchants and fishermen want the codfish from the seas around Newfoundland. I am told that the Beothuks fish only in the rivers and lakes, never in the sea, so why did they come here? Were they brought to Newfoundland by the unknown European people who lie in the sinister graves in the forest?

Are the Beothuks themselves the descendants of some other winter crew of long ago, cast away here and abandoned for ever?

It reminds me of the tale that the Gypsies tell. Their fate is not to be bound to one place, but the opposite, to travel about on a lifelong journey with no destination.

The Gypsies say that they have been condemned to this perpetual travelling as a penance for some terrible sin against Christ when He was on earth.

The Beothuks have hardly heard of Christ yet, but perhaps they have some other myth to explain why there are here. They may well never have known that there were any other lands or peoples in the world before the first English, Basque, and Portuguese ships came.

I swallowed the last piece of meat in triumph. Outside, there came the loud whistling wail of the freezing wind. I longed to be back in our hut beside the sea.

I addressed myself to Timaskatek.

"Have you finished with us?" I asked him. "May we go?"

I gestured to Gilbert and pointed to myself, and then out to the snows and the wind.

"We want to go back to the English fishermen."

I suddenly realised that I did not know the way after the end of the rocky path, and that Gilbert would probably not be able to remember it either. We would need a guide.

The Beothuks muttered among themselves. It was a sound as frightening and wild as the wind.

Aguthut rose up and forced his way towards me. I tried not to flinch.

He pulled the hood of his smock up over his head, and I realised that he was going to come outside with us as he pulled on his surprisingly skilfully-made mittens.

I tugged at Gilbert's shoulder.

"Come along, Gilbert, we must go back."

Gilbert rose, and we followed Aguthut out of the tent. Both Gilbert and I gasped in the cold air. Hard snowflakes stung our faces.

Aguthut had gone a little way ahead of us, so Gilbert sidled up to me with an urgent question.

"What did they want, Father?"

"They wanted to find out whether I was part of Harry Chard's conspiracy. They also wanted to make sure that Anasaquit would not be married to you against her will. They also wanted Christmas."

"Why do they want Christmas, Father?" Gilbert asked.

"I still don't know, although it is certainly not for religious reasons. Now let's catch up to Aguthut before he becomes suspicious of us talking together. I'm never sure how much English the Beothuks understand."

We followed Aguthut through the blowing snow. I think that we would have lost sight of him if it had not been for the maroon designs embroidered on his smock.

I kept my eyes on those pictures and patterns. Aguthut's pale smock blended in with the paleness of the whirling snowflakes, so that the embroidery seemed to be dancing in space in front of me, a pattern of animals and geometrical figures dancing in the air like a vision.

Every few moments I made sure that Gilbert was still walking beside me or behind me. The wind was growing ever stronger and I could not hear him breathing or the sound of his boots fighting against the snow.

Suddenly I realised that Aguthut had vanished. Before I could panic the wind dropped for a moment. The snowflakes slumped to the ground like a falling curtain, and in the distance I saw the fishing buildings and the grey sea beyond.

"This way, Gilbert," I called, trying to keep walking in the same direction even though the wind rose again and the snow veiled my sight.

When Gilbert and I tugged the door open, we expected the hut to be empty, but instead the whole winter crew was assembled. Boots, caps, and mittens steamed by the fire. A stinking pot of vegetables simmered reluctantly on the stove.

Peter Slade sat upon one of the benches like a king enthroned. Perhaps he was accustomed to sitting in such state in the days of his wealth and high social position.

"Where have you been?" he demanded.

Gilbert was going to answer, but I held my arm out to keep him quiet.

We took off our wet clothes and hung them up to dry out. I served Gilbert a plate of the mess from the pot on the stove, and then helped myself.

I settled myself comfortably on the floor with the plate in my lap and my spoon in my hand.

The spoon caught the firelight, and for the first time since coming to Newfoundland I noticed what a ludicrously expensive spoon it is, fussily engraved. The spoon came from my father's house. When it was there, it was so suited to a rich man's home that it would have been approved of the philosopher Aristotle, who believed that even inanimate objects had a moral duty to carry out their designated functions properly. Here, in a rough hut in a remote land, my spoon is a silly bauble, but it is the only spoon I have, so I must continue to use it.

When I judged that I had kept Peter waiting long enough, I answered his question.

"We have been to visit the Beothuks, at their invitation. They wanted an assurance that I was not on Harry Chard's side, and that the young woman Anasaquit would not be the victim of a forced marriage to Gilbert."

Peter was not pleased.

"Such hospitality might have been dangerous."

"Even so," I told him, "it must be returned. The Beothuks will be visiting in a few days' time to help celebrate Christmas."

At that, all the men shouted, but I reminded them of Harry Chard's demand concerning the twelve days of Christmas.

"Harry Chard decreed that Timaskatek the Beothuk should be the Lord of Misrule over Christmas, didn't he?

Well, then, so he shall be," I declared while I took another spoonful of whatever the mess was.

If Harry Chard wanted misrule, he will receive it. I am sure that this will be the most misruled Christmas ever.

Chapter Fourteen

As Advent approaches its end, I must spend more time meditating on the religious meaning of this season of the year. The fishermen divide their lives into the summer, when the fleet is here, and the winter, when only the poor lost winter crew are left behind.

Everyone knows how peasants must organise their lives around the seasons. Even the Beothuks seem to divide their year into two parts: the winter, which they spend inland, and the summer, which they spend by the coast. It is we who have made at least a few of them change their ways by spending the winter near the sea. Perhaps they have been selected to watch us, while the rest of their people wander through the snows of the interior, chasing the great deer.

Only we priests observe a year which is seamless, because there is always some feast to observe, and every day has it prescribed readings and prayers.

The men have left me in peace since Gilbert and I paid our visit to the Beothuks. Harry Chard has not appeared. He must be sulking in his palace, like a Roman emperor. Surely no Roman emperor was ever so proud and angry as Harry is.

I did ask Peter Slade how the winter crew were planning to celebrate Christmas.

"Most of them have always been too poor to celebrate Christmas as you and I have been used to doing, Father," he said.

"If they are used to poor Christmases, then this one will be less hardship to them," I suggested.

"Oh, they will find ways to make merry," he replied, "probably in ways that will displease you, Father."

"Merriment is not necessarily a sign of sin, you know," I said. "One does not need to be glum to be virtuous."

I have the advantage that I do not have to devise my part in the celebration of Christmas. It is all set out for me in the rituals of the Church.

I have to prepare some homilies to preach, and I do take care of those, because I believe that it is important to give my best even to an audience which does not want to listen. Indeed, such hostile congregations probably need good preaching more than others, and the winter crew are the most difficult congregation I have ever faced, unless I one day end up preaching to the Beothuks.

The men will have no difficulty in finding a Yule log to burn in the fire over Christmas. Newfoundland may lack birds and reptiles and warm weather, but this land does not lack for trees.

I once watched from an upstairs window of my father's house in London as a fir tree was carried past by a crowd of Hanseatic merchants. They were taking it to be set up in their private enclave at the Steelyard, by the place where the river Walbrook flows into the Thames. Apparently it is the custom in central Europe to set up a fir tree at Christmas and to festoon it with decorations.

I remember how impressed I was by that exotic fir tree, which those German merchants had brought over from their homeland. If we were to decide to adopt that tradition here, it would be simple enough to find the tree. I can see dozens of them from the window as I write this entry in my book.

Well, there will be no goose and no plum porridge, so the meals will not be very festive. We also have very little in the way of drink, other than beer, unless the men of the winter crew brought more with them than I know about.

I am writing this in the evening, using the last two inches of one of my best candles, but not a church candle, of course. I am glad that my father had his servants pack those best-quality candles in my chest.

I shall never learn to be as practical as he is. It never occurred to me that I would need candles. Did I imagine that there would be oil lamps here, with servants to tend them? No wonder my father despairs of me, but at least he has not abandoned me to darkness.

The candle is to my left as I write, and the fire is to my right. The ink makes a wonderful perfect black river as it flows from the pen, with no glints or reflections from the flames. My written words come out in absolute black. It is like writing with the substance of night itself.

The other men have gone into the hut where the boats are kept. One of the tasks of the winter crew is to repair and maintain the boats over the winter, since nobody is going to go out on the sea at this time of year. I ought to suggest making sledges, except that we have no horses to pull them, and the Beothuks have no draft animals.

I had to stop writing when there was an urgent pounding on the door, like the constables of the night Watch in London, but there are no constables here. They would not lack for work, but instead when I opened the door Harry Chard stood there, shaking with cold, and holding up a great sack.

For an instant of madness, my mind was filled with a torrent of terrifying speculations. I had seen so much since I had come to Newfoundland that I would truly not have been surprised if Harry had produced the head of Timaskatek from the sack.

Harry is a man of action rather than a man of meditation. While I stood in baffled panic he pushed past me.

"Let me in, you damned fool. Do you know how cold it is out there?"

The sack struck my leg, and there was something horribly misshapen and hard inside it.

Harry flung the sack down to the floor while he basked before the fire.

"A fine welcome for a poor cold Christian man, Father Fletcher!" he bellowed over his shoulder. "You haven't even said a word of greeting yet. It's a good thing that you weren't an innkeeper in Bethlehem on the icy night that Joseph and Mary came to the door."

"I'm sorry, Harry," I said, and indeed I had been rude and inhospitable. Even Harry Chard is entitled to receive civil treatment, although I have never known him to give a kind word to anyone.

"Don't you want to know what's in the sack?" Harry asked.

"I thought it would be rude to ask," I replied.

"You mean you were afraid to ask!" Harry said. "It's your goose for Christmas dinner."

"Goose?" I exclaimed. "Do you mean that you've been keeping a goose here all this time?"

I had seen a cathedral, a king's palace, and an ivory carving from a strange man's grave, but I could not believe that there had ever been a goose here.

"It's a Newfoundland goose," Harry replied, opening the sack. He used both hands to lift out a vast joint of meat.

"The Beothuks gave me this," Harry said. "It's from one of the great deer that they hunt in the forest."

I was impressed by the size of the huge haunch of venison, but I could not restrain myself from asking "Do the Beothuks know that they are illegally hunting in your king's royal forests?"

Harry grunted, and instead of answering my question he proceeded to give me cooking instructions.

"This is a fresh kill, so it should be hung for as long as possible. The shack where we gut and salt the fish in the summertime will do very well."

"You mean the splitting house," I said, just to let him know that I am not unaware of the arcane terminology of the fishing trade. "Why didn't you take it straight there, then, instead of bringing it in here?"

"Why, Father Fletcher, it was a courtesy. I thought you might care to bless the meat."

"I can bless only living humans, not dead beasts," I said, "although of course I'm grateful to both God and yourself for providing the food."

"The Beothuks provided it, not me," Harry replied. "Thank them instead."

"We must show our gratitude by entertaining them well over the Twelve Days of Christmas," I said.

"That is no part of your function," Harry said. "You are there to carry out the serious religious side of Christmas."

"Don't you think the Beothuks should see the religious rituals as well as the rough games?" I asked him.

"Timaskatek has seen it already, in England. He has seen the games as well. It is the games that he wants to see again, not the Masses and prayers."

"I will ask him that myself," I declared. "Meanwhile, I'm going to take your haunch of meat to the splitting house."

Although I am taller than Harry, I found it hard to lift up the great lump of meat and bone. I had hoped to leave the room with an air of superior dignity, but instead I had to struggle with the joint of meat in my arms while I got a hand free to open the door.

Outside, the cold struck me like a lash, because I had not thought to put my outer clothes on, but it is only a short way to the splitting house.

I found William Durdle and Horsfall sitting in there around a small fire.

They looked up in astonishment, and William shouted at me.

"What have you got there, Father?"

"Our Christmas dinner," I replied. "It is a gift from the Beothuks, just now delivered by Harry Chard."

Both William and Horsfall were impressed.

Horsfall ran his hand over the hard meat, which was frozen by the cold.

"I won't be surprised if a goose arrives next, and plum porridge too," he said.

"You may see things which are far more surprising," I told him.

"Who knows what the Beothuks will bring us?"

Horsfall snatched his hand away from the meat and clasped both his hands behind his back, as though he were afraid to touch the gift again.

"Father, I sometimes wonder whether these savages are really men and women like us," he said.

William Durdle rebuked him.

"They may not be Christians, but they are men and women all the same."

"I hope that one day they will be Christians," I said, "but even while they are still pagans they are as human as we are. I have seen savage men and women in England, and so have you."

"We have seen more savagery than you ever have, Father," Horsfall said.

"I know," I conceded, "which is why you should not despise the Beothuks, whom you know only as distant brown faces flitting among the trees."

Horsfall and William Durdle both looked down suspiciously at the haunch of meat, as though it were poisoned or bewitched, or as if it might suddenly move or speak.

William Durdle at least was prepared to give a fair chance to the mute flesh of the dead beast.

"Let's lay it on the tables where we put the split fish in the summertime," he said.

I thought he would put the meat there himself, but he stood aside and Horsfall stepped forward to lift up the haunch of meat as though this were a drill which they had rehearsed.

Horsfall dropped the meat onto the table with a thump.

I am not a practical man, but I was worried about one thing.

"Is it not too warm in here?" I asked William Durdle. "If you are going to keep this fire, the meat will go bad."

"Don't worry, Father, we don't often light a fire in here. Anyway, it is not true that freezing meat preserves it. That is a foolish superstition."

"Well, there are no flies at this time of year," I conceded, "and if the door is kept shut the wolves and catamounts will not be able to get in."

"Is your mind at rest, Father?" William Durdle asked.

"Not at all. I am concerned about much which is happening here."

Horsfall interrupted.

"He means about the meat, Father."

"The meat! No, I'm not worried about the meat. I'll say Grace over it on Christmas Day."

"Then may William and I return to our work?"

I had seen well enough that they were not doing any work, but then I know of no work for them to be doing at this moment.

I ignored their rudeness, because I was happy enough to return to our living hut, where there was a bigger fire and no ghostly smell of the summer's fish.

The Beothuks have given us a fine joint for our Christmas dinner. What are we to give them?

If we were in England we could give them English Christmas fare. Perhaps Timaskatek was given goose and plum porridge in Westminster Palace. I should certainly hope that someone remembered to show the poor captive some hospitality and charity.

Well, we can give them first beer, and keep the second beer for ourselves. I would wickedly like to give Harry Chard only the small beer, and the bone of the great deer to chew on.

I closed up my book when I had written those words, and spent the rest of the day meditating upon Christmas, as I should be doing.

The next morning Anasaquit came again. I happened to be looking out of the window towards the forest when she appeared. For the first time she was walking confidently, not approaching shyly, and she did not look over her shoulder to the trees of her native forest, which must be a symbol of familiarity and comfort to her.

As I got up and opened the door to welcome her, I made a silent prayer of gratitude for the presence here of the harsh and fearsome Timaskatek. What would the Beothuks have made of us? We must seem like creatures from some other world to them.

We are lucky that Timaskatek was brought back from England by Harry Chard, so that he could explain to his fellows that we are only ordinary men and women like them. Women, did I write? There are no English women in Newfoundland yet.

When the first English lady (or, more likely, fisher girl) arrives on this coast, I am sure she will lack the natural grace of Anasaquit.

She came in smiling, and sat down at the table without being asked. For the first time, I realised that the table must have been made here, out of native Newfoundland wood, by some former winter crew. I cannot believe that it was brought over all the way from England.

I looked at Anasaquit's brown hands folded together on the rough wood. The Beothuks have no tables. Does she realise that it was made out of the trees of her own forests? For that matter, so were our huts and the fish flakes.

I wondered how to begin the day's instruction. If I had known that I would have to convert a Beothuk, I would have prepared myself by finding out how the Spaniards approached the inhabitants of the warm lands to the south.

The Spanish friars boast of their converts, but they never explain how the first move was made.

"Anasaquit," I began, "I am a priest of God. This is His symbol," I continued, holding up the cross which of course lies upon my breast every day.

I needed to establish whether she had any idea of a god. We do not even know whether the Beothuks worship any divinities. No fisherman, nor even a ship's captain or a Fishing Admiral, has ever thought of asking them.

"Come to the window, Anasaquit," I said, taking her hand and making her stand up.

I drew her to the window. The day was cloudy, with a blustery wind. The sun could not be seen, which suited my purpose.

I pointed to the figure of Christ upon my cross.

"This is God when He was on earth as a man," I said.

Using the same hand, I pointed up into the sky.

"Now He is in Heaven, but He will return one day and heal the world for ever."

Anasaquit reached over and ran her fingers over the little carved figure of Christ crucified. The way she caressed the carving was disturbing, but she is still a pagan who does not understand what she is seeing and touching.

She looked up at the window, and pointed up into the clouds while her face broke into the most astonishing expression of joy and hope.

Lord, I prayed, I hope that this is a good sign. Please help me. I don't know what to do.

Anasaquit kept her face radiant and her hand pointing upwards for a long moment, as if she were posing for a painting.

She dropped her hand and looked at me expectantly.

I thought of explaining that we would soon be celebrating Christ's birthday, but I could think of no way of expressing the idea of birth by any gesture which would not be unseemly and impious.

That idea made me laugh. I was embarrassed at laughing about such a subject, and the embarrassment made me laugh even more, and Anasaquit began laughing with me, or perhaps at me. I do not care.

The startled face of Young Martin passed by the window as we laughed ourselves into painfulness. What he will make of that I cannot imagine.

Anasaquit, still laughing helplessly, took both my hands in hers, so that our hands shook together in our mirth. I do not remember having felt such joy since I first came to Newfoundland.

When I could control myself again, I once more pointed at the image of Christ upon the crucifix.

"Again, Anasaquit, Christ is in the sky, and yet He is with us wherever we are in the world."

Anasaquit stared at the tiny slumped figure, and then she knelt upon the rough floor and put her face down upon the bare boards.

What did she mean? I feared that she was bowing down to me, and I bent down to draw her up, and then I asked myself whether she was submitting herself to God.

How could I tell the difference? I took off the cross and its fine chain (another gift from my father, who has set me up well in the priest's trade).

I hung the cross from one of the nails above the window from which we hang the dirty rags which serve us as curtains. Then I did pull Anasaquit up, and let her go while I moved across to the opposite side of the room, as far away as possible from the hanging image of Christ which swung gently on its rich chain in the same rhythm as a beckoning hand.

Anasaquit took three paces across the room, and knelt before the cross.

I lifted her up again gently, and led her back to the table. I gave her a lump of our rugged bread and a cup of my third-best wine. (The second-best is for Christmas, and the best is for the Eucharist.)

The bread and wine were more symbols that Anasaquit could not yet understand, but I wanted her to become accustomed to them.

She chewed the bread vigorously, and looked in surprise at the wine after she had tried a sip. After I had taken a drink of the same wine myself, she took some more of hers. How new and strange wine must be to one who has never known it. How strong and strange Christ must be to one who has never known Him.

I hoped that Anasaquit had not been bowing down in fear to what she thought was some primitive angry god like the classical gods of Olympus. I will be able to tell when I know her better.

Anasaquit had the next word.

"I, Anasaquit—I?"

"Yes, that's right, Anasaquit."

"I, friend, Gilbert."

"I am glad to hear it," I told her. She had hardly met Gilbert, but I have no right to bar friendship between any two people, no matter how different their origins.

Another face rolled past the window, and then stopped and peered in. It was Harry Chard.

He stepped out of sight, and then the door opened.

"Good morning, Father Fletcher," he said.

"Anasaquit is here, too," I pointed out to him.

"Good morning to Anasaquit as well. How is the preaching and conversion going?"

"I hope it is going well, Harry. Have you come to join us, so that I can try to convert you into a Christian as well?"

"You are the kind of man who tells old jokes badly, Father."

I noticed that Anasaquit had shrunk back against the table, where my cross still hung. It had begun swinging again in the cold draught which Harry had let in when he had opened the door.

"Anasaquit does not want you here," I said. "If you have no business with us, please go away. I am sure that Peter Slade could use an extra man to help with his maintenance work."

"I am the ship's master!" Harry roared. "I am the Fishing Admiral!"

"The rule of the Fishing Admiral ends with the fishing season," I replied, "and you are the master of no ship. Your ship is far across the sea in Devon, and you will not see her again until the spring."

Harry came up close to me, and his red face glared up at mine.

"Beware of me, Sir Ralph," he said. "I am a dangerous man."

"I know that very well, Harry," I replied, "but the other men will not allow you to harm me."

Anasaquit struck across the room like a snake, and she leapt onto Harry's back.

They both fell together onto the floor, and I saw something dark and misshapen in Anasaquit's hand.

I grasped her wrist just as I recognised that what she was holding was a stone knife.

"No, Anasaquit!" I cried while she tugged against my restraining hand.

"Harry, get up," I urged him when I had forced Anasaquit to release her hold.

Harry bounced upright like a toy. He spun round to strike Anasaquit.

"No, Harry, don't hurt her!" I shouted. "You'll raise all the Beothuks against us."

He had still spoken no word, but he dropped his arms, panting heavily. His face was redder than ever.

While he was silent, I took the chance to try to calm him.

"Anasaquit thought you were going to attack me because you were standing so close," I explained. "She was trying to defend me."

"Why did you let her come in here with a knife?" Harry demanded.

"I didn't know she had a knife, and how could I forbid it? This is her country. Perhaps all women are armed here. With men like you about, I could not condemn that."

I was still holding Anasaquit's wrist. She and I were standing together like a pair of classical statues representing some incident from Greek mythology.

I released her, but she kept holding out her knife as a threat. She backed away towards the wall. As she passed the window a shaft of sunlight caught the blade of her knife, so that it glistened suddenly like a wicked gift. Her eyes were so bright with hatred that they seemed to be lit from within.

When Anasaquit felt the wall against her back, she spoke.

"Harry Chard. I, Anasaquit, friend, no."

Harry merely glowered at her, so I attacked him with my own weapon, words, where she had used a knife.

"There you are, Harry. The future Queen of England, as you would have it, is no friend of yours."

"She misunderstood me. It is all your fault."

"My fault, Harry? It was you who came at me in a rage."

For an instant I thought of telling him that the Beothuks had called me to their encampment to let me know that they were not part of his plan, but I realised that they expect me to keep that a secret. They will reveal their feelings at a moment which they choose.

"Harry, go," I urged him. "We cannot stand here all day as if we were presenting a tableau in a Mystery Play."

In the way that foolish thoughts come to one's mind in the most solemn of moments (who has not been forced to prevent himself laughing during a funeral Mass?), I had the idea of putting on a Mystery Play here. It will intrigue the Beothuks, and it will give the winter crew something else to do. Harry tore himself out of the room and slammed the door behind him so hard that the coarse glass in the window nearly fell out. I had to go and close the door properly, and then I went to calm Anasaquit.

As soon as I turned to her, I saw that she had no need of reassurance. She had hidden her stone knife away again, and she stood still and serene.

"Come to the table again," I said, and I took her arm to draw her across the room. She came willingly, but there seemed to be no strength in her arm either to comply or to resist. It was like moving a perfectly balanced statue.

I poured her more wine, and also some for myself. I needed it even if she did not. I hope that she had frightened Harry into being less harsh in his dealings with the Beothuks, and into being less sure that they would do whatever he wanted them to do.

"Never mind Harry," I said. "I, Harry, friend, no."

Anasaquit gave a bitter laugh. For once I was certain that I had communicated my exact meaning to her.

I picked up my cross and put it once more around my neck. I shall not try using it again as a symbol, until I am sure that Anasaquit was not bowing down in fear to propitiate a god of anger and punishment.

Just as I was wondering what to do next to carry on Anasaquit's lessons, the door opened and Gilbert came in.

"Peter Slade sent me," he announced. "Harry Chard told him to. He says that Anasaquit attacked him with a knife."

"She was defending me, because she thought that Harry was threatening me. Anyway, why should Harry send for you?"

"He thought that I might be able to calm Anasaquit."

I did not know whether to laugh at Gilbert or to pity him. His innocence is even deeper than the innocence of Young Martin, or indeed of myself.

"Gilbert," I told him, "I think it would have taken half the soldiers of the London train-bands to calm Anasaquit."

Even while I was saying that, I saw Gilbert smile. It was not the open smile of an innocent, but a knowing smile. Then I saw that the smile was not for me. He was looking at Anasaquit, and she was smiling too, as she held out her stone knife to show him.

"What is it made of?" he asked.

"Stone, Gilbert, finely worked stone," I said, as Anasaquit handed Gilbert the knife for him to admire.

Gilbert and I both examined the knife closely. It was shaped for the hand, and cruelly sharp. Whoever had made it had spent many hours chipping away at the uneven lump of rock from which the knife had been made.

Gilbert tried the balance of the knife in his own hand.

"I have found knives like this at home in Devon, in the stones beside rivers," he said. "Do you think the Beothuks have ever been in England, Father?"

"No, Gilbert. The Beothuks have no ships. They must have come to Newfoundland in small boats, by a short crossing from the mainland of the continent."

"Then who left such knives in England?"

"I don't know, Gilbert. Perhaps they are thousands of years old, and are left over from the time before the Great Flood. It will probably always be a mystery to us, just as that grave in the forest is a mystery to the Beothuks."

"I think the Beothuks know more than they are telling us, Father," Gilbert said, glancing at Anasaquit.

"In fairness, Gilbert," I replied, "the Beothuks cannot tell us very much, since they know very little of our language and we know nothing of theirs."

Anasaquit interrupted us.

"I, friend Gilbert. I, friend Ralph Lecher."

"We are friends of yours too, Anasaquit," I told her. "I, friend, Anasaquit."

Gilbert copied my example.

"I, friend Anasaquit."

"Well, Gilbert," I said, "Harry has judged well for once. You have succeeded in calming Anasaquit."

I suddenly had an idea.

"Gilbert, look at my pectoral cross. There, hanging on the wall."

"Yes, Father."

"Please kneel down before it. Don't kneel to me. I am unworthy of any man's homage. Kneel to Christ."

Gilbert was baffled, but he is not called Holy Gilbert for nothing, and he knelt at once.

Anasaquit leapt over and knelt beside him, so that she and Gilbert were pressed against each other. I put my hands on their heads and muttered a blessing.

"Please rise now."

Gilbert stood up, and then tugged at Anasaquit so that she rose, too.

Gilbert realised that he was still holding Anasaquit's stone knife, so he offered it back to her.

Anasaquit took the knife, and then to my horror she wrenched Gilbert's shirt open and plunged her hand inside, still holding the knife.

I was about to clutch at her arm when she withdrew her hand. It was empty.

Gilbert had been so startled that he had not had time to do anything. Now he put his hand into his shirt, and fumbled about until he found the knife.

Anasaquit was smiling at him again.

I spoke before Gilbert.

"Gilbert, leave the knife there. I think it's meant as a gift. It must be very valuable and precious to Anasaquit."

"She will have nothing with which to defend herself," Gilbert objected.

"That's the other meaning of the gift," I said. "Anasaquit is showing her trust in your goodwill, and in mine, and in the whole of the winter crew."

"Does that include Harry Chard?" Gilbert wondered.

"I, Harry, friend, no," Anasaquit replied.

Chapter Fifteen

Better people than me have received unexpected visitors on Christmas Eve, but not since the Wise Men came to that profound stable in Bethlehem have stranger visitors arrived on this exciting and mysterious night of the year.

The winter crew were trying to keep pious expressions on their faces for my benefit. I was not convinced, because while I was preparing to celebrate Mass they were setting up the traditional games as best they could in a single small room half a world away from England.

Young Martin was laughing and giggling as he worked, but nobody, including himself, knew why. That is Young Martin's way, and it is not his fault. I thought of my poor mute sister, and wondered whether anybody will try to give her as good a Christmas as she can understand.

A rough voice began singing a song which I did not know. Another voice joined it, and then two or three more.

All the men in the room fell silent, even Young Martin, as they and I realised that the singing was outside.

Peter Slade stepped over to the window. He always takes command when command is needed.

Peter glanced out into the night, and then called for Gilbert.

"It is Christmas, Gilbert," he said, as the rough roaring song continued in its wild throaty words that no Englishman can understand.

Gilbert was on the other side of the room, because he had been making festive drawings on the wall with a blackened stick, but the men stepped aside to let him pass.

As Gilbert timidly opened the door, I had an invigorating thought: whatever happens at this moment, I shall always remember it.

Of course we all knew that it was the Beothuks outside: but how many, and in what humour, and what did they want? Would Gilbert open the door to a burst of spears and arrows?

When Gilbert managed to tug the door open against the snow which had built up underneath it, the light from our fire fell upon the familiar faces of Aguthut, Timaskatek, and Anasaquit. Four other Beothuks stood behind them, two men and two women, and all the Beothuks were singing their rough song.

I stepped forward to welcome them.

"Come in, friends, come in," I said, beckoning.

I heard breaths being drawn in sharply from members of the winter crew, but although I knew that there was a risk in allowing the Beothuks into our simple little stronghold, it would probably prove far more dangerous to drive them away into the icy night.

Aguthut and Anasaquit strode in confidently. Anasaquit turned round and tugged at the smocks of the Beothuks behind her, who seemed reluctant to enter. I remembered that the Beothuks were uncomfortable with roofs over them. I hoped that Timaskatek would not be reminded of his stone cell in Westminster Palace.

All the Beothuks huddled together in the middle of the room, while the winter crew retreated to the walls. Gilbert closed the door again, a little too quickly and rather too hard, betraying his nervousness.

I waited a moment for someone else to make some gesture of welcome, but even Peter Slade seemed unwilling to take charge this time.

"Well," I cried, trying to sound hearty, "let's give our guests some beer—and not the small beer either," I added, hoping that Timaskatek did not know what small beer was, although I fear that he must have been given it to drink many times during his captivity.

The men rushed into movement like puppets lifted from their rack by their master's hand. That was nervousness too, of course: being given something to do was better than standing in immobile apprehension.

Horsfall and Young Martin went out to fetch the beer, and Peter Slade went with them. When they all came back with the jug, while the Beothuks had been politely waiting, I realised that we needed cups for our guests.

"We must share our cups," I commanded, "each one of us with one of our friends."

"There is no need, Father," Peter Slade interrupted. "What I bring with me, which I had been saving for tomorrow, will serve for all."

From behind his back he produced a marvellous wooden loving-cup, all carved from one piece of wood. The winter crew all gasped. Obviously they had never seen it before.

"What is this splendid cup, Peter?" I asked. "Did you bring it from England with you?"

I wondered whether it was some relic from Peter's former life of wealth and honour, but this was not so.

"I have been making it ever since the fleet sailed home at the end of the summer," Peter explained. "I put all my skill and care into it so that it would be fit to be used for the first time at a special occasion. Now that occasion has presented itself."

The Beothuks slowly broke up their huddled group and huddled around Peter. They were impressed by the cup, and so was I. Peter held out the cup again, and in the firelight I suddenly saw that the carvings all around the cup were of boars: the boar of the House of York.

Peter put the great cup down on the table, and called out to Horsfall.

"Fill up the cup, then, Horsfall," Peter ordered.

"Perhaps," I suggested, "it would be a good idea to add some water to the wine. Our guests may not be used to it."

Before Peter could answer Timaskatek answered for him, the first time that any of the Beothuks had spoken, unless one counted their loud wild singing outside in the snow.

"No water! Wine. No water."

"As you wish," I conceded, while Peter and I looked at each other, both realising that Timaskatek must have been initiated into the English liking for strong drink during his captivity in Westminster.

Horsfall had filled the cup with a care and grace of which I would not have believed him capable.

Peter picked up the cup and offered it first to me.

"Here, Father. You show them first, and then pass it back to me."

I took the cup, and was immediately astonished at how heavy it was. It would have been weighty even when it was empty, but it also had a whole jugful of wine inside it.

I drank a shallow sip of the wine, which was as harsh and coarse as the Beothuks' song had been.

There was some quality in common between the song and the wine. Is this another sign from God of why we are here in Newfoundland, or is the truth simply that this is a hard land of rocks and cold, and we cannot expect wine which has been carried halfway round the earth to remember its origins in the sunny ease of some southern vineyard?

As Peter had instructed me, I passed the cup on to him, and he drank from it as well.

I waited to see which of the Beothuks he would offer it to.

I expected that he would choose Timaskatek or Aguthut, but instead he held the cup out to Anasaquit.

She gripped the handles, and drank a long draught. Young Martin gave her a rough cheer, which the other men took up. I suppose they were acknowledging her enthusiasm as a drinker, a quality which they admire in whomever they find it.

Anasaquit looked round in puzzlement, and then passed on the cup to the old Beothuk woman. She took her first drink of wine, and then passed the cup on to Aguthut. I noticed that Timaskatek seemed to be scowling in disapproval, even though it was he who had demanded the full festivities of Christmas, but then his normal expression always looks menacing to me.

Finally the cup was passed to Timaskatek, who drank from it eagerly. He was the only one of the Beothuks who did not look surprised after drinking the wine. He has certainly been given wine before.

I expected Timaskatek to pass the cup to Peter Slade, but instead he handed it back to me.

When I took it, I immediately noticed how much lighter it was. Timaskatek must have drunk deep and fast.

I am sure he was taught that in England, too. I gave the cup to Horsfall.

"Now all of the winter crew must drink, to show our friendship to our guests."

Horsfall took the cup as gingerly as if it had been on fire. I feared for a moment that he would refuse to drink from it, and so offend the Beothuks that a great war would start between the Beothuks and the English. If that had happened, Horsfall's refusal of the loving-cup would become a famous incident in history.

Fortunately, his love of wine overcame his nervousness about the Beothuks, and he drank from it. He passed the cup on to his constant companion Young Martin, who passed it on to the even younger Gilbert, and so the loving-cup was passed around among all the men.

William Durdle was the last, and he put the cup down on the table.

Silence fell again, and the Beothuks, perhaps without being aware what they were doing it, started slowly huddling together in the middle of the room again.

I intervened quickly before someone like Horsfall should say something stupid.

"The Beothuks gave us a song when they arrived," I reminded the winter crew. "We must give them a song in return."

Young Martin muttered something too quietly for me to hear.

"What was that, Martin?" I asked him.

"Hail Father Christmas," he said.

I had hoped for something more religious, but at least it was not a song which was lewd, although I feared that we should hear more than one unseemly song before the night was out.

"A good choice!" I told him. "We all know the words. Gilbert, will you sing it first?"

"*Hail, Father Christmas, hail to thee*," Gilbert began. His voice will start to break on any day now, but thanks to the mercy of God he could still sing in his boy's voice that night, as pure and clear as the snows of Newfoundland.

One of the many valuable components of a priest's training is that they teach you to sing, even if you have always believed that you could not. When tutors as harsh and merciless as mine were order you to sing, you sing.

I joined in as loudly as I could, and I was delighted to see Anasaquit begin to smile. She turned to the older woman (her mother, perhaps?), who also began to smile with a mouthful of shipwrecked teeth.

When the song ended, the Beothuks seemed not to know how to respond, except for Timaskatek. He clapped his huge hands together, with no rhythm, but plenty of honest effort.

As the evening continued, Peter Slade surprised me by the amount of food and wine that he was able to produce from the huts around the fish flakes. I cannot imagine why he has been hiding it all this time.

The winter crew began trying to teach the Beothuks some of the traditional Christmas games. Once again it became obvious that Timaskatek has seen all this before. He gave rapid explanations to Aguthut in their own spiky language.

Aguthut became more enthusiastic as he drank more wine. I began to worry that the effect of too much wine might cause merriment to turn suddenly to quarrelling and fighting. I fear a fight between the English winter crew and the Beothuks more than I fear any of Harry Chard's clumsy conspiracies.

Anasaquit and her older companion kept out of the boisterous games, greatly to my relief. They stood together in the corner, until I realised with shame that I was sitting in the middle of the bench.

I went over to Anasaquit and took her arm.

"Here, come and sit on the bench," I invited her. "It's closer to the fire."

Anasaquit and the older woman sat down on the bench. Anasaquit's companion sat down awkwardly. She had obviously never sat on a bench before. Anasaquit has already mastered the trick of sitting down gracefully.

The Beothuk women looked at each other and laughed, at what I do not know. Anasaquit turned round and saw this book standing open, propped up against the wall. I had forgotten that it was there.

Anasaquit reached down and took the book. She ran her fingers over the black letters in my round handwriting. I favour the new Caroline writing, because it is so much clearer than the old Secretary hand, but it makes no difference to Anasaquit.

She said something to the other woman, and I intervened.

"Anasaquit," I said, and pointed to myself. "Ralph Fletcher."

I pointed to the older woman, and Anasaquit understood at once. She said something to her companion, who pointed to herself in the same way that I had done, and grinned with her disorderly teeth again.

"Desaditith," she said.

"I am pleased to meet you, Desaditith," I replied, hoping that it was indeed her name. I will be long remembered in both English and Beothuk memories if it turns out that 'Desaditith' means 'go away.'

Anasaquit pointed out a letter in the book to Desaditith.

"Ah," she said. "Ah."

I realised that Anasaquit was demonstrating to Desaditith that the curly wandering black trails of ink on the page were actually words, captured out of the air and fixed for ever like pictures.

Anasaquit pointed to another letter.

"Buh," she said. "Buh."

Anasaquit is learning more in our lessons than I have thought. She is learning her letters faster than William Durdle is.

I noticed that Horsfall was passing out more wine, so I asked Gilbert to go and get some water. Our water comes from melted ice. The ponds are frozen over, and the little streams have all ceased to flow as well, waiting immobile for the spring much as we all do.

When Gilbert brought in the water, he looked around to see if anyone wanted any, and when nobody showed any interest he placed the jug on the table.

Anasaquit noticed it. She set down the book carefully, and went to the table. She inspected the jug and sniffed the water, and then lifted the whole jug and brought it over to me.

"I don't want a drink, yet, Anasaquit," I told her, but instead of putting the jug of water into my hands she placed it on the floor in front of me.

She knelt down and took my pectoral cross into her hands.

She could tell that I did not understand what she meant by that, and the noise in the room fell silent as both the English fishermen and the Beothuks noticed this mysterious little tableau which the two of us had formed.

Anasaquit tugged at the cross, three times, and then she tugged at it again while she looked up at me with beseeching eyes.

She dipped her fingers into the jug of water and slapped her own brow with her wet hand, and at last I believed that I understood her.

It would be a great risk for me. I might be wrong. I might be in violation of canon law, and in my mind I ran through all I know of the applicable parts of Church law and ritual. I was thinking with the unnatural speed with which one can think in moments of crisis, when time stops as uncannily as the rivers in Newfoundland hold their positions all through the winter.

I decided that I could not refuse Anasaquit. It would have been better to have a Christian woman as a witness, but I would have to make to with two Christian men; or, that is, two men who called themselves Christians.

I chose the two oldest.

"Peter Slade and William Durdle, come here."

Both Peter and Slade stepped over to me, more surprised than curious. I was glad that neither of them was truly drunk yet. Even so, I am sure that this ceremony has been witnessed by the inebriated, performed upon the inebriated, and, I regret to say, performed by the inebriated. It makes no difference to its validity.

I now dipped my own fingers into the jug of water, and made the sign of the Cross upon Anasaquit's brow.

I suddenly remembered that I had to find a name for her.

"I baptise you," I said, making everyone else in the room start with astonishment, "Anna Mary, in the name of the Father, the Son, and the Holy Spirit."

Young Martin spoke first.

"Is she a Christian now?" he asked.

"She certainly is, even if she still has much to learn about the Faith," I replied.

Young Martin's innocent bluntness caused him to say what all the other men of the winter crew must have been thinking.

"Does this mean that she can marry Gilbert now?"

"She can marry any man she wants to," I replied.

Young Martin thought about that, and then, as is his way, he came up with a completely unrelated thought.

"Must we call her Anna Mary now?"

"No, that is simply her baptismal name. We can still call her Anasaquit."

William Durdle looked at the other Beothuks.

"What do they think of this, I wonder?" he said. "Do they consider it good or bad?"

Gilbert was scandalised.

"Baptism can't be bad!" he cried.

Timaskatek growled a few words to Aguthut and Desaditith. Once again I feared the worst, but Timaskatek spoke to me next.

"Good," he declared. "Anasaquit, good."

"Do you understand?" I asked him. "Have you seen this in England?"

"England, good, yes," Timaskatek replied, but I could not make out what he meant.

I wished I had some kind of gift to present to Anasaquit, and I had an idea which I put to Peter Slade.

"Peter, can you make me a little wooden cross for Anasaquit, which she could wear around her neck?"

"Of course, Father. I'll do it before Christmas is out."

Anasaquit tried to kneel before me again. I drew her up, and made her stand between Peter Slade and William Durdle.

"These are your baptismal sponsors," I told her. "You don't understand me, but I'll write it out, in the hope that one day you'll be able to read it."

I tore a page out of this book, and unpacked my pen and inkhorn to write out the words. Peter Slade signed it, and to my surprise so did William Durdle, in handwriting which was as square and spiky as St. Paul's Cathedral.

I waved the piece of paper in front of the fire to dry the ink, and then folded it and handed it to Anasaquit.

"This is yours to keep," I told her, gesturing that she should put it into her smock. She did so, plunging her hand into her garment so eagerly and roughly that some of the men had to hide their urge to laugh.

I withdrew into the corner to watch the Christmas games begin. Young Martin appointed himself to instruct the Beothuks in how to play them.

I expected that Timaskatek would know some of them already. Indeed, he did crow in appreciation whenever Young Martin announced the name of a new game, but he obviously did not know how to play, even though Harry Chard had appointed him as our Lord of Misrule.

Had he only seen games played at Christmas, and never been invited to join in? Did he sit as a spectator by the wall in England as I now sat in Newfoundland?

I hope that he did not see these games only from the hole in the door of his cell. Even the beasts in the menagerie at the Tower of London are allowed out into the air from time to time.

There had been no need for me to worry that the festivities would go to excess and lead to a fight. The Beothuks became tired even before the winter crew did. Like us, they are not used to staying awake for long after sunset. We are trying to live in the evenings as men did in classical times, but in those days they were playing games and telling stories and philosophising with laurel wreaths on their brows, far into warm Mediterranean nights, by the light of perfumed candles.

Peter Slade and Horsfall fetched some sacks and sail-cloth from the store huts, and made them up as rough beds for the Beothuks to sleep on. Gilbert and Young Martin brought in more wood so that the fire could burn all night, which meant that someone would have to tend it for safety's sake.

I am the priest, the man who does the least work, and also the man who remained the most sober, so the duty of firewatching fell to me. I occupied the time by writing up this book. The scratching of my pen sounded wondrously loud in the middle hours of the night, but the snoring and even more unseemly noises from the sleepers were louder still.

I had no difficulty in staying awake. I had so much to meditate upon.

I have christened Anasaquit, in good faith, in the hope that her faith is true and good as well.

Timaskatek has another eleven days to reign as Lord of Misrule, until Twelfth Night. I wonder whether we shall have a traditional Twelfth Night cake, with a pea and a bean concealed in it. I expect that Peter Slade even thought of that before we left England, and that he has been hiding a pea and a bean all this time. It would not greatly amaze me now if he were to produce a great bowl of plum por-ridge tomorrow.

What worries me most, and is keeping me alert through the night, is not whether Anasaquit knows that she is a Christian, or what japes Timaskatek may be plan-ning as manifestations of his fitness to misrule, or whether we shall have Twelfth Night cake to follow a miraculous plum porridge. I am puzzled by the absence of Harry Chard.

For the first time in my life I fell asleep sitting down, and sitting on an uneven stub of log at that. I cannot understand why I did not fall to the floor, but I woke up still balanced on my stool.

If I had tipped over onto the floor, my fall would have been broken by a clutch of sleeping bodies, English fishermen and Beothuks mingled together in a pretty picture of friendship. Well, perhaps not that pretty.

Holy Gilbert was the first to wake up, and he struggled across the room to me, trying not to disturb anyone.

He looked down at the snoring brown bodies. It was like surveying a landscape of hills and valleys. This agreeable brown and green countryside was made up of an assortment of backs and bottoms.

"Is this right for Christmas, Father?" Gilbert asked.

"Nobody has done anything wrong, yet, Gilbert," I replied. "The Church does not condemn happiness and good cheer, you know. Have you never seen this before?"

"I have always spent Christmas and all the other feasts of the year alone with my mother," Gilbert explained, and I knew that there was nothing I could say in reply to that.

While Gilbert went in search of some beer, bread, and cheese for breakfast, I imagined how Christmas was being spent in my father's home.

Oh, there will be wine, and plum porridge, and ruder games than will be played here. There will be music, and a tired old priest to conduct the religious services. One of the servants will be made Lord of Misrule, but he will understand very well that his misrule must be kept within limits.

My poor sister's nurse will bring her down from her bedroom, in the hope that she will be amused by the noise and lights. I fear that instead she will cry with nervousness and fright, and the nurse will have to take her back to the quiet austere room in which she is likely to spend all her life.

I fear that one day my father will have the idea of sending her to Newfoundland so that she will shame him no longer. My father is a man of duty but not of kindness.

Holy Gilbert brought in the provisions for breakfast. The second cold draught of the morning from the open door made the sleepers begin painful awakenings.

Before Gilbert closed the door again, I had a glimpse of fresh snow lying and big snowflakes settling respectfully onto their predecessors. Sometimes I forget that I am a priest, with a daily routine and special rituals to perform at the high points of the year. Gilbert reminded me.

"Will you say Mass, Father?"

"Of course, Gilbert, but I will wait until my congregation are in better condition to hear it."

Gilbert persisted, with the question which I feared but which I knew that I must answer.

"Will you give Communion to Anasaquit as well? Has she confessed her sins?"

"I believe that she means to lead a new life," I told him. "If I am wrong, it is I who will be punished by God, not Anasaquit."

Gilbert watched as Anasaquit and Desaditith helped each other to stand up.

"I like her," Gilbert announced.

"Who, Desaditith?" I answered to tease the poor boy. "Harry Chard will be very angry with you."

"I am sure I would like Desaditith too," Gilbert replied. "You know who I mean, Father."

"Of course I do, Gilbert," I said. "I'm sorry," and indeed I was contrite for having treated him like a simple schoolboy. I do not believe that Gilbert is my rightful king, but he is turning out to be graver and more intelligent than I had thought for so long.

I said a Mass quietly to myself, while some of the others watched me curiously and others fell upon their breakfast.

I had been pleased to note that none of the Beothuks seemed to be feeling unwell because of the drink. They might have misinterpreted it as the result of an attempt to poison them. Such dangerous errors will always be a danger between us until we learn each other's languages and customs.

Gradually everyone began talking. I was concentrating on the private words which I had to say to myself and to God, but I could not help noticing that the conversations became louder.

I nearly forgot my text when I noticed that Timaskatek and Horsfall, of all people, were now engaged in a simple but enthusiastic conversation. Horsfall, who had so denounced the 'savages' who lay in wait out in the forest!

I never found out what they were discussing, because we all noticed at once that the room had gone suddenly very cold, as though a spirit were about to manifest itself.

Harry Chard had entered so silently that none of us had heard him. He had not even shaken the snow off his clothes and hat, so that he stood encased in thick white snow like a model figure smothered in sugar as the centrepiece of a grand banquet.

William Durdle moved behind Harry to close the door which he had left open to the whirling snowstorm.

"So this is misrule," Harry remarked as he took off his cap and shook the snow off it into the fire. "It looks merry enough to me."

"So it should be," I said. "Christmas is a celebration, and why should we not enjoy merriment and fellowship, especially with our special guests?"

Timaskatek was glowering at Harry Chard. The stare was not simply Timaskatek's usual forbidding aspect: it was true anger and hate. Something has passed between them, either back in England or here in Newfoundland, of which I know nothing, but it is playing with all our lives as if we were chessmen.

"I, lord," Timaskatek reminded Harry.

"If you are truly Lord of Misrule, then Misrule!" Harry shouted. "Never mind that foolish young priest. You are to rule throughout the Twelve Days of Christmas."

I interrupted him, "And are you, then, to rule us after that?"

"The king shall rule," Harry replied.

"So he shall," I said, "and I shall proclaim him myself."

All the winter crew gasped at that. Even Peter Slade lost his composure for a moment.

"This is Christmas," I said, "a time when kings came to hail a greater king. I do not know how many people in England are part of your foolish and dangerous plot. Because of that, I believe it would be too dangerous for Gilbert to return to England with the fleet at the end of next summer."

"How will you stop me?" Harry Chard demanded.

"By setting up a king here," I said. "Let Gilbert marry Anasaquit, if they are both willing. Let them be proclaimed a king and queen here in Newfoundland, sovereigns over the Beothuks."

Timaskatek could clearly understand a few important words of what I was saying, and his face opened into that terrifying smile of his.

"The Beothuks have no king!" Harry Chard shouted.

"They will now," I said. "Whether they choose to recognise him is entirely their affair. You have built a palace for the king and a cathedral in which to anoint and crown him."

Timaskatek growled something to the other Beothuks, and they all fell into excited chattering.

Harry Chard watched them disapprovingly.

"Now see what mischief you have started, you foolish meddling boy! You are playing with sharp weapons that you do not know how to use."

"Let the Beothuks decide for themselves what they want to do," I replied. "For my part, I will decide for myself how I conduct my duties as the only priest in Newfoundland. It was you who placed me here for with the winter crew, Harry. Remember that."

Timaskatek, Aguthut, and Anasaquit all turned to face me. Aguthut spoke for them all.

"Anasaquit, Gilbert, yes. Gilbert, king, yes."

"There!" I exclaimed, but Aguthut clutched my arm to show me that he had not yet finished speaking.

"Timaskatek, England, yes."

"What?" I replied. "Timaskatek wants to go back to England?"

Timaskatek grinned again. It was a grin of triumph at having made himself understood to me.

"Timaskatek, England, yes."

Harry Chard flung his fur mittens onto the floor. He was too angry to speak, so I spoke instead.

"There you are, Harry. You told us that we must all obey the Lord of Misrule. He commands you to send him back to England."

It had taken such a long time, but looking back I now saw how obvious it had been that Harry Chard had not brought Timaskatek back to Newfoundland as an act of kindness. It had been a forcible abduction, making Timaskatek return as an instrument of Harry's plot to overthrow the king. The intended rebel had played his part as well as in a Mystery Play, but now Timaskatek would not act or obey any more.

Chapter Sixteen

Is not Easter supposed to be a symbolic greeting of what may be spring in the Holy Land, but here in Newfoundland we are still in winter, and the merry month of May will bring not flowers but the return of the icebergs.

As Lent draws to its glorious end, the marriage of Anasaquit and Gilbert draws closer. Easter falls on the twenty-third. day of March this year, so the new year of 1505 will begin only two days later.

A new year, a new Christian woman, a new marriage, and a new fishing season. The fishing fleet will come back, to reassure us that there really are other people in the world beside ourselves, and that England is not a dream land like Lyonesse. What poet or romancer could have imagined England?

Harry Chard has been sulking wherever he goes since Christmas. We have rarely seen him. I have looked for him in his cathedral, but he is never there. Indeed we had to repair and tidy the cathedral ourselves in preparation for the wedding.

I shall celebrate Easter there myself. If Easter is a symbol, then I shall make my own symbol. The painful day of Good Friday and the darkness of Holy Saturday will be observed in our home on the shore, but I shall announce the joy of Easter in Harry Chard's wooden cathedral, which is now Gilbert's cathedral.

When I realised that Timaskatek had not been brought back to Newfoundland as an act of kindness, but that he had been forced to return by Harry Chard, everything became clear to me in the same way as a mental puzzle can shiver into simple transparency as soon as one solves a part of it.

The Beothuks agreed that Anasaquit could be their queen, and that Gilbert could be her consort. I suspect that she already had some high status among her own people. In return, I have made Harry Chard promise to take Timaskatek back to England at the end of next summer.

Harry's conspiracy cannot proceed, because he has no claimant to the throne to put forward. Gilbert wants to remain in Newfoundland with Anasaquit for the time being.

The winter crew are relieved that they can go back to England in safety, because I have vowed to them that I will tell nobody about Harry Chard's plot against the king.

I will maintain the same vow for Harry Chard, although he does not deserve it. He will have enough trouble explaining why he chose to spend the winter here, a thing which no Fishing Admiral has ever done before.

Young Martin was worried about how far my promises of secrecy went.

"Will you tell anyone about the sins which Horsfall and I have admitted to you, Father?" he asked me.

"Of course not," I reassured him. "The secrets of your confessions are literally sacred."

I have advised Peter Slade that he should reconcile himself to King Henry, and that whatever his private feelings, there is no chance of the new Tudor dynasty being overthrown.

"Peter, you are an educated man," I told him. "I know you have lost the lands and wealth which you once possessed, but you still have your learning. Why not set up as a schoolmaster?"

"Myself, teaching Latin, and flogging boys?"

"Just so, Peter, but I hope you would flog only gently and only upon outrageous provocation. It is a pity that you are too old to become a priest."

"Ah, Father, I thought about it when I was young, but my father would not allow it."

"We have something in common, then Peter," I said, and I reminded him of my father's disapproval, as I had described it on the night so long ago when I had told the winter crew my short life story.

"I am his only son," I explained, "and neither I nor my sister can ever be married. Our line ends with us."

"Perhaps you cannot really understand his disappointment," Peter said. "Try to speak about it to him when you see him again."

That struck me as an extraordinary thing to say. For the first time since last summer, I find myself believing, indeed, expecting, to see England again.

Suddenly I had a great longing to see my father and sister again, to visit our house in the country, and to walk through the narrow streets of London, with windows hanging over me on both sides, and pigs trying to push me aside to gain the right of way.

"How shall I tell my father that I have given away the beautiful little silver Mass bell which he presented to me at my ordination?" I asked.

"Tell him how it happened, and let him judge," Peter said, and he left me thinking about a return to England which is still many months away.

I must keep my mind on my duties here in Newfoundland. I begin to understand now what a burden I have laid upon Gilbert by persuading him to stay here, even if his patient and enduring mother comes to join him.

Of course, Gilbert will be a king here, a king of forests and granite rocks. I remember how I used to imagine that Newfoundland was indeed a New World, created in innocence so that Man might be put to the test again.

Our ancestor Adam was created to be king of a beautiful garden, filled with flowers and fruit and every kind of beast. If Gilbert is a new Adam, then his Garden of Eden has only dark evergreen forests, few flowers, and fewer birds, and the only fruits are strange little yellow berries which grown on the barren lands beyond the trees. Perhaps this harsh Eden will see less sin than the beautiful Eden of thousands of years ago.

Rehearsals are going well for the Mystery Play which is to be performed at Easter. This book in which I write is sadly mutilated. It was so skilfully crafted by the bookbinder, but I have had to tear rough handfuls of pages out of it, rending the marvellous little stitches and defacing the leather spine. There are no shops here where I could buy paper, and I have no idea how to make it, so I had to provide the paper for the Mystery Play myself.

I asked Peter Slade to help me to write it, but he claimed that he had no skill in pretty writing.

"Neither have I," I told him. "A play is not a work of literature, but an entertainment, either for high moral purposes or for low amusement."

"I know how to study the writings of other men," Peter replied. "I could have written it in Latin, but I have no idea how to write well in English."

"The masters at Winchester College taught us composition in English as well as Latin," I said.

"That was a waste of time," Peter replied. "There is no point in learning to write well in English. Have you ever seen any English writings from the old days? You can hardly understand it. In two or three hundred years from now, nobody will be able to make out the meaning of your English. If you write in Latin, men will be able to read your words forever."

Peter walked away, strangely angry. Perhaps he feels that I was suggesting that his school was inferior to mine. Grown men can be peculiarly sensitive about such things.

I finally settled upon a play in two parts. The first part is to be the expulsion of Adam and Eve from the Garden of Eden, and the second part is to be how God made a covenant with Abraham, and set him wandering to a strange new land.

The two youngest men of the winter crew will act the female parts. Gilbert is to be Abraham's wife Sarah, which displeases him, because he does not want to play a woman, but he agrees to do it out of duty.

Young Martin, on the contrary, is unhealthily delighted to be cast as Eve, whom he will play opposite Horsfall as Adam. Those two can represent the Fall of Man better than any other two actors at my disposal.

In the interests of spreading peace, I did offer a part to Harry Chard. He ought to be the Serpent, of course, but four days ago I asked him to play God the Father.

"Go to the Devil," he replied, storming off towards the forest, and I have not seen him since. William Durdle is to play God the Father now, and very well he will do it too. His long beard and wavy white hair make him the very picture of God from a wall-painting in any country church.

Anasaquit has been continuing to try to learn English, and Desaditith always comes with her. I understand that the two of them try to practise conversations in English when they are on their own, and that Timaskatek laughs at them.

We did progress far enough for me to ask Anasaquit whether Desaditith was her mother, but she is not. Whether she is an aunt or an older sister I cannot make out, but she is some kind of relative. The Beothuks seem to live in small bands which rarely meet, so they must all be quite close kin to each other.

I have told Gilbert that when he and Anasaquit have children, he must speak only English to them while Anasaquit must speak only Beothuk. In this way we shall one day have people who can understand both ways of life and can interpret us one to another.

The days draw longer, though not as fast as they do in England. The time of the great fogbanks is approaching, and the days when the mountains of ice sail down ponderously from the north. What great ice there must be along those unseen shores.

I see now that I am having to tear out so many leaves from this book, that I must be sparing with my words for the next few months. I am scattering pages of the Mystery Play around our huts as pale substitutes for the leaves of spring which I would be looking for at home.

The need to husband my paper carefully meant that I did not write anything in this book until after the Mystery Play was over.

Peter Slade created a wonder of a Gate of Paradise out of spare timber and old sailcloths and boat-covers. We set up the Gate of Paradise in front of the forest.

First of all, among the trees, Adam and Eve acted out their original happiness. Then they played out the Fall of Man, and I, as the Archangel Michael, drove them out through the grim gate into our world of sin and pain and suffering, where we must all languish until the Saviour comes again.

Aguthut and Timaskatek, who did not appear in the play but willingly helped, carried the gate away while the audience (the winter crew, our Beothuk friends, and a frighteningly silent Harry Chard) walked over to an expanse of bare rocks. It was almost like an English audience in a town following the carts of a Mystery Play through the streets.

I had chosen the harsh rock to represent the deserts of the East, where the city of Ur of the Chaldees was. Abraham's home city lay in a hot desert, but the cold and grimness of the Newfoundland landscape make a suitably forbidding substitute.

The winds from the sea set off our actors' words as effectively as the hot howling winds of the sandy desert would have done.

The Beothuks watched in unreadable silence. I know that they have an idea of a God. They must have some ancient story of a first man and a first woman, because otherwise how can humanity have come to be?

Yet again I am impatient for the days when we can communicate with each other properly. Do the Beothuks, too, know that we were expelled from Paradise because we fell into sin? The Beothuks must have come here from the great continent. How did they come here from Eden?

The play continued, with the actors playing many parts as is the tradition, until Abraham received his covenant with God and history was once more set upon a right course.

For the last few days the winter crew have been reminiscing about the games which are played in their villages around Easter. Most of them are so violent and unseemly that I do not want them taught to the Beothuks, but some of the more innocent ones might help to build fellowship and good cheer.

After I had written those last words, fellowship and good cheer were interrupted by the malign intervention of Harry Chard. I had only just raised my worn-out pen for yet another sharpening, when Harry burst in through the door.

Rather, it was not Harry himself bursting in through the door. It was the point and axe of a great halberd, with Harry coming afterwards, wielding it from the other end.

In the way that one notices and remembers foolishly unimportant details in moments of high crisis, instead of seeing only what matters most, I found myself for an instant wondering how Harry could balance the halberd while he was holding it at the very bottom of the shaft.

When my mind cleared away this nonsense, I saw that Harry was staring at my with eyes so bright that I seemed to be looking straight through his skull at the sunlit snowscape beyond the open door.

It was me that he had come to kill, and with a weapon that is meant for fighting against heavy war-horses.

I leapt up from the bench, still holding the penknife with which I had been sharpening my goose-quill. I stepped out of the way of Harry's first lunge with the point of the halberd.

Harry was between me and the door. He lunged at me again as I scurried around the room. I had little space to move, but then neither did he. He drew back the halberd for another lunge, and the shaft broke our only window.

The noise of the glass breaking, so loud and noticeable a sound in our silent wilderness, must have been heard by the winter crew. I heard voices coming closer.

I could not rely on outside help. I kept skipping like a schoolboy to evade the cruel sharp blade, and then I realised that Harry, much wiser and more learned in fighting than I am, had forced me into a corner.

I did not expect the words which he now spoke to me.

"In the name of the king of England, Father Fletcher, I will execute you for treason."

"Treason?" I replied, hoping to distract him while someone, anyone, came to my aid from outside the door. I could hear more voices, but no hero stepped in to save me. "I have committed no treason against King Henry, and there is no other rightful king in England."

"You know very well that I mean the true king, of the House of York. I will set him up here in Newfoundland, and he will cross the ocean and reign in England hereafter."

"The Beothuks are not with you," I said, "and neither are the winter crew. Even Gilbert does not want to act in your play, because he knows that it will end in his cruel death in the Tower of London, and probably the innocent Anasaquit with him."

"Damn you, boy, these are great matters of state," Harry answered, and I noticed that he was being forced to lower the halberd because of its weight. "You know nothing of the ways of men and of kingdoms."

"I know that you are the most friendless man since Judas Iscariot," I said. "This Yorkist plot has only one conspirator, yourself, and all those whom you suppose to be your allies are either indifferent or hostile."

"There is a plot against me, and you have led it from the beginning!" Harry shouted.

"I would never have spoken against you if you had not stranded me here with the winter crew on the coast of Newfoundland, Harry," I replied, although I was gasping with anxiety. Would I die in a state of sin? I hoped that I would remember that I would have to forgive Harry before he struck the blow that would kill me.

Harry's eyes burned into mine again, and slowly he lifted the point of the halberd towards me again.

"I forgive you, Harry!" I shouted.

He roared with rage, and instead of rushing at me with the point of the halberd, he lifted it so that he could strike me with the heavy axe and cleave me in two.

The point buried itself in the uneven timbers of the ceiling, and for a brief eternity he and I were frozen as in a scene in a painting.

I wanted to run past him for the door, but there was no space. I had to run at him with my little penknife in my hand, and that is my excuse before God and man, because although it was only a penknife the blade was just long enough to go through Harry's thick smock and shirts, and beyond into the flesh beneath.

I felt no resistance at all. Fear must have given me strength, or perhaps my onward rush could have been stopped only by a coat of armour.

Harry cried out in pain and astonishment, and we froze again as I became crazily aware of faces in the door and faces pushing through the broken window.

I was in such agitation that I could not have named the faces even if there had been time to think.

I leapt back in both relief at my survival and in horror at what I had done.

Harry crumpled forward onto the floor, his hands fumbling among his torn clothes to find the pain of the wound.

As his face struck the planking, the halberd was jarred loose from the ceiling, and the axe fell upon his own head and buried itself in his skull.

Peter Slade led the winter crew and the Beothuk men as they all pushed one another through the door and looked down upon Harry Chard, who was convulsing upon the floor as blood burst out of his head and horribly delicate brains climbed out of the split bones.

Everyone looked at me, but only Peter Slade had the possession to be able to speak to me.

"You've killed him, Father!"

He snatched the penknife from my unresisting hand, which seemed not to belong to me.

I fell hard upon the floor next to Harry, bringing a shock of pain to my knees, but the pain seemed not to belong to me, either.

I seized Harry's right hand, which was clenching and opening, over and over. I bent down and spoke to his nearest ear.

"Harry, I know you can't speak. I know that you trust in God. I have no time to carry out the full rites, so I bless you in the name of the Father and the Son and the Holy Spirit. Please, Harry, depart from this world in peace."

I wanted his own suffering to end, and I wanted us not to have to watch any more of it.

Harry's right hand stretched out its fingers in a gesture of mysterious and fascinating grace, and then collapsed.

"I've killed him," I said stupidly.

Peter Slade and William Durdle stepped forward and began arranging Harry's body decently.

Peter tried to reassure me, even while he and William were tugging the axe of the halberd out of Harry's head.

"No, you didn't kill him, Father. It was an accident. Your little knife couldn't have done him a real hurt, not through all those heavy clothes. It was his own fault for trying to kill you. You have no guilt in this."

I know that it is true. I hope that my faith is strong enough that I can be comforted by a confessor, if I ever live to speak to another priest.

The men of the winter crew carried Harry's body out, while Horsfall briskly washed down the floor with a seriousness and efficiency which I have never seen in him before.

Aguthut and Timaskatek watched as the corpse was borne out into the snow and taken into one of the curing houses. The Beothuks may have an imperfect understanding of our language and religion, but death is a foreigner to no nation.

I had wanted to stand while I recovered myself, but I began shaking. Aguthut led me over to the bench where I had been sitting only a little while before, blamelessly writing Latin words into this book.

My own familiar round schoolboy handwriting was still on the page (and why should it not be?), stopping at the point where my pen had become too blunt and I had been moved to take out my penknife.

For several days, I could not face writing in this book again. It was the very act of writing which brought back the memory of what I had done.

Of course I had to perform the rites of burial for Harry Chard. There was no consecrated ground in which to bury him. The Beothuks seemed surprised when they understood how we were going to put him to rest, and I suspect that they do not bury their dead.

I thought about burying Harry next to his grotesque wooden cathedral in the forest. It may be what he would have wanted, but the idea made me uncomfortable. I could not bring myself to treat his monstrous toy of a cathedral as if it were a real church.

Then I remembered that there was already a graveyard nearby.

We buried Harry with the mysterious European dead who lay in the secret grave among the trees.

As I recited the Latin words with their terrible power to awe even men who cannot understand them, I wondered whether the ground in which we were laying Harry was already consecrated. Had these people, whoever they were, been Christians too? Am I really the first priest to come to Newfoundland?

Angrily, I forced my thoughts back to the burial service. Harry was buried decently. The men of the winter crew each threw a handful of stony soil into the grave. Harry lies now among the strange fishermen and warriors who came to Newfoundland before us. Like them, he will never see his home again.

The Beothuks watched the service impassively, except for Anasaquit, who clutched at Gilbert, and Desaditith, who looked with concern upon Anasaquit until the grave was filled and we all walked away.

Easter came with cruel snowstorms followed by ice. The new year of 1505 began in as wintry a fashion as if we had renewed the old Roman custom and started the year on the first day of January.

I carried out my duties, not in a spirit of grim obligation, but with growing hope for the year to come. For myself, it means only that I will return to England, that mythical land as strange and as desirable as the Arcadia of the Greeks.

What use the Church will find for me there, I cannot imagine, but I can be certain that employment will be found for me somewhere.

When Easter was over, the next ceremony was the wedding of Gilbert and Anasaquit. One of the witnesses was Timaskatek, who caught me out in the forest a few days before and pushed me against a tree.

"Ralph Lecher, battize Timaskatek," he demanded, and I have done so. Of all the Beothuks, he is the one who has the most understanding of what baptism means. I wonder how many priests have conducted a christening under the threat of violence by the aspiring new Christian?

I had asked Gilbert where he and Anasaquit wanted to be married, and he surprised me by choosing Harry Chard's wooden palace. Because that was Gilbert's wish, that was where we held the wedding, but I had the superstitious feeling that the angry spirit of Harry Chard was watching us.

Our contribution to the feast was salted codfish and second beer. The Beothuks brought meat of the great deer, and skin bags of the little yellow berries from the barren lands outside the trees.

It had been agreed that the Beothuks would take Gilbert and Anasaquit, as their king and queen, to a place in the interior of the land where Gilbert could be introduced to his new relatives in accordance with the customs of the Beothuks.

The winter crew and I gathered to wave them goodbye as their friends and relatives and their 'loyal subjects' now, if one took Harry Chard's mad view of the world, led them away.

The column of Beothuks wound away with a solitary English boy in the middle of it. He looked half joyful, half fearful. Timaskatek remained behind, by his own choice, I am told. He wanted to stay near us. Perhaps he hopes for an English May Day after enjoying his English Christmas.

Gilbert and the Beothuks had promised that he and Anasaquit would be back in the summer, when the Beothuks return from the interior to the coast.

The winter crew began to prepare for the return of the English fishing fleet. The snow still came, but now we began to see ice floating down from the north, which is the first sign of spring. I settled into the routine of my priestly duties, and ceased to write in this book until the fleet came into sight one day.

We heard a great and strange cry of "England, England!" from Young Martin, who was working by the seashore.

Peter Slade stopped checking the supports of the fish flakes and turned to Young Martin.

"England? You can't see England from here, Martin, even though the fog and ice have gone."

"Not England!" Young Martin replied, shouting just as loudly as before. "The English ships! The fleet is back!"

All the winter crew had heard him, and all of them ran to the shore, and I with them, to see the miracle of masts and sails on the horizon.

None of us did anything. We stood like Roman statues on the rocks, watching the ships come closer, until they anchored offshore and put their boats out.

I had looked forward to seeing the traditional race between the ships' captains to see who could land on the shore first and claim the status and privileges of the Fishing Admiral for the whole season.

Instead, four boats approached slowly, and the first boat suddenly sported the flag of England, raised by a short sailor with a long beard which the wind blew over his face.

When I looked past the sailor, I was amazed to see a familiar face behind him, a face which looked much less smug and comfortable than when I had last seen it. It was the Dominican friar from the Palace of Westminster, the one who had given me my pay for this venture.

Behind him in the boat sat some men in breastplates with swords. They could not be fishermen, or even soldiers. They must be gentlemen. What could this mean?

All at once I understood everything, and I laughed long and loud, as I have not laughed since I first came to Newfoundland a year ago.

These creatures were to have been the retinue of the new Yorkist king, the pretender who was to have been set up by Harry Chard.

As the boat came closer, I could see that the friar and the gentlemen were scanning our own faces, obviously looking for Harry Chard.

Their eyes settled upon Peter Slade, whom they obviously knew, but he stepped back and walked away behind our huts, waving to me to go and greet the newcomers.

I must confess that I took a wicked delight in it.

The gentlemen leapt into the water, and strode up the rocks towards me.

I came forward and took the hand of the first gentleman.

"Welcome to Newfoundland! I am sorry to tell you that Harry Chard has died, but I have good news as well. The youngest of our winter crew, Gilbert, has married a noble maiden of the local people."

"Harry Chard, dead?" the gentleman asked stupidly, and then he realised that the Dominican had splashed awkwardly ashore as well and was standing at his shoulder, glowering at me like a rebuked sinner.

The gentleman introduced him.

"Father Fletcher, this is Father Wratten, of the Dominican order. He is to replace you as the priest here."

I think that it was with the help of God that I did not laugh again. I believe that I would never have been able to stop.

At last I know the Dominican's name. He must have high influence, to have been ordained priest so young.

"Welcome, Father Wratten," I told him. "I will tell you all you need to know for your stay here. But if you are going to replace me, what am I going to do here all summer?"

It was the gentleman who answered me.

"One of the ships came only to transport us. It will return to England, and you with it. Father Wratten has been sent here for the whole year, as you were."

We showed the whole party to our huts, sailors, fishermen, gentleman, friar, and all. In truth, it was they who showed more hospitality, giving us food and drink such as we had not known for several months.

The ship which had brought the gentlemen will take the whole winter crew, including me, back to England in two days' time, after the captain has taken on water and carried out some minor repairs.

The conspiracy has failed, and for that reason the conspirators dare not return to England yet. I hope the gentlemen will be made to work alongside the fishermen and then be made to stay with the winter crew, as I was.

Father Wratten will be ill-advised to try his arrogance upon my new Beothuk Christians, and I have tried to warn him so.

This first great task of my young life is finished now. I have saved Gilbert from certain death upon a block in the Tower of London. I have had a hand in stopping Harry's dangerous plot.

Most of all, I have baptised two new Christians.

I went into the forest and brought back Timaskatek. We are fulfilling our promise to him, and he will return to England with us.

I now need only to pack up all my belongings, including my pen, my inkhorn, this very book, and the chest containing my forty testoons.

I believe that I have earned them.

Waking the Messiah

JoAnne Soper-Cook
ISBN 1-55081-143-6 / $16.95 (sc)
5" x 8" / 168 pp.

The engaging plot of this novel focuses on Moriah, a character with multiple personality disorder, and her four distinct personalities— the Little Girl; Leslie, the domineering Lesbian; Moriah as an adult; and Jesus Christ. After a life of physical, sexual, and emotional abuses, Moriah attempts to break free from the bonds of the Pentecostal Assembly and form a new life in Newfoundland by whatever means necessary, even murder. Adult material.

All Gone Widdun

Annamarie Beckel
ISBN 1-55081-147-9 / $19.95 (sc)
5" x 8" / 280 pp.

This is a novel of one man's quixotic mission to save the Beothuk of Newfoundland from extinction, his love for Shawnadithit, and the tragedy of her life and the lives of her people. Based on true accounts, the novel is told in the alternating first-person narratives of William Epps Cormack, an eccentric Newfoundland-born Scottish merchant, and Shawnadithit, a young Beothuk woman captured by English settlers in 1823 who proved to be the last Beothuk.